"Do I have to spell it out for you, Jade?"

Magnus snarled. "I've spent two long, loveless years waiting for you—waiting for us to get our lives back. And now—" He swung away from her suddenly, going to the window and thudding a hand against the wooden frame.

"I'm sorry." Jade's voice was hushed. It was no wonder he'd lost control. "I thought...that you wanted somehow to...punish me for something.... I should have understood."

He spun around to face her then. His eyes were somber, and the color had receded from his face, leaving his cheeks sallow.

"What the hell are you apologizing for?" he asked her roughly. "You understand, all right. Why do you think I've been so reluctant to make love to you? Make no mistake, Jade. You're damn right to be afraid of me...."

Dear Reader,

Welcome to Silhouette **Special Edition**...welcome to romance.

Fall is in full swing and so are some of your favorite authors, who have some delightful and romantic stories in store.

Our THAT SPECIAL WOMAN! title for the month is *Babies on Board,* by Gina Ferris. On a dangerous assignment, an independent heroine becomes an instant mom to three orphans in need of her help.

Also in store for you in October is the beginning of LOVE LETTERS, an exciting new series from Lisa Jackson. These emotional stories have a hint of mystery, as well...and it all begins in *A Is for Always.*

Rounding out the month are *Bachelor Dad* by Carole Halston, *An Interrupted Marriage* by Laurey Bright and *Hesitant Hero* by Christina Dair. Sandra Moore makes her Silhouette debut with her book, *High Country Cowboy,* as **Special Edition**'s PREMIERE author.

I hope you enjoy this book, and all of the stories to come!

Sincerely,

Tara Gavin
Senior Editor
Silhouette Books

Please address questions and book requests to:
Silhouette Reader Service
U.S.: 3010 Walden Ave., P.O. Box 1325, Buffalo, NY 14269
Canadian: P.O. Box 609, Fort Erie, Ont. L2A 5X3

LAUREY BRIGHT

AN INTERRUPTED MARRIAGE

Published by Silhouette Books
America's Publisher of Contemporary Romance

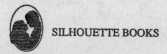 SILHOUETTE BOOKS

ISBN 0-373-09916-9

AN INTERRUPTED MARRIAGE

Copyright © 1994 by Daphne Clair de Jong

This edition published by arrangement with Harlequin Enterprises B. V.

Printed in U.S.A.

Books by Laurey Bright

Silhouette Special Edition

Deep Waters #62
When Morning Comes #143
Fetters of the Past #213
A Sudden Sunlight #516
Games of Chance #564
A Guilty Passion #586
The Older Man #761
The Kindness of Strangers #820
An Interrupted Marriage #916

Silhouette Romance

Tears of Morning #107
Sweet Vengeance #125
Long Way from Home #356
The Rainbow Way #525
Jacinth #568

Silhouette Intimate Moments

Summers Past #470

LAUREY BRIGHT

has held a number of different jobs, but has never wanted to be anything but a writer. She lives in New Zealand, where she creates the stories of contemporary people in love that have won her a following all over the world.

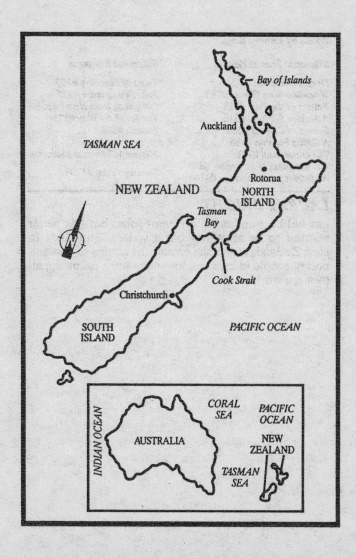

Chapter One

Everything seemed brighter than Jade remembered. The light was harsh on painted roofs, and the trees, shimmering under the beat of the sun, were implausibly green. Power poles whizzed past the car, the wires gleamed in long streaming lines, and other traffic shot by in blurs of colour.

Clenching her hands in her lap, she peeked at the dashboard in front of Magnus. The needle was steady and just within the legal speed limit.

Magnus slowed to allow room for a white van cruising onto the motorway from the side, and she gazed at his hands—strong hands, fastened tight on the steering wheel so that his knuckles showed pale against the tanned skin. She glanced at his face then, wondering if he, too, was nervous.

He turned his head slightly, his expression aloof, the deepset eyes in the clever, lean face the colour of gunmetal.

Sometimes they became softer, like a dusky evening sky, but it was a long time since she'd witnessed that sea change.

"All right?" he queried abruptly, his dark brows fractionally rising.

"Yes." Jade deliberately loosened her fingers and gave him a shaky smile.

Something flickered in his eyes and was gone. Then he returned his attention to his driving, smoothly changing lanes and accelerating. It was a new car, with comfortably moulded velour seats and plenty of leg room. Magnus needed that to accommodate his length. He was over six foot when he stood.

She said, "I'm not used to traffic anymore."

He looked at her with faint surprise. "I've taken you out a few times recently."

"Short trips," she said. "This is different."

A brief frown creased the skin between his brows. The car slowed a little as he eased his foot back on the accelerator. "Is it worrying you?"

Jade shook her head. "No, it's just . . . I have to get adjusted to things."

"We'll be there in about an hour or so."

It would be a bit more, but she supposed he was trying to reassure her. "I'm all right," she said vehemently, "really."

"I know. I wouldn't be taking you home if you weren't."

She wondered if he really believed it, but the last thing she wanted was to start an argument. Trying to be positive, she said, "I'm looking forward to being at Waititapu again."

"You'll find there have been changes."

A small chill cooled her skin. "What changes?" She knew, of course, that the younger children had left home— Danella married, Laurence attending an agricultural college down south, Andrew at boarding school.

Magnus shrugged. "The trees you planted have grown, for one thing. And there's the housekeeper."

"She won't be needed now."

But Magnus, his lips thinning, said in a carefully expressionless voice, "I think she'd better stay. For a while, at least."

Jade breathed twice, slowly. Matching his reasoned tone, she argued, "They've said I'm perfectly okay, you know. There's no need to coddle me."

"I'm sure they're right," he agreed, "but we don't want to take any risks. We'll leave the question for a few months."

That seemed to be his final word. Jade briefly dug her teeth into her lower lip, then turned her head to look out of the window. They were already approaching the Auckland Harbour Bridge, the long, upward curve rising ahead, the waters of the Waitemata below sizzling with sun sparks, and randomly sprinkled with dipping and twirling sails—white, blue, red, striped.

"How is your mother?" Jade asked as they left the bridge and headed north.

"Much the same."

Jade said after a while, "And the new nurse-aide?"

"What about her?"

"Is your mother getting on with her?"

A large maroon sedan swung too closely in front of them and Magnus braked, letting slip a violent swear-word in a savage undertone.

"Your mother doesn't like new people in the house," Jade observed when they had picked up speed again.

Magnus moved his head sharply but when she looked at him he was staring at the road ahead. His voice clipped, he said, "I'm aware it wasn't easy for you. Things are different, now. It's a big enough house."

And it should be simple for Magnus's mother and Jade to avoid each other.

Her mouth turned down in a wry grimace. She suddenly felt tired, and laid her head back against the soft upholstery. "Do you mind if I sleep?"

"Not at all."

She thought she detected relief in his voice. A sense of panic assailed her, similar to the one that had made her eyes prick with tears and her stomach churn earlier when she'd heard the big wooden door shut behind them and watched Magnus swing her suitcase into the luggage compartment of the car. She'd remained on the step, stifling a ridiculous urge to pound on the door and ask to be taken back inside, telling them she wasn't ready to leave after all. And then Magnus had slammed the lid down on her case and turned to her and said, "Coming?"

And she'd reminded herself that this was what she'd been waiting for, fighting towards. Going home with Magnus.

She dozed until they were almost halfway to Waititapu, opening her eyes when the car slowed to a crawl and then halted, the engine idling. They were passing through Orewa, a beach town where the sea was separated from the main shopping street by a grassy park or, further along, a single row of housing. Magnus had stopped to let a group of children walk over the road on a pedestrian crossing. She closed her eyes again.

Next time the car slowed on the outskirts of a small town, Jade sat up. Her neck was stiff and her mouth dry. She said, "Could we stop for a drink?"

He answered without looking at her. "Of course, if you're thirsty."

She raked back heavy honey-blond hair with her fingers, and thought restlessly that soon she'd get it decently cut.

Magnus drew up outside a dairy and said, "What would you like? A soft drink or milkshake? Or coffee?"

She looked at the shop, small and clean with high stools and a narrow bar along one wall. Across the road was a hotel with a door marked Bistro Bar. "Could we go over there?" she suggested. "For a proper drink?"

His hesitation was only momentary. "Okay," he said. "I don't suppose it will do any harm."

She bit back a retort, reminding herself that he'd got used to thinking of her as someone who had to be stopped from doing things that might harm her. She gave him a bright smile and said, "Oh, good! Thank you."

Immediately she was aware that it had sounded a wrong note, either childish or facetious. She saw the quick drawing in of his lips before he turned away from her to open the car door.

The bar was dim and almost deserted but for two men conducting a low-voiced conversation in one corner. A faint smell of stale beer mingled with the over-sweet scent of a floral air-freshener, and there was no one behind the counter.

Magnus saw her seated on a curved leather banquette in a bay window, and said, "I'll try to rustle up some service. What do you want?"

"Um . . ." She hadn't thought of what she wanted, except to express some sort of independence, celebrate her new freedom. "What is there?"

He glanced at the array of bottles over the bar. "A white wine? Or gin and lime with tonic?"

"That sounds good," she said over-eagerly. "I'll try it."

He gave her an odd look but nodded silently and went over to the bar, firmly pressing the bell-push on the counter. A man appeared from somewhere at the back and took the order.

A few minutes later Magnus put the tall glass, pleasantly bubbling and with a slice of lime on the side, before her. "Here you are." He sat opposite her with a glass of beer in front of him.

Jade picked up her glass and sipped tentatively. "This is delicious."

"Your favourite tipple."

Jade's head came up, and Magnus caught the look on her face.

"You don't remember," he said. And then, rather gently, "It doesn't matter."

She gazed back at him in dumb dismay, and swallowed a sudden rush of tears. She couldn't show that kind of weakness now, not today. He might think ... heaven knew what he might think. Fiercely, she fought for control.

"After all," Magnus said, "it's been a long time."

"Yes." She dipped her head and took a long draught of effervescent liquid. The sweet-sour taste of lime and bitter tonic underlaid with the bite of gin steadied her.

She put the glass down on the table, stained and pock-marked under dark, polished varnish, and looked out the window. A sheep truck rumbled by, making the building shiver, the closed window mercifully shutting out the inevitable smell. Through the truck's slatted sides she glimpsed a quivering nose, a dark shining eye and twitching pink ear lifted above the tightly packed huddle of stained white wool. It was safer for them to travel squeezed in like that, less chance of falling and getting injured. She hoped the closeness of others was a comfort to them. "Poor things," she murmured.

Magnus had been staring into his untouched beer. "What?"

"Nothing." She pulled her gaze away from the window. The bartender was rattling glasses, clinking bottles as he tidied the shelves. "I've never been in here before...." She paused. "Have I?"

Magnus shook his head. "Not that I know of." He picked up the glass and began to drink. She watched his head tip back, his eyes half closing, his throat taut. And had a sudden clear picture of him lying naked over her in their bed at Waititapu, his head lifted like that momentarily before he lowered it and laid his mouth on hers.

A sweet rush of longing warmed her skin, her body, setting it tingling with desire. Magnus put down the glass and as he caught her eyes she saw the quick shock in his, and the sudden colour that overlaid his cheekbones. Her lips parted and trembled on a smile, welcoming, acknowledging, promising.

His face changed and he deliberately turned away from her, idly watching as the two men in the far corner rose from their table and ambled towards the counter to chat to the bartender.

Jade felt the rebuff as though he'd physically repulsed her. She said quietly, "What's the matter, Magnus?" Her hands were cupped about her glass, the ice in her drink making them cold, and damp.

"Nothing." His eyes met hers again, and there was no emotion in them, nothing but faint boredom and a hint of impatience. He lifted the glass to his lips again, and half drained it. "Do you want some peanuts or something to go with that?" he asked her, glancing at her drink.

Jade shook her head, almost laughing at the banality of the question. But perhaps he'd been right to deliberately expunge the unexpected flare of sexual anticipation. This was hardly the place for a passionate interlude. Tonight . . .

Her blood stirred and she concentrated rigorously on her drink, half horrified and half amused at her thoughts. She peeked at Magnus, but he wasn't looking at her. It was a temptation to keep on looking at *him,* to take pleasure in the firm line of his chin, the supple skin of his neck with the slight thrust of the Adam's apple, the hollowed throat bared by the open neck of his casual shirt. If she opened the other buttons she'd find a solid masculine chest, bone and muscle firmly encased in warm skin with a teasing of wiry dark curls to tickle her palms.

Jade shook her head and quickly finished her drink. Soon they would be home, and later they would have the opportunity to rediscover each other. It would be like a second honeymoon, with the bonus that now she knew a lot more than she had the first time, about her own body and his. That was something she thanked heaven she hadn't forgotten—the deep, delicious pleasure that she and Magnus found in each other when they made love.

"Ready to go?" His voice broke in on her thoughts.

Nodding, Jade edged herself out of the banquette. He didn't touch her as he walked by her side to the car and unlocked it, opening her door. She smiled at him but he didn't seem to see it before he closed the door behind her.

"I could take a turn driving if you like," she offered as he slid into the seat beside her. "I should have mentioned it before."

"No need," he said, buckling himself in. "Anyway, you're out of practice."

"I'll have to start again sometime." Driving herself would probably be less nerve-racking, she thought, than being a passenger, and already she had lost much of her earlier anxiety.

"Let's not rush things." He started the engine, glanced behind them and moved the car out onto the roadway.

"I'm sure I'm perfectly safe behind the wheel of a car," she said as they picked up speed, feeling a perverse need to prove herself in some way. "At least I would be, given the chance."

"You'll have your chance," he assured her. "You're being over-sensitive, Jade."

She supposed she was—something she ought to watch. It wouldn't do to see implications that didn't exist.

He said, "Why don't you go to sleep again?"

"I'm not tired."

Magnus gave a small shrug. "Suit yourself."

They left the town, and the road wound through plumped-cushion hills with leftovers of blue-green bush folded into the clefts and post-and-wire fences marching across the rounded humps. A yellow-eyed hawk tearing at a dead possum on the road lifted itself reluctantly over the windscreen as the car approached, the feathers at the ends of its wide wings spread like fingers.

Taller hills rose ahead, dark, billowing cloud boiling into the sky behind them. Magnus negotiated carefully around a temporary fence erected to keep traffic safe from where the road had cracked away and was sliding into the gully on the other side.

"Has there been a lot of rain up here?" Jade asked. She'd noticed how green the hills were, the rich, emerald-green of lush pasture.

"Our tanks are still quite full," Magnus answered, "and the grass is growing well. It should be a good year for the cattle. We've had to watch the sheep and keep them on the high ground." Sheep were better on drier land, where they were less likely to get eczema and foot-rot. Waititapu was a group of farms running beef cattle and sheep as well as a large dairy herd.

They turned off the main highway and soon the smooth road gave way to a narrower, unsealed portion. The engine note changed as the road curled about the hillside, becoming steeper where ponga and manuka and shivering flags of white toetoe and silky purple pampas grass overhung it from the high banks.

Magnus slowed to a near-crawl on the steeper corners that were corrugated by previous traffic, and the dusty ferns alongside brushed the windscreen and the roof.

The entrance to Waititapu was marked by heavy posts and an open gate. The car rattled over the metal bars of the cattle stop and followed the winding driveway between totara and English oaks shading azaleas, daphne and blue hydrangeas. In spring daffodils and jonquils and scented creamy freesias fringed the drive, but now the grass edges were neatly shorn.

At the end of the drive, the house stood white, high and sprawling, and the paddocks ended in a six-wire fence at the top of a steep sandy slope to the sea.

Magnus swept the car into the big new garage and opened the door for her, and immediately Jade smelt the salty wind. When he'd got out her case they walked onto the cobbled patio behind the arched trellis connecting the house and the garage, and Jade halted, her mesmerized gaze on the riffled blue expanse lying from headland to headland and stretching to a distant, purple-limned horizon.

"I'd forgotten," she said, "how beautiful it is." Magnus was looking at her curiously as she turned to him. "Magnus—do you remember when you first brought me here?"

He said, "Yes." And then, as though he hadn't meant to, "Do you?"

"Of course I do!"

His eyelids flickered. He looked at her with a strange, probing expression and then said abruptly, "We'd better go in. You'll be getting cold out here."

There was a brisk sea breeze, but she wasn't cold. He didn't give her a chance to argue, swinging away from her with the suitcase and pushing wide the side door for her to precede him.

She stepped inside and paused, so that Magnus almost cannoned into her. She felt his steadying hand on her arm as he muttered, "Sorry. You remember your way?"

"Yes, it's just a bit dark after the sun outside." She walked along the passageway to the front hall, an impressive entry with a glass-panelled door, and a chandelier hanging from the high ceiling. A broad stairway curved down on one side.

A voice, clear and feminine but not young, called, "Magnus? You're back?"

There was a faint thudding on carpeted floorboards, and a grey-haired woman appeared in a doorway opposite the stairs. Slim and neatly groomed in a navy blue dress, she was leaning on two sticks. "And Jade," she said, her gaze resting coolly on her daughter-in-law. "Welcome home."

With genuine gratitude, Jade said, "Thank you very much. It's... nice to see you again, Mother Riordan." She crossed the hall and leaned forward to kiss a dry but scarcely lined cheek.

"You're too thin." The grey, aloof eyes were very like her son's, although a shade lighter. "That dress doesn't fit you."

Jade managed to smile. She'd specially requested that Magnus bring the flared coral linen dress for her to come home in, and a pair of high heels to go with it. "I'll have to alter some of my clothes."

"Or eat more."

"It's good of you to be concerned."

Magnus said, "Should you be standing around, Mother? Where's Ginette?"

"I told her to take some time off. I didn't want a stranger around when you brought Jade back."

Jade wondered who she had been trying to save from possible embarrassment.

"Ginny's hardly a stranger," Magnus protested mildly. "She's part of the household."

His mother's head lifted. "She's not family."

"Yes, well, why don't you sit down," Magnus suggested. "And I'll take Jade and her luggage upstairs."

"I told Mrs. Gaines you'd both have a cup of tea with me. She'll have heard the car."

"We won't be long," Magnus promised. "Come on, Jade."

He had already started up the stairs, and she followed as Mrs. Riordan returned to her sitting-room.

He glanced back and, reaching the top of the stairs, led Jade along the passageway to the room he had brought her to as his new wife. The door was open, and Jade walked in and straight over to the window, to the view she'd always loved. From here she could see the breakers lift and curve and gallop towards the shore, then unfold along the sand with lazy precision.

She heard Magnus put down the heavy case, and hoped that he would come and slide his arms about her as he often had when they'd shared the room before, nuzzling her hair or her neck, sometimes inviting her to return to the wide, white-covered bed that faced the window and the sea.

Instead, he said, "We'd better go down pretty soon or she'll start to fret."

Jade dragged her gaze away from the smooth dun of the beach, the circling gulls, the shiver of sunlight on the sea. She turned and pushed back her hair.

"Do you need to freshen up?" Magnus asked. His eyes looked remote and didn't quite meet hers. "I'll wait for you."

There was a bathroom shared with a spare bedroom next door. She said, "Would you mind putting my case on the bed for me? I'll unpack properly later, but it's got my toilet bag in it."

He did as she asked, and she opened up the suitcase, rummaging for the flowered bag. The room looked strangely empty and unlived in, the dressing table holding only a small bowl of pansies, the polished bedside tables bare. Magnus had always been a tidy person.

In the bathroom there was one toothbrush on the rack over the basin. Jade opened the mirrored cupboard above and saw a safety razor, a comb, some masculine deodorant and a bottle of aftershave lotion, finding them oddly reassuring. After rinsing her face she combed her hair and used a pink lipstick, not too bright. Mrs. Riordan didn't approve of obvious make-up.

Her cheekbones were more noticeable than when she'd last looked into this mirror, and her sea-green eyes looked larger, the lids shadowed under finely curved brows. Oddly, she didn't think she looked any older. But maybe that was something that happened so slowly you didn't notice it yourself. Certainly she felt older inside, indelibly marked by bitter experience.

Mrs. Riordan's hair had been more grey, her body rather more stooped than before, her eyes more hollowed under strong brows. And Magnus? He was the same, yet different. She couldn't read Magnus any more. Didn't know what he was thinking, feeling.

She swallowed on a sudden upwelling of grief. Magnus had suffered, too.

She would make it up to him, somehow. Starting tonight, she would make it all worthwhile for him.

Opening the door, she smiled at him, and his muscles moved in answer as though he'd forgotten what a smile was.

With a sudden surge of compassion and love, she walked over to him and put her hand against his cheek and kissed him on the lips. "It's so nice to be here, with you," she said softly.

He didn't move. His eyes seemed to grow hot, then cold. His voice harsh, he said, "We're keeping my mother waiting."

"I'm ready." Confused, she stood back from him.

"Right." He clamped a hand on her arm and marched her to the door. It was the first time he'd voluntarily touched her today, except for a perfunctory brush of his lips on her cheek when he'd come to fetch her.

All the way down the stairs he didn't look at her once. When they reached the bottom she made an uneasy movement, and he looked down at his hand on her arm and dropped it as though he hadn't realised he was holding her at all.

A solidly built middle-aged woman wearing an apron was bearing a laden tray across the hallway. Seeing them, she asked, "Did you have a good trip, Mr. Riordan?" Her gaze, discreetly curious, skimmed over Jade.

"Yes," he answered perfunctorily. "Mrs. Gaines, this is my wife. Jade, Mrs. Gaines is our housekeeper, and a great asset to us."

The woman smiled politely. "How do you do, Mrs. Riordan? I can't shake hands, I'm afraid."

"I'll take that for you," Magnus offered, relieving the housekeeper of the tray.

"Oh, thank you. If there's anything else you need—"

"This looks fine," Magnus said. "I'll bring it along to the kitchen when we've finished."

He carried the tray into the room and set it down on a round table near his mother, who had her feet up and cushions piled behind her on an antique chaise.

She said, "Thank you, Magnus. Sit down, Jade. Do you still take sugar?"

"Yes, I do."

"I'll fix it," Magnus said. He'd never had much patience with his mother's ritualistic afternoon teas. Jade hid a smile as she saw the resigned look on the older woman's face.

She sat in the chair Mrs. Riordan had waved her to, and took the cup of tea that Magnus handed to her. She'd have preferred coffee, but tea was what Mrs. Riordan always had at this time of day, and it was easier to conform.

After serving his mother, Magnus proffered a plate of sandwiches to Jade. She shook her head, too tense to be hungry.

"How are you feeling now, Jade?" Mrs. Riordan asked her.

"I'm perfectly well, thank you. And you?"

Mrs. Riordan sipped her tea. "I don't get any better."

"Aren't the new pills helping?" Magnus asked her.

"They ease the pain a little. You should eat something, Jade."

Jade reached over to the table and took a small chocolate-iced square from a glass dish and nibbled at it. It was sickly sweet and she wished she'd taken a sandwich when it was offered, but at least the chocolate square gave her an excuse not to talk. She took a mouthful of tea to wash it down.

Mrs. Riordan said to Magnus, "Danella phoned while you were away. She and Glen are coming for the weekend, with the baby."

Magnus frowned. "*This* weekend?"

His mother looked frosty. "Is it a problem?"

"Jade needs some time to settle—"

"It's all right." Jade swallowed disappointment and a flutter of trepidation. "I'll look forward to seeing the baby."

Magnus cast her a swift glance, and his mother said, "It's only right that Danella should come and introduce her family to Jade, now that she's back. A courtesy."

A new departure for Danella, then. Jade quickly stifled the thought.

"They might have waited a bit longer," Magnus said. "Are you sure you don't mind, Jade?"

"I'm not an invalid," she reminded him, keeping her voice low and even. "There's nothing to worry about." Turning to his mother, she said, "Magnus told me Danella and the baby are both doing well. I'll be interested to meet Glen, too."

"He's her choice. She wouldn't listen to anyone. I hope she won't live to regret throwing herself away."

Jade said carefully, "I suppose no one ever seems good enough for your daughter—or your son."

Magnus asked his mother, "Have you told Mrs. Gaines there'll be extra people for the weekend?"

"Yes. She's going to ask the farm manager to bring over some meat."

"Mrs. Gaines seems to be a nice woman," Jade commented.

Mrs. Riordan gave her a look of surprise. "She's very capable, and able to take direction."

Unable to think of any reply, Jade sipped at her tea in silence. Magnus said, "We were lucky to find her. Not too many women are keen on living and working out here." He glanced at Jade.

His mother said, "It's not in the wilds, Magnus. Mrs. Gaines has a very comfortable position here. And she's well paid."

Jade thought the housekeeper probably earned every cent, but refrained from giving an opinion. She allowed her mind to wander as Mrs. Riordan returned to the subject of her granddaughter. It had been an exciting, tiring day, and the room was rather stuffy. She found herself almost dozing. Blinking herself awake, she drained her cup and lowered it to her lap, and Magnus immediately stood up and said, "Finished?"

She put the cup into his outstretched hand and he replaced it on the tray. Adding his mother's cup and his own, he said, "I'll take these to Mrs. Gaines. I have some work to finish in my study, and Jade hasn't unpacked yet. Is there anything else you want before Ginette gets back?"

"Nothing, thank you, I have my book." Mrs. Riordan fumbled at her side and produced it. "I'll see you at dinner, Jade."

Jade stood up with relief, and Magnus retrieved the tray and stepped back for her to precede him to the door.

In the hallway he said, "If you need help I'm sure Mrs. Gaines won't mind—"

"I can manage," Jade assured him. Erasing any hint of complaint from her voice, she added, "Will you be long, working?"

"I may not be finished before dinner. You should probably rest for a while when you've unpacked."

"I slept in the car."

"Not for long."

"I might go for a walk on the beach later."

"Be careful," he said, but didn't offer to accompany her, and after a moment she turned to go up the stairs while he carried the tray to the kitchen.

When she was alone, the bedroom seemed larger than she remembered it. She had become accustomed to having a very small space to herself.

The suitcase was on the bed as she had left it. Kicking off her elegant high heels, she fished out a pair of comfortable sandals and put them on.

When she opened one of the matching built-in wardrobes that flanked the door to the bathroom, a scent of roses and lavender met her. Someone had placed a bowl of potpourri on the shelf above the hangers.

Most of them were empty, those clothes still left on them mostly formal or party dresses, and the lower shelf near the floor held several pairs of high-heeled shoes. She went back to the suitcase and emptied out jeans, sweatshirts and blouses, skirts and low-heeled shoes.

With a pile of undies in her hands she crossed to the long dressing table, pulling out the top drawer to put them in. She closed it and knelt to open the second drawer, sinking back on her heels.

The drawer shimmered and frothed and glowed with silk and lace and ribbons, with peach and apricot and emerald and wine-red garments that weighed next to nothing as she lifted them, that were low-cut and narrow-strapped and exceedingly sexy. She remembered the way Magnus would look at her when she waited for him, wearing one of them, her hair shiny with brushing, her skin fresh and warm from the bath and scented at throat, wrists, between her breasts and behind her knees.

She found a pale green wrap, delicately hand-embroidered, that Magnus had bought for her birthday, and laid her cheek against its soft lustre, closing her eyes. When she'd put it on for the first time, after a bath, and re-entered the bedroom, he'd drawn her to the bed and stroked her body through the fabric, then eased the garment away from her until his hand met her bare skin and kept on stroking. "Satin," he'd murmured. "You're all satin."

* * *

A creaking sound made her eyes fly open, her cheeks flushing. She stumbled to her feet, recalling that the house talked quietly in the late afternoon, its joints making small protesting noises as the sun cooled. It had been built in the thirties, replacing a homestead that had stood on the property since the last century. There had been alterations over the years—extra bathrooms and, of course, kitchen renovations, and the old garage had been turned into a bedsitting-room for Mrs. Riordan's nurse-aide when Magnus had the new four-car garage erected.

Jade put the satin robe on the bed beside the modest, opaque garments she'd removed from the suitcase. The lovely nightgowns she'd worn at home had hardly been suitable for institutional living; they were meant for the intimacy of a bedroom shared with a lover—a husband.

Picking up the small heap of cotton nightwear, she dumped them on the floor of the wardrobe. She'd give them to the Red Cross or the Salvation Army.

She turned to close the empty suitcase. It had probably come from the spare room on the other side of the bathroom, where they had used to store such things. She went through, carrying the case.

The bedspread had been changed. Jade remembered a quilt heavily patterned with dusky pink roses. The new cover featured an abstract design in dark blues and reds with streaks of gold. Interesting and dramatic. She supposed that male guests might have found the overblown roses a bit much for their taste.

She turned to open one of the wardrobes that twinned the pair in the main bedroom, and stepped back in surprise.

The hangers were fully occupied with shirts, trousers, suits and jackets, and several pairs of men's shoes were on the lower shelf. She made to hastily close the door, a reflex action to the unintentional invasion of someone's privacy. Then she paused, her heart thudding, and raised a hand to touch a jacket sleeve, her eyes puzzled. She looked down at the shoes, and swung round to survey the room, that she now realised had a distinct air of being lived in.

No wonder the other bedroom had seemed larger, barer. The tallboy that had always been there had been moved in here. How stupid, she thought, not to have noticed. A man's brush and comb sat atop the chest, alongside the small tooled-leather box where Magnus habitually kept his cuff-links and tie-pins. On the bedside table a pair of burnished metal bookends held several paperbacks and two volumes with library numbers on their spines, and lying beside them was a magazine. She walked over to inspect the date and found it was this week's.

Jade swallowed hard, and went back to the master bedroom, flinging open the doors of the second wardrobe there.

It was empty but for a few forlorn hangers and a couple of bags stowed on the top shelf.

When had Magnus moved out of their room?

And *why?*

Chapter Two

Jade backed away from the wardrobe and slumped down on the bed, her brain grabbing at snatches of logic, of comfort. He'd been unable to bear sleeping in the bed they'd shared, without her? He'd moved out temporarily to accommodate some guests and just never bothered to bring his things back? But surely there was plenty of room for guests without such an upheaval.

Other possible answers didn't bear thinking of. She got up, hurrying into the other room again, closing the wardrobe, removing the suitcase, breathing quickly with relief as she reached her own room, before she realised the absurdity of her anxiety to hide her knowledge of where Magnus had obviously been sleeping lately. Nothing had been locked, after all. And certainly Magnus was no Bluebeard.

The thought made her smile, and steadied her. There must be a perfectly ordinary, understandable explanation. She only had to ask him.

She was out of the room and had run down the stairs before she hesitated in sudden doubt, her hand still on the smooth polished rail. He might not welcome the interruption.

Too bad. She needed an answer. Removing her hand from the stair rail, she lifted her head and walked across the hall.

Mrs. Riordan's voice called, "Is that you, Ginette?"

"No," Jade answered reluctantly, stopping at the open doorway. "It's me," she said. "Did you want something, Mother Riordan? I don't think Ginette's around."

"Jade." The book she'd been reading lay open on Mrs. Riordan's lap. The sun had left the room, and it seemed gloomy. "Come in."

Jade advanced a few steps. "Is there something I can do for you?"

"It's getting cool. My knee-rug—it's on the chair over there."

A wheelchair stood in one corner, a checked mohair rug folded on the seat. Jade fetched the rug and placed it over Mrs. Riordan's legs. "Anything else?"

"Not at the moment. Why don't you sit down?" she suggested.

"I . . . was going to see Magnus," Jade said.

"Is it so urgent?"

Jade shook her head and took one of the high-backed chairs. "Did you want to talk to me?"

Mrs. Riordan closed the book on her lap and sat holding it tightly. "I wonder if you realise," she said, "how fortunate you are in having Magnus as your husband."

"I assure you I do," Jade answered her. "I know that Magnus has made great sacrifices for me, that things have been . . . hard for him."

"It's something that you acknowledge that. I should tell you," the older woman said, looking straight at her, "that I advised him to divorce you."

Jade paled. "It would have been understandable."

"Magnus has a very strong sense of loyalty."

That cuts more than one way, Jade thought grimly.

Mrs. Riordan continued, "He's never shirked a responsibility. And he feels responsible for you, as his wife."

Jade met the penetrating gaze and said calmly, "I think he feels a good deal more than that. Magnus and I love each other."

A look of remote scorn crossed the other woman's face. "Love! Is that what you call it?"

Her head lifting, Jade said, "I don't know what else to call it. It's why we married each other."

A faint colour came into Mrs. Riordan's sallow cheeks. "Magnus married you because he needed someone to give him practical help after his father died and I became—as I am now. He knew you were efficient as his secretary and I suppose he'd already discovered that you were equally so in his bed. I thought at one time that you were genuinely in love with him, and even felt a little sorry for you because of it. You were, after all, very young at the time."

"I was twenty-one."

"Very young," Mrs. Riordan repeated, "to be married to a man ten years older."

"Nine."

Mrs. Riordan made a dismissive gesture. "I suppose he thought you would give him children."

Jade's hands clenched tightly before she deliberately relaxed them. She said, "There's still time. Actually, Magnus didn't w—"

Mrs. Riordan's gaze sharpened as Jade halted in mid-sentence, but she said nothing.

"Things will be different now," Jade said firmly. "And I'm afraid I don't think it's... appropriate to discuss my marriage—with anyone." She stood up. "If that's all you wanted...?"

A door opened and closed and light, quick footsteps traversed the uncarpeted passageway. A young woman appeared in the doorway of the room. Her dark hair was swept back into a knot, her brown eyes questioning as they met Jade's.

She wore jeans that showed off a nicely proportioned, curvy figure, and a cropped top displaying a firm tanned midriff. In one hand she had a large plastic carrybag with a shop logo printed on it. "I'm back, Mrs. Riordan," she said. "Sorry, am I interrupting?"

"I was just leaving," Jade said. "You're Ginette?"

The young woman gave her an alert, curious look. "That's right. You must be—"

"This is my son's wife," Mrs. Riordan said.

Ginette held out her hand. "Hello. I'm pleased to meet you at last, Mrs. Riordan." Her clasp was firm and seemed friendly.

"Call me Jade, please."

"Thanks. With two of you in the house it could get confusing." Turning to the older woman, Ginette added, "I'll just go and get changed, then I'll be right with you."

"Yes." Mrs. Riordan was eyeing the skimpy top. "You'd better change."

Ginette stood back for Jade to go out first, and threw her a wry look before hurrying off down the passageway.

Shaken by the confrontation with his mother, Jade found herself wavering in her decision to confront Magnus. She hesitated, then walked to the front door, down the broad steps and across the springy short grass to the ragged edge above the beach. Here it was not fenced, and she kicked off her shoes and went on down the uneven, sandy slope, her feet sinking into warmth and gritty softness.

The beach had a slight downward slope, and she found firmer, cooler sand to walk on where the tide had recently receded, leaving behind glistening bits of driftwood and scattered shells.

A small breeze ruffled her skirt and her hair, and she shook her head back, then gave in to an impulse and ran— ran along the curving tide line, with the wind on her face and the sand under her feet, for the sheer joy of being there.

She didn't stop running until she reached the water-worn grey rocks at the base of the headland, and then she climbed them until she found one that was almost flat on top, and sat there with the flared skirt of her dress drawn round her knees, hugging them and staring out at the sea until her breathing was perfectly steady and the sky was washed faintly with pink, the horizon gradually darkening.

She stood up at last, discovering that her limbs had stiffened, and looked towards the house. It gleamed white, the windows dark and opaque, and as she gazed at it a man came out of the door and stood looking about him. Magnus.

He was too far away for Jade to hail him. She scrambled down the rocks and briskly retraced her steps along the sand. From there she could see the top storey of the house, but knew that she'd be invisible to Magnus unless he came to the edge of the grass where he could look down on the beach.

She had nearly reached the spot where she'd climbed down before she saw him there. She waved, and he lifted a hand in return, but didn't come to meet her. When she paused at the foot of the slope, she saw that he had her shoes in one hand, and only then did he come down a short way and stretch out his free hand to help her to the top.

He released her as soon as her feet reached the grass, and stepped back, holding out her shoes. Jade took them but didn't put them on. The coarse grass would help to get the clinging sand off her feet.

"Were you looking for me?" she asked him, tucking her hand into his as they walked.

For a moment his fingers were rigid in hers before they curled about her hand. "It's dinner time," he said. "We wondered where you were."

She had a watch, but she wasn't used to checking the time for meals. It hadn't occurred to her. "I'm sorry, I suppose I should have come in earlier. I didn't notice the time."

"You enjoyed the beach?"

"It's as beautiful as I remember."

He glanced down at her and seemed to think better of whatever he'd been going to say. "Ginette's back—Mother's nurse-aide. You'll meet her at dinner."

"We've already met. I was talking to your mother when she arrived this afternoon. She's young."

"She's about your age."

She looked younger, Jade thought.

They were nearing the door, and Magnus loosed her fingers and opened it for her. "If you want to go up and change, I'll let them know you're on the way."

"I don't need to change—do I?" Her dress might have got slightly creased but it was still presentable. As he shook his head, she added, "I'll wash my hands and get the sand off my feet, and be down in five minutes. Don't wait for me."

She ran up the stairs, and was as good as her word. When she hurried into the dining-room with the big bay windows overlooking the sea, the housekeeper was just serving the first course.

"I'm sorry, Mrs. Gaines," Jade said as the woman passed her on the way out of the room. "I didn't realise how late it was."

"It's mostly cold anyway," the housekeeper said.

There was salad and cold roast pork, but also steaming new potatoes and fresh peas boiled with mint and sugar. Mrs. Riordan, in her wheelchair, sat at the foot of the large dining table, opposite her son. Ginette was on Magnus's right, and Jade slipped into the empty chair on his left with a murmur of apology.

Magnus passed her a dish of potatoes and turned to Ginette. "How was your afternoon?"

Ginette had an elusive dimple by her mouth, Jade noticed, making her smile particularly attractive. "I had a lovely time, thank you. I went to Warkworth and did some shopping. Found some quite nice things. This dress, for instance." She looked down at the low-cut cotton dress, sleeveless and smothered with tiny blue flowers.

"It's very nice," Magnus said, inspecting what he could see of it.

The dimple flashed. "Thank you, Magnus."

Jade stiffened in the act of forking a piece of meat from its platter. The housekeeper had called Magnus "Mr. Riordan." The two women were of different generations, of course, she reminded herself. Carefully she lowered the pork to her plate. It would be stupid to get upset just because an attractive young woman called her husband by his first name.

She smiled across the table at Ginette. "What else did you buy?"

"Oh, not much. Couldn't afford to—not that I'm not well paid," she added hastily, with another glance at Magnus, "but I'm saving to buy a car."

"You don't have one?"

Ginette shook her head. "Magnus gave me the use of one."

"It goes with the job," Magnus explained.

"I see."

Mrs. Riordan said precisely, "Magnus bought another car so that Ginette could take me about, and so she needn't bother him to provide transport for her on her days off."

Jade tried not to flush. She hadn't been criticising, merely making conversation. "It sounds like a very sensible arrangement."

She busied herself with her meal, letting the conversation drift around her. They spoke of ongoing household and farm matters that she'd had no chance to learn about, and people she didn't know. But Magnus turned to her as they were discussing a family whose eldest son had apparently won a scholarship to study in America. "You'd remember the Beazleys, Jade," he said.

She frowned blankly. The name meant nothing. "No," she said, "I'm afraid I don't. How long have they lived around here?"

Mrs. Riordan said dryly, "About twelve years."

"They have the Mediterranean-style house about four miles down the road," Magnus said, "and a large family. Terry is the same age as Andrew."

Andrew, the youngest Riordan, had been twelve the year that Jade arrived at Waititapu. She recalled vaguely a number of seemingly interchangeable youngsters who used to arrive on horseback or bicycle with him at odd times, always apparently in dire need of immediate sustenance, no matter what the time of day. Had one of them been Terry Beazley?

"I remember the house," Jade said, recalling that they'd passed it on the way here, and it had been quite familiar to her. "But the people—" She shook her head. "Perhaps when I see them...."

Mrs. Riordan said, "They're practically our neighbours!"

Magnus said, "I explained to you, Mother. Don't worry about it, Jade. As you say, it will probably come back to you when you meet them again."

Jade nodded, still frowning. "It's rather hit-or-miss, I'm afraid," she said. "I'm sorry."

"Not your fault," Magnus told her. "We know that." He was looking at his mother. He turned his attention to Ginette, asking if she needed more petrol for the car.

Jade's eyes wandered about the familiar room. There was a new picture on the cream-papered wall, a vase she didn't recognise on the sideboard, and the sideboard itself had been shifted to make room for the small tea-trolley that used to be kept in the main living-room.

She realised that she was very sleepy, and blinked, giving herself a little shake.

"Something wrong, Jade?" Magnus asked her.

Her head jerked up, her eyes wide. "I'm a bit tired, that's all."

She wished immediately that she hadn't said it. Magnus was inspecting her face rather thoroughly. He said, "You'd better have an early night."

Her voice was higher than she'd meant it to be. "I've had enough early nights, thank you. And enough of people deciding for me what to do and when to go to bed."

There was a short silence, broken by Ginette's light, pretty laugh. "Well, that's telling you, Magnus." Turning to Jade, she added, "All the same, he could be right, you know. It's a stressful experience, coming home." Her brown eyes were compassionate, her smile understanding. It wasn't fair that her sensible advice made Jade's teeth clench. Ginette was a nurse and no doubt was accustomed to summing up patients' needs.

But Jade wasn't her patient. She was no one's. It took some willpower to bite back the urge to tell Ginette so. "I suppose it is," she said. "More so than I realised."

Perhaps she'd expected too much of her homecoming. More of Magnus's time, for instance. When she ought to have known that Magnus rarely had time to spare. That hadn't changed, she reflected rather caustically.

Mrs. Riordan hadn't mellowed, either—the reverse, if anything. Before, she had usually accepted Jade's presence with dignified tolerance if little warmth. This afternoon she had shown real dislike and antagonism. Although she'd made a reasonable recovery from the stroke she'd suffered after her husband's death, the after-effects, coupled with the pain from her chronic arthritis, had left her highly irritable, and that obviously had not improved with time.

Mrs. Gaines came in to clear the plates and place a dessert decorated with cream and strawberries on the table. When Mrs. Riordan had helped herself and Magnus passed the bowl to her, Jade shook her head. "I've had enough, really. I'll just wait for coffee." It was true she was feeling unusually well fed. The meat and vegetables, while plain and wholesome, had been deliciously fresh and neither overcooked nor barely warm.

Mrs. Riordan said, "Nonsense. Give her some pudding, Magnus. It'll do her good."

Jade felt her hands fasten hard on the seat of her chair. "I don't want pudding, thank you," she said clearly. "Pass it to Ginette, Magnus."

She met his eyes, held them with hers. And after a moment he silently placed the bowl on the other side of the table in front of the nurse.

Ginette said brightly, "I wish I had your willpower, Jade. Mrs. Gaines makes such superb sweets and cakes."

"It's not willpower," Jade said, her stomach churning with tension. "I'll have to get used to eating good food again."

"I thought the food was all right?" Magnus said, his voice sharp. "You told me it was."

"It was wholesome and adequate," Jade said wearily. "There wasn't anything wrong with it."

Ginette, pushing the bowl towards Magnus, made a sympathetic face. "Food cooked in bulk does tend to be bland and stodgy. And keeping it warm dries it out."

Jade said, "Exactly."

Thankfully, the others soon finished their dessert, and Mrs. Gaines brought in coffee and the plate of chocolate biscuits with which Mrs. Riordan liked to finish the evening meal. No one commented this time when Jade declined to take one.

She was glad when they were able to leave the table. Magnus went round to push his mother's wheelchair. She said, "Take me to my sitting-room, Magnus, thank you."

He obeyed without comment, Ginette following along behind, and Jade stood uncertainly at the doorway of the dining-room. Mrs. Gaines came hurrying along from the kitchen, a large tray in her hands. Moving aside for her, Jade said, "Can I help?"

"That's all right, Mrs. Riordan. I can manage," the woman said.

"You'd better call me Jade, don't you think? We could have some confusion, otherwise."

"If you like," the housekeeper agreed equably. Unexpectedly, she added, "My name's Netta."

"Thank you."

Magnus came out of his mother's room. He said, "Do you want to sit in the lounge for a while, Jade? Ginette may join us later."

"I was hoping to talk to you," she said. "Could we go for a walk?"

"In the dark?"

They'd often walked in the dark before, arms about each other in the moonlight, with the spent sea swaying and hushing beside them and the night air cooling their skin. Sometimes they'd even swum together, naked in the concealing blackness, and sometimes they'd made love on the beach, spreading towels or discarded clothing beneath them, and later laughing together at the gritty sand that nevertheless clung to their damp limbs and had to be washed off in the waves.

"We can find our way," Jade said. "Can't we?"

Some expression lit his eyes for a moment, and she thought he, too, was remembering. But he quickly doused it. "All right," he said. "Will you be warm enough?" He eyed the short sleeves of her dress, the scooped neckline.

"It can't be that cold outside." She turned towards the door so that he had no choice but to follow.

They walked side by side, their feet making no sound on the cushioning grass. She wanted to hook her arm into his, but he seemed distant, almost a stranger, keeping nearly a foot of space between them, his hands thrust into his pockets.

The water gleamed in the light of an egg-shaped orange moon. Jade paused at the top of the sand to take off her shoes while Magnus waited, his eyes on her but his body half-turned away. When she ran down the slope, her feet sinking into the soft, now cooled sand, he followed more slowly, joining her at the bottom.

"What did you want to talk about?" he asked her as they found the firmer part of the beach and walked parallel to the restless, white-glimmering waves.

"Us," Jade said. It was a large subject that might occupy the rest of their lives.

Magnus said, "I know it's necessary, but... tonight?"

Jade took a quick step ahead so that she could turn and face him. She said provocatively, "You have a better idea?"

He didn't laugh, or reach for her, or react visibly in any way. Perhaps the moon didn't give enough light for him to read the flirtatious challenge in her eyes, the curve of her lips. Standing rock-still, he said, "You've only just got here. Wouldn't it be wiser to postpone any heavy discussions for a day or two? Give yourself a chance to adjust?"

"Myself," she said, "or you?"

"Both of us, perhaps."

"Magnus—why have you moved out of our room?"

It seemed a long time before he answered. "I thought... you might prefer it."

Her heart thudding uncomfortably, Jade said, "Prefer to sleep apart from you?"

He seemed to be studying her carefully. "You wouldn't?"

Jade made a helpless gesture, not understanding him. "You're my husband, Magnus."

"Yes," Magnus said, and then he added, unbelievably, "Has it occurred to you that since we've spent the requisite two years living apart, it would be quite easy to get a divorce?"

Chapter Three

Divorce? The word echoed in her head, louder than the sound of the breakers rolling in from the sea. His mother had advised Magnus to divorce her, she remembered. Apparently he was ready to take the advice.

And he was still speaking, his voice composed, even. "Sharing a room would muddy the waters as far as the court is concerned. You hadn't considered that?"

Jade opened her mouth, her lips moved. Her voice seemed distant, hardly her own. "No, I hadn't. The thought never crossed my mind." She felt numb. Somewhere there was an enormous pain waiting to crash over her, but for the moment the numbness mercifully held it at bay.

"Never?"

Jade shook her head. It was difficult to say anything. Had she been stupid? It was entirely possible that Magnus had found someone else. Not only possible, probable. She ought to have expected this.

Who is she? was the question screaming in her mind, but her lips refused to form the words. Instead she said, grasping at random thoughts, "You've been so faithful!" Immediately shaking her head, she amended, "I mean, you visited so regularly."

"Once you could bear me to."

She whispered, "I didn't mean to—"

"Forget it."

"But I am grateful," she said stumblingly. She hadn't thought she'd ever have to say that. Not to Magnus. It was the kind of thing that people who loved each other didn't need to put into words.

He took a sharp breath. Without moving he seemed to have withdrawn to a greater distance. "Gratitude is the last thing I want. You needn't feel obligated to me in any way."

Obligated. Was that how he felt? "Your visits, the fact that you cared enough, helped me get well—"

"'In sickness and in health,'" he reminded her.

"A duty?"

The sound of the waves filled the pause that he allowed to elapse. "I happen to take the promises of the marriage service very seriously."

Jade gulped in a breath. She mustn't scream at him. *"Then why are you talking about divorce?"*

Magnus hesitated. Then he said, "It's an option."

She wanted to dispute that, hotly. It had never been an option for her. So far as she was concerned, marriage was for life. Then she thought she was being selfish. And unrealistic. "I know that I've made things very difficult, that you've put up with tremendous pressures, made sacrifices that no man should be asked to make. I can't blame you if you've found—" She couldn't go any further, gagging on the words, *someone else.*

And somewhere deep inside quiet rage mingled with the pain—rage that his love hadn't withstood the test after all, hadn't been strong enough to sustain itself.

Magnus said harshly, "That's not the point. I suppose I wasn't entirely blameless—"

"It wasn't your fault."

"You're generous. I wouldn't have been surprised if you'd accused me of gross neglect, and laid all your... failures at my door."

"Failures?" Jade winced.

Magnus said swiftly, "A bad choice of words. And not quite what I meant."

Jade swallowed. She accepted the apology, but the remark had wounded. Was their marriage one of the failures?

Yesterday she'd have said it wasn't. To be fair, she could hardly expect their relationship to pick up where it had left off—or rather, at some point before that. But naïvely, she'd supposed that since they had weathered the past couple of years, the readjustment would be relatively easy, that nothing now could part them or thwart their love.

She'd been wrong, it seemed. Magnus had been chafing for his freedom—for how long she could only guess. What, then, had brought him to her side every weekend, and led him to bring her back to his home now? Guilt? Compassion? A sense of obligation, a determination to keep to the letter of his marriage vows until he had irrevocably cast them off? Had he felt trapped, wanting to free himself but bound by his conscience to wait until she could fend for herself?

The paling moon had turned cold. Jade shivered in its merciless light. "I don't know... how to answer you," she said painfully. "I wasn't prepared for this."

"I'd hoped to postpone this discussion, not spring it on you right away, but you have rather forced it on me." He paused again. "We can't just put the clock back, Jade."

To match his self-sacrifice, she ought to let him go without a murmur, as reparation for the time and the emotional investment he had expended on her, on helping her get well.

She couldn't. He was her husband and with her dying breath she would fight to win back his love, the love they had shared with such passion, and joy, and mutual commitment. They'd had more than sex to bind them. Much more. Impossible to believe that all that had died.

He hadn't moved, only a faint flutter of his shirt indicating that he'd taken a quick, silent breath.

A chill shock swirling round her feet reminded her of the incoming tide. Magnus hadn't seemed to notice, although his shoes were wet.

She stepped back, feeling a little dizzy. "I don't think I can deal with this at the moment. I *am* tired, after all," she said truthfully. "I think I'll take your advice and go to bed early. You needn't come back to the house with me."

He accepted the hint, only moving a few feet from the foaming, hissing water, then remaining there as she hurried away from him across the sand.

When she was sure he wouldn't see the gesture in the darkness, Jade scrubbed furtively at the tears streaming down her face. She stumbled onto the flat surface of the lawn and continued across the cool, harsh grass to the house, not remembering her sandals until she'd reached the door. She barely hesitated then, before letting herself in quietly, creeping along the darkened passageway and bolting up the stairs.

Thankful that no one had seen her, she shut herself into her room, and leaned on the door for a second or two before going to the bathroom. There she switched on the light and began sluicing her face with cold water.

Her eyes were only slightly reddened when she looked at herself in the mirror, but her cheeks looked pale and pinched, showing the effects of shock.

She laid her throbbing forehead against the cool glass, fighting down a sense of panic. She could cope. Everyone—she, the doctors, Magnus—had made sure she was thoroughly well before allowing her to return to Waititapu.

They'd warned her that if she felt she was regressing, she must not delay in seeking help. But she knew in her bones that she was as strong now as any other woman—stronger than she'd been before. She'd come through this—*they* would come through it, she and Magnus. Their marriage would survive.

She didn't know what time it was when Magnus returned to the house, but it was hours after she'd left him alone on the beach before he came upstairs. In spite of a feeling of utter weariness, Jade hadn't slept. She heard him walk to her door, and pause there.

Holding her breath, she waited. After a moment the door silently opened, and a shadow slipped through the gap, closing it behind him.

She said quietly, "Magnus?"

The shadow stilled. "I didn't intend to wake you."

"I couldn't sleep."

He moved forward, then stopped. "I found your shoes. Where do you want them?"

"Oh." She was emotionally drained, too much so to feel anything, even disappointment. "Leave them by the wardrobe—I'll put them away in the morning. Thank you."

He stooped and straightened again, and seemed to hesitate. She held her breath, wanting to break the silence, unable to think of anything to say. It was all very different from the fantasies she'd indulged in when they'd said she was ready to leave the hospital.

Then the moment passed, and he said, "Good night, Jade."

She watched him move towards the bathroom, saw the faint light that split the darkness as he opened the door. He closed it behind him, and was gone.

She woke late the next morning to a surreal sense of disconnection. Everything was very quiet, and instead of a curtained alcove, she was lying in a room that seemed at first sight vast. When she realised where it was, her eyes instinctively turned to the pillow next to her, finding it plump and untouched.

Maybe she'd dreamed yesterday. Maybe she wasn't home at all, but hallucinating. She sat up, clutching at the sheet, pushed back her hair and looked about her. She reached out and ran her fingers over the bedside table. The solid, grained wood seemed real enough.

Now she heard the distant, constant susurration of the sea, and a seagull's lifted scream. Downstairs a door snapped shut, and there was a faint hum that she identified as the sound of a vacuum cleaner.

But it was the sandals neatly placed side-by-side in front of the wardrobe that convinced her.

Yesterday, last night, hadn't been a dream. Magnus had brought her home, and evaded her for the remainder of the afternoon by shutting himself in his study, and Mrs. Riordan had told her that she'd advised a divorce. The suggestion had scarcely impinged, because she'd never have believed that Magnus would countenance the thought.

And then Magnus, walking with her on the beach but not touching her, had said that it was "an option." Magnus, her

beloved, her husband, who had unfailingly and unstint-
ingly given her all the support, and all the love—she'd
thought—that she'd needed so badly, had hinted that he
wanted a divorce.

For long minutes she was tempted to huddle under the
blankets again, deny everything to herself and hope that the
pain, the regrets, the disbelief, would go away.

But she knew where that could lead. Instead, she flung
back the covers and made herself wash, and dress in jeans
and a loose top, and comb her hair.

Her face was still pale, the skin about her eyes faintly
darkened. She rummaged in a drawer and found still us-
able foundation, blusher, eye shadow, and a defiantly bright
lipstick. The wand of mascara had dried up. Since she'd left
them here she'd scarcely cared enough to be bothered with
more than an occasional dash of lipstick.

She must find out if anyone was going to Warkworth.
Apart from a haircut there were several things she needed.

She made the bed with quick efficiency. It didn't need
much, looked scarcely used in fact. Not the way it would
have been if Magnus had shared it last night...

Closing her mind to the thought, she straightened with
flushed cheeks and left the room. He would share her bed
again one day. Somehow she would make sure of it.

Downstairs, the door to Mrs. Riordan's sitting-room was
closed. Relieved, Jade made her way to the kitchen.

There was no one there, the stainless-steel bench gleaming and the sink empty. A bowl of flowers stood on the
window-ledge between unfamiliar looped net curtains with
small orange spots. The café curtains printed with tiny blue
tulips must have worn out.

The dishwasher humming and swishing in one corner was
new, too. The big old table with the handsomely turned legs
in the centre of the room was the same, though, its scrubbed

and scarred surface covered with a cheerful orange ging-
ham cloth, and another bowl of flowers sat in the middle of
it.

Jade bent and sniffed at the frilled pinks. The scent
somehow cheered her. She looked about and found the
toaster with the bread bin beside it. And a new coffee-
maker.

When Mrs. Gaines came in Jade was sitting at the table
with an empty cereal bowl and a plate of toast crumbs before her, sipping her way through a second cup of coffee.

"Oh! Good morning." The housekeeper stopped in the
doorway.

"I hope you don't mind. I know breakfast was well over
when I got up. I'll wash my dishes and get out of your way."
Jade finished the coffee quickly, and rose.

"Mr. Riordan said not to disturb you. The vacuum
cleaner didn't wake you? I only used it downstairs."

Jade had turned on the hot tap and was rinsing the dishes,
placing the cup on the bench with the plates leaning on it.
"You didn't wake me." She reached for a tea-towel, only to
find that the rail on the wall had been replaced by a unit
holding paper towels and plastic cling film. Dismissing an
irrational dismay, she asked, "Where is the tea-towel kept
now?"

Mrs. Gaines opened a drawer and handed her one.

"Do you need any help?" Jade asked. "I'm used to
housework." At the hospital the patients who were not too
ill had been rostered to help with the cleaning. *"Rehabili-
tation, they call it,"* Annie had said, grinning at Jade from
the corner of her mouth, a spray of untidy red curls spring-
ing free from the edges of the cotton scarf that was supposed to confine them. *"Saving money, more like. Well,
personally I'd rather be polishing floors than plaiting bloody*

baskets with Miss Ivan the Cherrible. That's enough to send anyone nuts!"

Jade smiled, remembering. Miss Cherrible, the occupational therapist, had been relentlessly kind and implacably cheerful, and a major irritant to Annie. Jade had to agree that at times the relative boredom of cleaning wards was preferable to the firmly maintained *bonhomie* of the therapy room.

Magnus had been at first horrified and angry that she was wiping floors and changing beds and peeling the potatoes in the kitchen. Jade had to talk him out of complaining that the patients were being used as cheap labour. "I don't mind," she'd told him. "Really, it's better to have something to pass the time, and at least it's useful. You didn't object to my doing housework and cooking at Waititapu."

"That's an entirely different thing!" he'd exploded. "Waititapu was your home."

And then he'd fallen silent and grim-lipped when she laughed.

Mrs. Gaines seemed rather nonplussed by Jade's offer of help. "It's kind of you, Mrs.—er, Jade. But I have my routines, you know."

"Well, let me know if there's anything I can do. Do you know where my husband is?"

"Not exactly. He said he'd be back for lunch."

Magnus wasn't in the house, then. "Lunch will be at twelve?"

"Mrs. Riordan likes it dead on twelve. But I suppose if you wanted to change it—"

Jade said hastily, "There's no need to change anything."

When she re-entered the hall Ginette was closing the door of Mrs. Riordan's sitting-room. This morning she wore a simple button-through frock in small green-and-white hounds-tooth checks, almost like a uniform. She smiled at Jade. "Hello. Have a good sleep?"

"Too long," Jade said briefly. Hesitating, she added, "I wondered if I ought to say good morning to Mrs. Riordan."

"She's resting just now. She'll read a couple of chapters and then drop off for a little while before lunch. I'll come and wake her at about a quarter to twelve. It gives me time to do my aerobics, and take a walk down the drive to fetch the mail."

It seemed everyone had their routine. "I could get the mail," Jade said. "I wouldn't mind a walk."

"Oh, all right. The rural delivery van won't be here until about half past eleven, though."

"That's later than it used to be."

"Is it? I wouldn't know. See you at lunch." Flashing another dimpling smile, Ginette strolled off to her room.

Jade let herself out of the big door facing away from the sea. The concrete terrace, newly painted a terracotta colour, ended in several steps down to a wide path skirting the house.

She crossed the lawn to a gateway leading into a small fenced grove of trees and bushes, all natives, with a narrow gravelled path winding between them. The three kohuhu with crinkled, pink-edged leaves were almost twice her height, giving her a thrill of pleasure. When she'd planted them they had barely reached her waist. Another, shrubbier group with dark, wine-coloured leaves made a lovely foil, just as she'd pictured them.

Purple hebe brushed her jeans as she passed. The golden kowhai had long since finished flowering, but among the saw-edged leaves of the rewarewa she spied a red, spidery blossom. The kauri still stood straight and slender.

"For the grandchildren," she'd told Magnus when he teased her about its notoriously slow growth habit. "And great-grandchildren."

"Mmm," he'd said. "I suppose by then it might be a decent-sized tree."

Weeds had been allowed to spring up among the low creepers and ground-covers. Jade hauled some out, thinking that she'd have to get some tools later and do the job properly. But she managed to pile up quite a heap pulling them out by hand.

A distant toot made her glance at her watch. That was probably the rural delivery van, signalling that there was mail in the box at the gate.

She stood up from where she'd been kneeling on the ground, and dusted her jeans. But her hands were grubby, too, so it didn't do a lot of good.

She walked quickly down the drive, her feet scrunching on the gravel. Sunlight flittered through the moving leaves of the trees, dancing in dappled patches before her. A fantail looped through the air about her head, then retired to chirrup at her from a swaying, slender branch, regarding her with alert, unwinking eyes. She had a sudden sense of well-being, a lift of the heart.

The red mailbox held several envelopes. None, of course, was for her, but she riffled through them all the same. Two were addressed to Miss Ginette Fairfield. Jade wondered if Ginette got a lot of mail. Was that why she'd apparently made a habit of collecting it?

She went back to the house more slowly. Coming out of the shading trees of the drive, she saw Magnus seated on a tractor that had stopped by the fence surrounding the house. He wore a faded khaki shirt and trousers, one arm resting on the steering wheel as he grinned down at Ginette, who leaned on a fence post, smiling up at him.

Ginette's costume was a clinging pink satin leotard, worn with matching pink socks, and exercise shoes. Her breasts were rounded and full, her waist slim, and her hips trimly curved. A pink sweat-band confined her hair. An escapee from an exercise video, Jade thought, walking, unnoticed, towards them.

As she did so Ginette laughed, pulled off the sweat-band and shook out her dark curls, then stepped back from the fence. Magnus lightly jumped down from the tractor and vaulted the fence with one hand on the post.

He saw Jade, and the smile faded. Ginette, following his eyes, took another step back from him and waited.

"Any mail for me?" she asked as Jade neared them.

"Two." Jade's face felt stiff, but she managed a semblance of a smile. Ginette's letters were on top of the pile, and she handed them over, noticing how grubby her hands still were, with dirt under the fingernails.

Ginette glanced down at the envelopes. "I love getting letters, don't you?"

Did her tone sound forced? Jade quelled the thought. "You're lucky. Do you want the rest, Magnus?"

He took them from her. "You've been all the way to the gate?"

"It's still where the mailbox is."

"Are you sure that's wise, in this heat?"

"What do you think it will do to me? It's not that hot under the trees. You've been working in it. And without a hat."

"I haven't been ill."

Ginette said, "I'd better get changed before lunch. See you guys later." She set off for the house at a quick jog, the gleaming, high-cut leotard emphasising the movement of smooth thighs and a firm, neat behind. Magnus looked after her for a second or so before pulling his gaze away.

Jade said, "A walk in the sun certainly isn't going to cause a relapse. What were you talking about?"

"What?" He frowned.

"You and Ginette—what were you talking about?"

"Nothing much. Just chat." He looked down at the envelopes in his hand, and began to tear one open, at the same time starting towards the house. "Did you have a good sleep?"

"Yes, thank you. How long is it since Ginette came to work here?"

He was skimming the letter in his hand. It was a second or two before he looked up. "Ginette? It's coming up to three months, I think, since the first woman left and she took over. Why?"

"I couldn't remember when you'd first mentioned her."

"At the time you weren't particularly interested."

Jade bit her lip. "I'm sorry." Three months ago she'd begun a new treatment programme, the one that had finally worked.

"Understandable," Magnus said briefly. "It isn't important."

"I'll need some new clothes," she said as they approached the steps to the house. "I can use my own money, but could I have the car sometime?"

"I'll drive you," he said, "and pay for whatever you need. I told you, the farms and the business are both doing well now. Or have you forgotten that, too?"

"No, I hadn't forgotten. But you've no need to pay for my clothes. My savings account must be quite healthy." She'd had a modest but adequate amount of money in it before she got ill.

She made to go up the steps, but he stopped her, his hand on her arm. "Do you have an account with another bank?"

"Another bank?" Jade stared. "You know I have two accounts, the cheque account and a savings one. That's all."

Magnus drew in a breath. "You don't have enough in those accounts to buy more than a few undies, I should think."

"Oh, nonsense!" she said. "It wasn't an enormous amount, but I can certainly afford to buy some clothes. I'm sure there was at least—"

"Jade."

His voice silenced her. She looked at him, puzzled. "Unless you used it after all," she said uncertainly. "Did you?"

"No, I never used it. I told you, I didn't need to."

"Then the money must be—"

His grip tightened. "I had to take over your accounts, your bank-books," he said. "You do understand that?"

"Yes, of course I understand." She hadn't been capable of attending to them herself. "There'd have been a couple of bills outstanding, but nothing big!"

Magnus shook his head. "For some time before you got ill you were taking out fairly large sums of cash. You'd just about cleaned out your savings."

Chapter Four

Jade couldn't believe it. "I don't recall doing that."

"No?" He raised his brows, almost as though he didn't believe her. Then he said, "You don't recall quite a lot about that time, I gather." His eyes were searching.

Jade spread her hands in resigned acknowledgement. It was true. The period immediately before her hospitalisation carried hazy memories at best, and there were gaps even further back. "But—why? What did I spend it on?"

"I've no idea," Magnus answered grimly. "There was certainly no evidence that you'd bought anything with it. No new clothes, no receipts for any large expenses."

She shook her head. "I don't understand."

"Well, never mind. I'll arrange for an allowance to be paid to you."

"I don't want—"

"You're entitled," he said shortly. "And as I said, we're very comfortably situated now. No need to worry about money. Come on. You don't want to be late for another meal.''

Before lunch Ginette had changed back into her demure green-and-white dress, and Jade had dispensed with the grubby jeans in favour of a cotton shirtwaister. The belt was a little loose, but otherwise the style tended to disguise her loss of weight. Perhaps, she thought, spreading a scone with jam and fresh whipped cream that she didn't particularly want, Mrs. Riordan was right. She ought to eat more.

Ginette carried most of the conversation, with Mrs. Riordan interrupting occasionally to alter its direction. Magnus, who had changed from his farm gear into a white shirt and sand-coloured slacks, seemed preoccupied, and Jade was content to say very little.

Then Magnus turned to her and said, ''I could take you to Warkworth this afternoon, if you like.''

Surprised, Jade said, ''Thank you. How much time will I have?''

''As much as you want. When would you like to go?''

''Whenever it suits you,'' Jade replied. ''If I could use the phone, I'll try to make an appointment to have my hair done.''

''You don't need permission to use the phone,'' he pointed out with a hint of irritation. ''What's wrong with your hair?'' he added, looking at it.

Ginette laughed. ''Isn't that just like a man? If Jade is uncomfortable with her hair, Magnus,'' she reasoned, placing a hand briefly on his arm, ''it needs fixing.''

Jade said, ''It's too long. And it's out of condition.''

Magnus shrugged. ''If you say so.''

''Magnus,'' his mother said, ''if you're going to Warkworth, there are one or two things you could get for me, if you would.''

''Of course. Just let me know what you want.''

* * *

Magnus was waiting when she let herself out the front door, the car already standing on the drive. He straightened from his lounging position against it and opened the passenger door for her.

The car swept down the drive and onto the road, and Jade found her breath coming out in a sigh. She had only been at Waititapu for one day, and already it was a relief to get away for a while.

She said, "I didn't realize you still had to work on the farms yourself. Didn't you tell me you'd installed a manager?"

"Yes, I did, next door, and he and his son run the two farms with some help from the sharemilkers on the dairy unit and a couple of farm workers. But I give them a hand if they're short of labour or when I feel the need for some physical activity."

"You felt the need this morning?"

"I offered to do an urgent fence repair because the others are busy drenching cattle. Anyway, I like to keep an eye on things."

"So you're still doing two jobs?"

"As a matter of fact it's worked out rather well. When I left the partnership in Auckland and set up my own office at the house, I lost a few clients. But I also picked up some local business, particularly from farmers, because they feel that an accountant with his own farming operation just down the road from them might have a few clues about doing their books."

"You don't find it difficult, working from Waititapu?"

"I had clients before who were miles away from the office. Sometimes I travel to them. But I have a fax machine, and the phone and computer. Now the farms are on their feet again, I'm thinking of employing a part-time secretary...."

"I could do that," Jade offered. "I might be a bit rusty, but I'd soon pick it up again."

Magnus was staring straight ahead, his eyes on the road. "The thing is," he said, "how long will you be around for? And I don't want to put you under any stress."

"A bit of part-time secretarial work wouldn't be particularly stressful," Jade said, carefully ignoring the first part of his speech. "I can't sit about twiddling my thumbs all day. And it would make me feel better about living on your money."

He cast her a frowning glance. "You more than earned it in the year after we were married, acting as nurse, nanny, housekeeper...."

And wife, she added silently. It hadn't been an easy start to marriage, but she'd thought they would weather it, that their love would keep her strong. She'd been wrong. Magnus, trying to save the family farms while continuing to run his own business, providing for his family and worried sick about both his mother and his sister, had less and less time or emotional energy to spare for his wife. But it wasn't he who had finally cracked under the strain.

"You don't owe me anything," she said.

He flicked another glance at her as though he wanted to say something, and then had changed his mind. After a while he said, "We'll go to the bank first, and I'll transfer some money into your account. Will you need cash for the hairdresser?"

"I think I have enough for that," she said.

In the event she had barely sufficient. She emptied her purse of notes and handed them over to the girl who had shampooed and cut her hair, then emerged to find Magnus waiting for her.

"Very nice," he said, examining the shortened style. It felt light and soft, and a conditioning treatment had given it a new sheen. "Where to now?"

The hairdresser was on the main street. Many of the shops were built in colonial style with wide corrugated iron verandas shading the footpath. Some were refurbished old buildings, others new ones designed to reinforce the impression of a leftover corner of nineteenth-century New Zealand. Although the town was quite small, it seemed very busy, the road noisy with traffic.

Her ears jangling, Jade said, "You've done your mother's messages?"

"Yes. You wanted clothes, you said."

She hesitated, embarrassed. "I'm not sure how to pay for them."

"I told you I'd put some money in your account. And here's your cheque-book." He took it from his pocket and handed it to her. "They said it's okay to use it even though the account has been inactive for so long."

"Thank you." She stood holding it. "What are you going to do?"

"I've done all I need to. But there's no hurry. We could make a time to meet at the car—unless you'd like me to come with you?"

At the hairdresser's, she'd had to try twice before she could blurt out that she had an appointment, and she was sure the girl at the counter had thought she was odd. "I'd like you to come," she said.

Magnus quickly hid his surprise. "Okay, if it's what you prefer. We can use my credit card if you like."

"That isn't why I asked you."

"I wasn't saying that." He paused, looking at her. "You have a lot to get used to again, don't you?"

Jade nodded, grateful that she didn't need to explain.

Magnus unexpectedly took an active part in choosing the clothes.

"I like this," he told her, taking a sleeveless silk dress with a flowing skirt from a rack. "Do you?"

"It's lovely, but not what I'm looking for," she answered. A textured linen oatmeal-coloured skirt over one arm, she pulled out another in colourful stripes, a smart red-and-white dress with a slim skirt, then one of soft grey green with large pockets and a gold-buckled belt. "I'll try these on."

"What about this?" It was a full-skirted fuchsia cotton dress with tiny sleeves, the front demure but the back unexpectedly scooped.

"I don't think so," she said.

The shop assistant clipping tickets onto a pile of jackets on the counter said, "That's been marked down. Wish it would fit me!" She was plump and dark, her nails painted blood red and her abundant bosom encased in a cascade of scarlet ruffles.

"Try it," Magnus urged. "It's a bargain, apparently."

Looking at the tag, Jade privately thought that the new price was more appropriate than the crossed-out one, but it was very pretty, if a little impractical for everyday. She wouldn't buy it, of course, but she took it from Magnus so as not to make a fuss.

When she came out of the changing room he queried, "Any good?"

"This skirt," she said, turning to the hovering shop assistant and handing her the oatmeal one. "And..." Holding the two dresses she'd picked out she said doubtfully, "I don't know about these."

"Didn't they fit?" Magnus asked.

"Yes, and they both look good," she admitted, "but I only wanted one."

The assistant said, "They're about the same price, so that won't help you make up your mind." Smiling at Magnus, she said, "What does your husband think?"

"Take them both," Magnus responded on cue.

"No." Jade shook her head. "If I regain the weight I've lost it's a waste."

"What about the other dress?" Magnus asked.

She'd left the fuchsia cotton hanging in the booth. "I haven't tried it," she admitted. "I've no use for it, really."

The assistant persuaded, "It's the sort of dress you could wear anywhere. Day or night. And it doesn't have a snug fit. I'm sure you'd find it useful."

"Try it," Magnus urged her, drawing back the curtain. Taking the other garments from her, he added to the shop assistant, "We're taking both of these."

Jade made to protest, but she didn't want to argue in front of the woman who was now folding up the dresses and the skirt.

"Come on." Magnus reached up and took down the fuchsia dress from the hook, holding it out to her. "I want to see it on you."

She flashed him a look that brought his black brows up. Taking the dress, she stepped into the booth and pulled the curtain across between them, rattling the brass rings. She thought she heard a faint breath of laughter as she began unbuttoning her blouse.

The dress flattered the line of her shoulders and neck, complementing the uncluttered new hairstyle, making her skin appear creamy and warm, and moulding the rounded swell of her bust. The midsection skimmed her ribs and waist, and the hem of the gracefully flared skirt lightly brushed her legs.

She turned to look over her shoulder in the mirror, seeing how the back dipped almost to her waist, framing smooth skin and the faint hollow of her spine. It might have been made for her.

The curtain moved as Magnus opened it a few inches.

She was facing him, her eyes startled and wary, but his gaze was apparently riveted on the view in the mirror, before he turned it to her face, then thrust the curtain aside and let his eyes lower, examining the length of her body. He took a step back, and said, "Yes. Definitely, yes."

The shop assistant, her curiosity evidently having got the better of her, hovered at his elbow.

"There!" she said with satisfaction. "He was right, wasn't he? It's *lovely* on you!"

"I don't think—" Jade started.

He shook his head. "I'll give it to you," he said. "A coming-home present."

"Been away, have you?" the assistant enquired.

"Yes," Jade said after a moment. "For a while."

"He must have missed you." Casting a teasing glance at Magnus, the woman added, "I'd make the most of it, if I were you. Were you in hospital?"

"Why do you say that?" Jade asked sharply.

"You said something about regaining weight." Smiling at Magnus again, she said, "Though some of us would kill to be as slim as she is."

Magnus wasn't looking at her, but at Jade's suddenly whitened face. He stepped forward, and said dismissively to the woman, "Thank you." He gave her a smiling nod and jerked the curtain closed again.

Jade would have moved back, but his hand was on her arm. "Are you all right?" he said, his voice low, his eyes frowning.

"Yes." There was moisture on her upper lip. "It's hot in here." She drew a shaking hand over her clammy forehead. "I want to get changed."

"Turn around." He was turning her as he spoke, his hands firm but gentle. He slid down the short zip at the back of the dress.

"What are you doing?" She twisted to face him, and the loosened dress slipped off her shoulders. She snatched at it, holding it over her breasts.

"Helping you," Magnus answered tersely. "Don't be coy," he said under his breath, evidently conscious of the flimsy curtain between them and the woman in the shop. "I've seen you undressed before, remember? Or don't you?"

Her pallor was replaced by a quick flush. She presented her back to him again, letting the dress slide to the floor as she grabbed her bra and fumbled it on. Before she could fasten it, his fingers had grasped the catch and were doing it for her.

She bent to retrieve the dress, but Magnus said, "I'll get it." She moved out of the way and he picked it up, smoothing it over his arm as Jade reached for her blouse, and then he pushed her shaking fingers aside and did up the buttons.

He handed her the skirt she'd been wearing, and she said, "I can manage now."

"Sure?"

"I'm all right." She dropped the skirt over her head and groped behind her for the zip. Magnus, his eyes on her face, nodded and went out. She heard him say that he'd pay for all her purchases with his credit card.

"Is there anything more you need?" he asked her as they left the shop.

"I'll just stop at a chemist's," she said, "and meet you at the car."

He looked down at the two carrybags she'd insisted she could manage herself. "I thought you needed an entire new wardrobe."

"I have more than I need, now. And more than I can afford."

"You can afford it," he said firmly. "I can. I told you, money isn't a problem, Jade." He took her arm and they began to walk.

"You know I didn't mean to use your card."

"What's the difference?" he argued. "Forget it."

It was quibbling, she supposed. If she'd written a cheque she'd only have been spending the money he'd put into her bank account. "You must have done really well...."

"We were lucky with the wool prices last year. The dairy farm did well, too, and the company had a good payout. This year will probably be just as good."

"You thought it would take five years to pull the farms out of the red," she reminded him. "But you've done it in three?"

"It hasn't been easy, but selling off part of one of the farms gave us some working capital, and the bank was accommodating, fortunately. They were impressed by my accounting ability and I persuaded them that I knew something about farming as well." He paused. "I'm no millionaire, but within reason we can afford to spend on the things we want. But I'd never have managed it without your help over the first rocky bit. Whatever happens, Jade, I'll always be grateful for that."

Grateful. The word was a stone sinking into her mind. Was it gratitude that had kept him by her side every weekend, given him endless patience, led him to take her back to his home although not to his bed, and offer her free use of his money? Hurt translated to anger, and she said, "I don't want your *gratitude,* Magnus. And I don't want your money! As soon as I can, I'll be paying it back."

His hand dropped from her arm, and his face went blank, expressionless. Someone passing by jostled him, but he took no notice. His voice clipped, he said, "There's no need for that. I wouldn't take it. You're still my *wife,* " he added with a sudden vehemence, "for what it's worth!"

Which wasn't much, Jade reflected.

They had stopped outside a chemist's shop. He reached out and almost forcibly removed the carrybags from her hands. "Go on, then," he said. "I'll see you at the car, if you're sure you don't want anything more."

She hesitated. "I need a little bit of cash."

"Sure. I should have thought of it." He put down the bags and took some notes from his wallet. "Enough?"

"Plenty, thank you."

By the time she rejoined him he'd regained his calm, aloof demeanour. And on the way home he seemed preoccupied, driving all the way in near total silence.

When he'd driven into the garage, he said, "Did the doctors give you any medication to take?"

"Only if I need it," she said. "They weaned me off before I left. You know that."

He said, his expression carefully controlled, "Danella and her husband will be here tomorrow."

"I know. And their baby."

He glanced at her swiftly, and then away, frowning.

"You think maybe I should take a tranquilliser? Don't worry, Magnus. I'll know if I need one."

His lips tightened. "Good." He reached over to the back seat for her parcels.

"I'll carry them," she said, leaving him to pick up the packages he'd got for his mother. "Thank you for driving me."

She put away the new clothes in the wardrobe and stuffed the packaging into the wastebasket. Hearing footsteps she paused, listening, then opened the door. The door to Danella's old room across the passageway was open and the housekeeper was making up one of the twin beds.

"Can I help?" Jade walked forward and took one end of the sheet, tucking it efficiently into a hospital-type corner.

"Thank you." Mrs. Gaines pushed a pillow into its case and placed it on the bed.

"I meant to tell you," Jade said. "I appreciated the pot-pourri in my wardrobe."

"I make it myself," the housekeeper confided. "Every-thing comes from the garden. It's wonderful what you can do so close to the sea. Mr. Riordan told me you used to look after it all."

"I enjoyed it." She'd found the formal beds with their precise edges rather sterile but had meticulously main-tained them, only replacing some annuals with perennials and ground-covers to cut down on maintenance. Then she'd asked Magnus if she could use an adjoining corner of the neighbouring paddock, making an old misshapen totara and a couple of ragged pongas the nucleus of her own garden of native trees and shrubs.

Mrs. Gaines placed the pillow on the bed, then shook out a cotton cover. "I must pick some flowers for this room."

"I'll do it, if you like. I'm sure you've plenty of other things to attend to."

They finished making the beds in amicable silence, and Jade went out to find flowers. She had gathered a small bouquet of miniature roses, lavender and blue daisies when voices attracted her attention, and she saw Mrs. Riordan, leaning on Ginette's arm and with a walking stick in her other hand, walking between the flower-beds.

Jade fixed a smile on her face. "Good afternoon, Mother Riordan. Hello, Ginette."

Ginette smiled at her. "Hi."

"What are you doing?" Mrs. Riordan demanded.

"Picking a few flowers for Danella's room," Jade explained calmly. "The garden has grown since I've been away. Everything looks different."

"Of course. You didn't expect things to remain the same, did you?"

"You haven't changed much," Jade pointed out.

"I'm older," Mrs. Riordan said uncompromisingly, while Ginette raised her brows silently behind her. "And so are you. Though you don't look it. Even with your hair cut."

"I . . . er, thank you."

Mrs. Riordan said, "It wasn't a compliment, merely a fact. You've been buying clothes, Magnus says."

"You noticed yesterday that my clothes didn't fit." Why justify herself? Jade thought furiously. She tightened her lips, determined not to be drawn into a defensive stance.

"And insisted on him accompanying you," Mrs. Riordan went on as though Jade hadn't spoken at all.

Insisted? Keeping her voice even, Jade asked, "Did he say that?" She glanced at Ginette, watching with a gleam of perhaps sympathetic curiosity in her dark eyes.

"Well, how he spends his money is his own business," Mrs. Riordan said. "I'm glad that you're well enough to go shopping."

"So am I," Jade said.

There was no way she was going to try to explain to Mrs. Riordan what it was like to be taken shopping in a group, shepherded by a couple of nurses in mufti.

People hadn't been fooled by that. They'd stared, either laughing or pitying. When she'd screwed up enough courage to take a purchase to the counter the assistant had spoken to her as though she must be both deaf and retarded. After the third or fourth such expedition, Jade had stubbornly refused all offers to repeat the experience.

"You'd better put those flowers in some water," Mrs. Riordan said. "The daisies won't keep, anyway."

"They only need to keep for two days." Jade relaxed her grip on the flower stalks. They'd grown warm in her hand. "I'll see you at dinner, then."

She was thankful to get away.

After dinner the women sat in the big front lounge. Mrs. Riordan had a book, Ginette switched on the television set and watched a game show with the set on low volume, and Jade was glad to bury herself in the newspaper that Magnus offered her. She hadn't realised that he didn't intend to remain with them until he said, "If you'll all excuse me, I have some work to catch up on."

The newspaper was a local giveaway, full of advertising and personal and business items concerning the surrounding community, and a careful perusal gave her the chance to fill in some of the inexplicable gaps in her memory. Inexplicable because there seemed no discernible pattern to what she recalled and what she didn't. The cause of the haphazard memory losses was plain enough—her illness and the treatment that had been prescribed. Whatever she had lost was a small price to pay for the prospect of a normal life.

When the game show ended Ginette changed the channel. Mrs. Riordan was engrossed in her book, and Jade had finished the paper. As she folded it up, Ginette said, "Is there anything you'd like to watch?"

Jade shook her head. "You watch what you like." She got up, the newspaper in her hand.

Mrs. Riordan meticulously turned a page, then looked up. "You're not going to bother Magnus, are you? He doesn't like to be disturbed when he's working."

"I know." Jade stood undecided, then said rebelliously, "But I want to talk to him."

Mrs. Riordan looked thoroughly disapproving, but said nothing as Jade turned on her heel and marched out, her head high. She thought she heard a giggle, quickly suppressed, from Ginette. Then she was stalking along the passageway to the big room at the back of the house. She tapped on the door briefly and flung it open without waiting to be invited, then stood on the threshold.

Magnus turned in his swivel chair at the desk and looked at her with surprised enquiry. A computer screen glowed on the desk, and he lifted his hands from the keys.

"Jade!" He got up as though he might have come towards her, but after taking one step he halted. "What can I do for you?"

"Nothing," she said, closing the door behind her and standing just inside it. "I'm being childish." Clutching at the newspaper in her hands, she confessed, "Your mother told me not to disturb you, so I thought I would. I'm sorry."

Magnus sighed sharply, then unexpectedly laughed. "I'm sorry, too," he said. "I know she's difficult, sometimes. But it's not entirely her fault, you know."

"I know." When she had first come to Waititapu Magnus had explained the doctor's warning that stroke victims sometimes became abnormally moody or hostile, that character traits might be exaggerated or reversed, and social inhibitions on speech and behaviour lost. "I'll try to be patient. Heaven knows, I ought to understand."

She came into the room and dropped the newspaper on a chair. Another desk held an electronic typewriter, a filing cabinet stood near the window, and two walls were lined with shelves holding files and thick books on accounting practice. "You haven't been lucky with the women in your life," she said, and then bit her tongue. Perhaps he did feel lucky, now. Maybe he'd found someone healthy and uncomplicated and undemanding. Like Ginette. "I mean," she said, "between me, and your sister, and your mother—it hasn't been easy for you, has it?"

"Sympathy isn't necessary. It wasn't exactly a picnic for you, either. And I'm not sure that I'm the unlucky one. Having your own family around might have helped you a lot."

A faint stinging behind her eyes made her blink quickly and look away from him.

"You still miss them, don't you?"

She kept her eyes wide and looked at him. "What's the point? It won't bring them back." The doctors had taken her through all that, believing the trauma of losing her entire family in a matter of days might well have had something to do with her admission to a psychiatric ward seven years later.

You feel guilty that you weren't with them?

Who had asked her that? The question surfaced briefly, a flash of memory. The voice . . . but then it was gone. One of the doctors, no doubt. There had been so many of them.

Maybe, whoever he was, he'd been right. Maybe she had some unresolved guilt that when her father, with her mother sitting beside him and her younger sister in the rear seat, had in a moment of fatal inattention driven into the path of an oncoming train, she had been with her own friends at a party. Her parents had died instantly, and her sister had followed them in less than a week. But that wasn't what had sent her over the edge.

Magnus said, "You're right, there's no point in dwelling on the past. But somehow, the past has a way of catching up on the present." He indicated the chair she'd flung the newspaper onto. "Why don't you sit down?"

"I don't want to be a nuisance."

"You're not a nuisance. A distraction, maybe. . . ."

The note in his voice was one she hadn't heard since she'd come home, but as she looked up at him in quick, eager hope, the small, teasing smile on his mouth faded, and the once-familiar light in his eyes with it. He stepped back towards his desk, his face stiffening into a mask.

She picked up the paper and sat down, her gaze puzzled and questioning. "Magnus—what's the matter?"

Magnus sank back into his own chair, half-turned from her. He said, "You're not the only one who has things to get used to."

Carefully she lowered the folded newspaper to her lap. "You can get used to most things if you put your mind to it."

He steepled his hands, briefly looking down at them. "You should know."

Jade wondered if he was having second thoughts. She recalled the expression in his eyes when he'd come into the changing booth and looked over her shoulder at her reflected back, bared by the deceptively provocative dress.

She guessed that he'd started the afternoon by just being kindhearted, considerate. Perhaps faintly aware of the ordeal it was for her to do some simple shopping, he'd tried to make the experience easier. But if at first he'd play-acted his interest in her purchases, he hadn't been able to hide the darkening of his eyes at that moment, or the glint of male admiration when he'd stepped back to look at her.

He still found her desirable, at least occasionally when he was caught unaware. The thought quickened her pulse. She smoothed the paper on her knee, and it made a small crackling sound. She looked down, studying a picture of a smiling child leading a disgruntled white-faced calf with a black patch over one eye. "You were kind, today," she said. "I appreciated that."

"Don't count on my being kind!" The sudden harsh note that grated in his voice brought her head up, her eyes fixing on his.

He stood up again with a violent movement that set the swivel chair gently rotating behind him. His hands thrust into his pockets, he said curtly, "I'm sorry. I didn't mean to scare you."

She'd instinctively stiffened, her fingers tightening around the newspaper she held. Deliberately she relaxed them. "I'm not scared of you, Magnus."

He said, "There were times...."

A faint flush in her cheeks, she said, "I was sick, then. I didn't know what I was doing."

"So you wouldn't shrink back and scream if I touched you?"

"You fastened my bra for me today, and I didn't scream then."

"Did you want to?" His eyes were sombre, watchful.

Jade's lips parted. What did he want from her? Hadn't she invited his touch last night, and been rebuffed?

As she hesitated, he said, "You were certainly clutching at your dress like a startled virgin." He paused. "You did want to scream, didn't you?" His voice had flattened.

Jade shook her head. "No. I told you, the *doctors* have told you, I'm *better!* Why are you asking me this?"

She saw the quick rise and fall of his chest. "Because, God help me, maybe I'm wondering if you'd scream if I tried to *un*fasten it."

When they were first married he might have said something like that in fun, laughing, and she'd have laughed back and dared him to do it. Now there was no laughter in his face, his eyes. They looked almost tortured.

Hope and puzzlement and dread stirred her blood and shortened her breath.

She was his wife, she reminded herself. If she was going to have to fight for him, she had that advantage. And it *was* an advantage, because Magnus wasn't a man to take his marriage vows lightly. He'd said as much last night—proved it over the last two years. He must have been lonely, in need of companionship, comfort, the solace of sex. How could she blame him if he'd found those things with a sympathetic woman?

She said, "I wouldn't scream." And then, "There is such a thing as forgiveness. But..." She bit her lip. He hadn't asked her for forgiveness. He'd asked for—or at least hinted that he wanted—his freedom.

"*But...*" Magnus echoed. His mouth twisted. "Some things are difficult to forgive."

"That isn't really the issue, is it?"

Slowly, he agreed, "Perhaps not. You might say it's only the beginning."

Did he want her to forgive him so that he could start a new life with a clear conscience? A life that didn't include her?

Jade stood up, laying the paper alongside the electronic typewriter on the nearby desk. She might understand his defection, but that didn't mean she wasn't hurt by it, and that she didn't feel like lashing out and trying to hurt him in return.

But she didn't want him to think that she was reacting out of pique or anger. She lifted her head and directed a steady green gaze at him, keeping her voice calm. "I'll never agree to a divorce, Magnus. If it's what you want, you'll have to arrange it yourself. I believe that's possible. But I want no part of it."

She saw his face change, from a wary determination to some kind of shock. Obviously this wasn't what he'd expected. She didn't wait to say any more, but with her head still held high she went to the door and wrenched it open, closing it with a snap behind her.

Chapter Five

She heard Magnus come up the stairs some time later. She'd been trying to read, too tense to sleep, but this time he didn't pause at her door, his quiet footsteps going straight past. A few minutes later he was in the bathroom.

Unexpectedly the connecting door opened. Magnus seemed to hesitate, and then came towards the bed. "Jade—"

"Yes?" She closed the book.

"I don't want a divorce, either. I can't say I've never considered the question—I did, early on, when I—when I was having some trouble accepting...things. But last night, I was offering the choice to you. I thought you understood."

Jade closed her eyes. The room seemed to whirl about her. "You thought *I* might want it?" He must have been blaming himself, taking the responsibility for her eventual collapse, and she couldn't let him. He had borne enough burdens for other people in the past. "Things will be different, now," she said, "won't they? We can learn from our mistakes, both of us. That's the important thing."

Magnus said slowly, almost unwillingly, "Yes, you're right, of course."

She stirred, lifting herself against the pillow, her hand tight on the sheet that had fallen to her waist, revealing one of the flimsy, lace-trimmed nightgowns that he used to delight in removing from her. She said, "Magnus—do you want to come to bed...with me?"

For the longest time he stood immobile, so silent he didn't even seem to be breathing. Then at last he said, "You've only been home two days, and you've a lot to assimilate. It's a bit soon—"

"Not too soon. You don't have to handle me with velvet gloves—"

"It isn't just you," he interrupted. "I...need some time, too." His voice was rasping, but carried an underlying note almost of pleading.

Curbing her bewildered disappointment, Jade said, "If that's what you want."

"I *want*—" Magnus stopped abruptly, fiercely. "I think it's best."

It was a phrase calculated to set her teeth on edge. She bit back her instinctive objection and said, "Will you at least kiss me good-night?"

She wondered if he was going to refuse. He moved jerkily towards the bed, and when she held out a hand to him, took it in a crushing grip. Then he bent and kissed her forehead and stepped back, dropping her hand. "Good night, Jade," he said.

Mrs. Riordan breakfasted in bed, quite early. When Jade entered the dining-room at eight, she found Ginette nibbling on toast and drinking coffee, while Magnus had just started on a plate of bacon and eggs and grilled tomatoes.

"There's more here," he told her, indicating a covered dish on the table.

"I usually have cereal and toast," Jade said doubtfully, helping herself to cornflakes and milk.

Ginette finished her coffee and said, "Excuse me." As she rose, she asked Magnus, "What time is your sister expected to be here?"

"They said they'd make it before dinner. I'll be working in my office until they arrive."

As Ginette left, Jade offered, "Can I help?"

He looked as though he was about to refuse, and she said quickly, "I'd really like something to do, Magnus. Even if it's only tidying papers or opening the mail. Filing? There must be something I can help with."

"Bored already?" he asked her.

"I just hate doing nothing, and you know I always liked office work. It's what I trained for."

"And what you were good at," he said, the knife and fork in his hands stilled. "Then I brought you here and turned you into a nursemaid, cook-housekeeper and general drudge."

"I was never a drudge! No one forced me, Magnus. You know I offered of my own free will."

A look of angry pain passed across his face, and was replaced by bitterness. "Yes. You must have been—"

His expression changed again, to a guilty dismay, and Jade, smiling wryly, supplied the word. "Mad?"

The knife and fork clattered onto the plate before him, and he covered his eyes with one hand, dropping his head onto it.

"Not then, actually," Jade said. "That came later."

He looked up, his expression rueful in the extreme, and said, "I'm sorry." Then, catching her eyes, he said, "You can *laugh* about it?"

"Now I can. And please don't apologise to me, Magnus."

He made a small grimace and returned to his breakfast. "I'll try not to be so tactless in future."

"I told you last night," she said, flushing slightly as she recollected in what context, "there's no need to treat me with velvet gloves. It was a perfectly ordinary remark."

"Okay, I'll try to remember."

Jade gave an exaggerated sigh, and gazed at him with her chin on her hands, her elbows resting on the table.

Magnus winced. "I've just done it again, haven't I?"

Jade nodded, and he pushed away his emptied plate, smiling almost reluctantly at the long-suffering expression on her face. "I won't apologise yet again." He reached for a piece of toast. "Shall I ask Mrs. Gaines to make some fresh toast?"

"No, not for me."

She had finished her cornflakes, and Magnus said, "Have some bacon and eggs, then." He lifted the cover.

They did look and smell delicious, and it would be a pity to waste Mrs. Gaines's efforts. Later, though, she'd tell the housekeeper that there was no need to make a cooked breakfast for her.

Magnus poured coffee as she took a crisp rasher and an orange-yolked farm egg from the dish. "There are a couple of things you could do," he told her. "I've got behind with the filing, and there are letters that need typing. I've made notes on a tape recorder. I usually send them to a secretarial bureau in Auckland."

"I'll deal with them."

By the time he'd finished a second cup of coffee she was ready to accompany him to the office. He gave her a pile of paper and indicated the filing cabinet. "Ask me if you're not sure where to put any of them. And there's a tape player on the desk over there with the typewriter."

"Earphones?"

"In the drawer."

He switched on the computer and settled himself in front of it while Jade quietly went about slotting papers into the filing cabinet. She put aside the queries to be dealt with later, now and then stealing a glance at the apparently oblivious man sharing the room, his fingers tapping on the keys, his head bent slightly towards the screen as he concentrated on the figures that moved about it.

It was a familiar scenario, although formerly his office had been in a glass-walled building in the heart of Auckland city.

During a preliminary interview before hiring Jade, he had expressed both surprise and some reservations about her youth, but Jade had deliberately cultivated a mature appearance and manner, and her qualifications and ability had been impeccable.

They'd been a good team, she and Magnus. After her first few weeks working for him, she'd never felt like an inferior staff member, a minion, and once he'd ensured she was thoroughly acquainted with her duties, Magnus had treated her like an equal.

The job had been challenging, exciting, because they complemented each other, he with his brilliance with figures and knowledge of the intricacies of accountancy, and she with her meticulous spelling, grammar, layout and keyboarding skills, her talent for organisation, her ability to take care of time-consuming details and deal with difficult clients who wanted an appointment yesterday, or got fidgety when the person before them took up more than the allotted time.

Always a perfectionist, she'd been constantly striving for the role of office paragon, never a foot wrong or a hair out of place. She had exerted herself to more than live up to expectation, a byword for efficiency and thoroughness.

When his father died of a heart attack with no warning at all, Jade had been the first person Magnus told. He'd taken the call, and then asked her to come into his office and said calmly, "I've had bad news. My father collapsed and died about half an hour ago."

She'd thought at first that he was completely unemotional about it. He'd asked her to cancel his appointments or refer them to his partners, firing instructions about unfinished business so fast she could scarcely keep up as she scribbled notes. "Phone me at home if you need to," he'd said, and stood up. "I know I can rely on you to deal with most things for the next couple of days."

She'd looked up then and seen him frowning at the neat piles of ledgers and papers on his desk. Then he'd raised his head and his eyes met hers and she instinctively stood, too, her notebook still clasped in one hand, the other outstretched to him as she whispered, "I'm so sorry!"

He'd taken her hand as though it was a lifeline, the strength of his grip almost cracking the bones. Staring down at their entwined fingers, he muttered, "He's my father, you see. . . ." He looked up at her, and she saw the baffled disbelief in his eyes.

"Yes," she said softly. "I know." She'd wanted to take him in her arms, but this wasn't the right moment. There were things he had to do for his mother, his family—his father. He would have to remain in control for them. "I'll look after things here for you," she'd assured him, and then, crisply, to steady him, "Can you drive? Or shall I get someone to...?"

"No." He'd dropped her hand then. "I'll drive myself. Take my mind off it," he added without hope.

"If there's any way I can help," she said, "do let me, please."

"Thank you, Jade. It's a help just to know you're here." He'd stooped and kissed her cheek before striding out.

It had been the first time they'd touched, and the first time she'd seen a hint of emotional vulnerability in Magnus. It wasn't something he allowed to show very often. To this day she didn't know if he'd ever let go his rigid control and cried for his father.

Jade slid the last drawer closed, and turned to see Magnus flex his shoulders and push his chair a little way from the desk. As she left the metal cabinet he enquired, "Finished?"

"Nearly. I'm not sure what to file these under." She took the small sheaf of queries over to him and put them into his outstretched hand.

He went through them quickly, giving instructions, and then passed them back. "Can you remember all that?"

"Yes. Thank you." She paused before turning away, and he looked up at her.

Jade smiled. "Just like old times."

He said on a harsh note, "You must tell me if you're tired."

"I'll tell you," she promised, inwardly sighing.

He pressed a couple of keys on the computer and removed a disk from the drive, slotting in another. Jade finished the filing and went to the other desk, slipping on earphones so that she could transcribe the tapes he'd recorded without disturbing him.

At ten-thirty Mrs. Gaines tapped on the door and brought in a tray with one cup of tea on it. Seeing Jade, she went away to fetch another.

"Thanks, Netta," Jade said when she returned with it and placed the cup before her.

Mrs. Gaines jerked her head in the direction of her employer. "He forgets to drink it, quite often," she murmured. "Do you think you...?"

Jade promised, "I'll remind him."

When the housekeeper had closed the door, Jade took her cup and strolled over to her husband's side, leaning back on the desk so she could face him.

She saw him press the save keys and picked her moment. "Mrs. Gaines is afraid you'll forget your tea."

He glanced up, then reached for the cup. He pushed his chair away from the desk, sipping the hot drink. "How's the typing?"

"I'm a bit out of practice, but it comes back. I'm enjoying it. And I feel..."

His eyes lifted to hers. "What?"

"Well—useful, as if I'm earning the money you spent on me yesterday—at least, part of it."

He didn't look pleased. "I told you, that money *was* earned."

Jade's fingers tightened on the cup in her hands. "You know I didn't want payment."

Shortly after their wedding—a hastily arranged, muted celebration because of his recent bereavement, Magnus had confided his shock discovery that his father's apparent prosperity had been an illusion. He'd left behind huge debts. "The farms may have to go," Magnus had said.

Jade had been shocked. "No, Magnus!" The farms had been in the family for generations. "It's your heritage, and your mother's home! What would it do to her, on top of the stroke?"

"I know. I could divert some of the profits from my business to the farms, try to rebuild them into a viable enterprise, but there isn't enough income to provide the household help and nursing that my mother needs, and send the twins and young Andrew to university as my father had planned. That's quite apart from normal living expenses. I'm sorry," he'd said then. "It isn't fair to involve you in this mess. I should never have married you."

"Don't be silly," she'd told him. "I want to help, Magnus. You must let me."

Three years on, it hurt her that he seemed unwilling to acknowledge that his love had been all the reward she needed.

Magnus said now, "If you didn't want payment for all that you did for me—and my family—then why can't you accept the clothes and whatever other necessities I can give you in the same spirit, instead of being so damned difficult about it?"

Jade sipped thoughtfully at her drink. "I suppose you're right," she said. "I'll stop being difficult. Magnus—"

His eyes were alert, as though something in her voice had warned him.

Her eyes fixed firmly on the quarter cup of now luke-warm tea in her hands, she said in a low but steady voice, "Is there someone you should... tell... about the decision we agreed on last night?"

There was a heartbeat's silence, and then she heard the thud of his cup as he placed it forcefully on the desk. "*No*, damn you!" he said, making her gaze fly to his face in astonishment, seeing it bleak and angry and taut. "There isn't anyone I need tell. Now, if you don't mind, I'd like to get back to work."

Startled, Jade straightened from her perch against the desk, staring at him, but he wasn't looking at her. Calling up some more numbers to the screen with quick keystrokes, he was ignoring her completely, his eyes fiercely concentrated, a scowl on his forehead.

She walked back to her own desk, and sat there looking at his rigid back for some time.

Where had that got her? she wondered. Exactly nowhere, of course. His anger could mean any one of a number of things, and she had no idea which. She put her cup on the corner of the desk, picked up the earphones and flicked a switch. Magnus's voice filled her ears, and she concentrated hard on transforming the verbal notes that he'd made into neatly printed copy.

By lunchtime she'd typed a small pile of letters for Magnus to sign. He wrote his strongly looped signature at the bottom of each, and said, "Enough for today. You've been a great help." He seemed to have got over his spurt of temper.

Jade said, "I've enjoyed it. It's good to feel like a useful member of society again."

She got up, took a deep, relaxing breath and lifted her hands to briefly massage her scalp, her fingers pushing under her hair and fluffing out the new short style. Magnus's eyes were drawn to her taut body, and for an instant she was held still in his dark, riveted gaze, until he dragged it away.

She lowered her arms slowly, a small spark of triumph warming her. No matter how he might try to pretend, he wasn't indifferent to her. On a basic, sensual level she had a measure of power over his emotions. It was a power that she would exploit if she had to.

"Lunch," Magnus said curtly. He strode to the door and opened it, waiting for her.

"Coming." She gave him the sweetest smile she could muster as she preceded him from the room.

Mrs. Riordan's eyes flicked from Jade to Magnus as they entered the dining-room together. Ginette, too, gave them a curious glance.

"How are you, Mother Riordan?" Jade asked as she seated herself.

Mrs. Riordan took a fork and picked up a piece of cold beef to slide it onto her plate. "The same as usual. What have you been doing with yourself all morning?"

Magnus said, "She's been working."

"Working?"

"With me," he expanded. "In the office."

"Is that wise?" Mrs. Riordan asked. "Be careful not to overtax her, Magnus."

Jade said, a little more loudly than necessary, "I'm not being overtaxed. It's been good for me."

"She's finished for the day, anyway," Magnus decreed, picking up several unopened letters that sat beside his place. "You'd better take it easy this afternoon, Jade."

Jade was opening her mouth to protest when he added, "You might find Danella and family a bit wearing."

Jade closed her lips rather tightly, and Ginette sent her a glance of humorous understanding.

Reluctantly, Jade returned a wry smile.

"This one's for you." Magnus was handing her a letter, and she saw her name on it in large, sprawled handwriting.

She picked up a knife and slit the flap, drawing out three pages covered in the same scrawl. "It's from Annie!" she exclaimed.

Magnus had been studying one of his own letters, although it looked less like a letter than a bill of some kind.

He looked up, and she thought a flash of relief lit his eyes. "Really?"

She must have written almost immediately after Jade had left. "I'm so glad she changed her mind."

I'll visit you, Jade had promised as she packed.

Annie, perched on Jade's bed, had vehemently shaken her head. "Don't you come back here," she advised her. "You don't want to remember all this."

"I won't forget you," Jade had replied, and kissed her friend's cheek, giving her a long, warm hug. "You've done me more good than all the nursing staff and the doctors combined. Come and see me when you're out. I'll give you my address—"

But Annie had at first refused to let her. "They reckon you're cured," she said. "You won't need anything to do with loonies like me."

"Don't you dare say that!" Jade scolded.

Annie said gruffly, "Okay, but I'm not much of a letter writer, anyway. And I warn you, if you come visiting, I'll tell them I don't want to see you! You shake the dust of this place off your feet and get on with it."

"Changed her mind?" Magnus queried.

"She wouldn't promise me she'd write." Jade scanned the page eagerly, and gave a gurgle of laughter. Glancing up, she found Magnus regarding her with a look of enquiry, Ginette smiling curiously, and Mrs. Riordan wearing an aloof air of impending disapproval.

"I'm sorry," she said, folding the letter and replacing it in the envelope. "I'll read it later."

There was no way this audience could appreciate the humour of Annie's account of old Mrs. Penny's trenchant exchanges with a nurse determined to give her an unwanted though much-needed bath, or of the havoc one of the younger patients, who insisted on being called Madonna although her file said her name was Maryanne, had wreaked in Miss Cherrible's therapy room during an inspired attempt at fashioning a costume for a rock video.

"This Annie," Mrs. Riordan said precisely, "is an inmate of that place?"

"A patient," Jade said. "And my very good friend."

Mrs. Riordan's brows rose. "And you gave her *our* address?"

Jade stared at her, nonplussed. Before she could speak, Magnus said, "Jade and I took Annie out with us a few times. I liked her."

His mother cast him a look of sheer disbelief. Jade said, "I asked her to come and see me when she's well enough." Glancing at Mrs. Riordan, she added, "But she didn't want to do that."

Ginette put a hand over her mouth, making a little choking sound. Mrs. Riordan's expression was a mixture of relief and chagrin.

Magnus, apparently unnoticing, said smoothly, "Well, we'll have to try to persuade her."

"Magnus!"

He looked down the table at his mother. "Any of Jade's friends are welcome in this house—aren't they, Mother?"

Their eyes locked, hers outraged, his unflinching. Jade was holding her breath, a small flutter of apprehension in her throat. She had never noticed before how very alike these two were, their uncompromising profiles remarkably similar.

"Your father's will stipulated that the house was to be my home for my lifetime," Mrs. Riordan reminded her son.

"Certainly," Magnus replied. "That's why I'm doing you the courtesy of asking for your endorsement. No member of this family has ever been refused hospitality for their friends.''

For a second or two his mother maintained her stubborn stare, then she turned aside, saying pettishly, ''Oh, do as you like. You always have.'' With a brief return of acid spirit, she added, ''But the responsibility is yours—yours and hers!'' Her gaze swung to Jade.

Magnus said quietly, ''Yes, of course. Thank you.''

Ginette's lips moved in a tiny, silent, ''Whew!'' She cast a glance of deep respect at Magnus.

Jade sat silent. Perhaps she ought to have felt triumphant, but instead she was conscious of a stirring of sympathy. Once Mrs. Riordan had held total sway over her family, undisputed mistress of this big house and wife of one of the most respected landowners in the district. But she had reared a son who was at least her equal in strength of will, and who had been forced to provide for her needs by installing other women under her roof, one to keep the house in order and another to nurse her, a constant reminder of her physical dependence.

Jade herself had for a short time filled both those functions, and more. No wonder Mrs. Riordan had resented her, and perhaps still did. Neither of them had been given an easy road.

Turning to her mother-in-law, Jade said warmly, ''Thank you very much, Mother Riordan. I appreciate that. But I don't think Annie will accept the invitation.''

If Mrs. Riordan was surprised, she didn't show it. But after Ginette had wheeled her out of the room, declining help from Magnus, he said, ''That was graciously done.''

Not pretending to misunderstand, Jade answered, ''It must be difficult for her, having to depend on others for almost everything.''

''You didn't realise that before?''

"I did, but not so well. I was younger," Jade said. "Too young, your mother says."

"She was right."

Was she? Mrs. Riordan had also said that Magnus had married Jade because of his practical, not emotional, needs. She hadn't been right about that, too, had she? For the first time, Jade felt a shiver of doubt.

Magnus said, "I expected too much of you."

"No more than you did of yourself."

"But I could take it. I was older, and—"

"And a man?" She looked at him sardonically. He knew her feminist views.

He smiled, shaking his head. "I'm not going to fall into that trap."

Jade gave a quiet laugh. His smile widened, and momentarily it seemed that the time they'd spent apart might never have happened. They sat looking at each other, and Magnus made a small movement as if he might have reached out, touched her.

Then Mrs. Gaines came hurrying in, a tray in her hand for the dishes, and Magnus pushed back his chair and got up.

"See you later," he said, giving Jade an impersonal nod.

"All right." She watched him leave, and then got up in her turn and started helping Mrs. Gaines to remove the plates from the table.

Chapter Six

Jade did some serious weeding after lunch, and then decided to go down to the beach for a swim. Today the sea was calm, the waves hardly rippling as they swept onto the beach in glassy, foam-bracketed curves. The water felt cool and soothing, and on coming out she wrapped a big towel about her waist and climbed back to the house, crossing the lawn to the back door.

She could hear voices coming from Mrs. Riordan's ground-floor sitting-room, and tried to use the stairs without being noticed, but as she made her way up Magnus appeared at the top, looking down at her damp hair and shoulders, the swimsuit dipping low between her breasts, the towel draped saronglike to her ankles above bare, sand-dusted feet.

"We wondered where you were," he said. "I came up to look for you. You've been swimming alone?"

"Yes," she answered, hackles rising at the faintly censorious note in his voice. She reached the last step and stood level with him, but still had to look up several inches to meet his eyes. "I don't need a keeper," she said. "Not any more."

"Don't be so touchy." He reached out and with one finger flicked a droplet of water from her shoulder. "Danella's here."

"Yes, I gathered that. They're early, aren't they? I'll...change and be right down."

Perhaps he noticed her nervous reluctance to walk into a room full of people, especially when one of them was his younger sister. "I'll wait for you," he said.

"Thank you." She was surprised but grateful.

She thought he would remain at the head of the stairs, but instead he accompanied her to the door of her room and walked into it after her. Then he went to stand with his back to her at the window, throwing over his shoulder, "Don't be too long."

She dragged jeans and a shirt from the wardrobe, bra and pants from a drawer, and went into the bathroom, rinsing the sand off under a lightning-fast shower before putting on the clothes.

When she came out of the bathroom Magnus said, "That was quick."

His gaze slipped over her as she crossed to the dressing-table and ran a comb through her hair. The ends had nearly dried already. She turned to the wardrobe and took out a pair of Brazilian sandals, sliding her feet into them.

"Right," she said. "Let's go."

On the stairs he didn't touch her, but as they approached the open door to their left she was glad to feel his fingers lightly resting on her waist.

There seemed at first glance to be a lot of people in the little sitting-room, but as the group resolved itself into component parts she saw that Mrs. Riordan was in her favourite place on the chaise by the window, with Ginette standing by, while a young man with hazel eyes and curly brown hair was talking to her. Magnus's sister sat on a chair facing her mother, a plump, bald-headed baby on her knee.

Danella's blue eyes met Jade's as she broke off in midsentence. She changed her grip on the baby, cradling it against her, and said, "Hello, Jade."

Jade's smile felt stiff. "Danella, it's nice to see you again."

Magnus's hand on her back urged her into the room. "And here is your niece," he said, gently touching the baby's cheek. "This is Rose-Lee."

"She's lovely," Jade said automatically as the baby turned its head towards Magnus, one dimpled hand flung out in a groping reflex. Jade proffered a finger, and the little hand fastened onto it, the blue eyes finding her with a surprised stare.

Jade laughed. "Hello, Rose-Lee. You're a little charmer, aren't you?"

Rose-Lee gave a sociable gurgle, still gazing at her, and then bestowed on her a wide, toothless and totally beatific smile.

"She's taken to you," a male voice said.

"You haven't met Danella's husband, have you?" Magnus said as she turned. "This is Glen," he told her.

Rose-Lee relinquished her finger, and the young man held out a hand. "And you're Jade, of course," he said. "Pleased to meet you at last."

Jade returned his firm grip and open smile with relief. At least here was someone who had no previous baggage to bring to their meeting. He looked nice and seemed anxious to be friendly.

Mrs. Gaines came in bearing a teapot and several cups on a tray, along with freshly baked scones and a date loaf. The conversation centred about the baby, the news in today's paper, and Glen's recent promotion to second-in-charge of the sales division of the manufacturing company he worked for.

Glen addressed a couple of remarks to Jade, and Magnus cast a glance her way now and then—just checking, she thought—while Danella and her mother ignored her. Perhaps not deliberately. Despite their past differences they seemed to be finding plenty to talk about. With Danella and Glen living down in the centre of the North Island, she supposed that mother and daughter didn't see each other very often.

The baby began to fuss and wriggle, and Glen retrieved her from her mother's lap. "Come on," he said, squatting in front of Jade, "talk to your auntie."

The baby blew a bubble and made a grab for the flowered cup in Jade's hand. She lifted it out of the way, and found it taken from her by Magnus. He said nothing but his eyes were piercing.

Coolly, she passed him the saucer, too, and held out her arms to Rose-Lee.

Glen handed the child over without hesitation, and Rose-Lee grinned up at her, waving her arms. Jade laughed, holding the warm little bundle firmly safe.

"She knows a sucker when she sees one." Glen smiled.

Danella said, "Will you get our stuff out of the car, Glen, and I'll feed her." She rose and came to take the baby from Jade.

"I'll come and help, Glen," Magnus offered.

Jade stood up and began gathering the empty cups.

Mrs. Riordan said, "Mrs. Gaines will deal with those, Jade."

"It's okay," Jade said pleasantly. "I don't mind. You and Danella will want to talk." She piled the dishes onto the tray, adding the remains of the scones and date loaf. Giving the other women a meaningless smile, she lifted the tray and walked to the door. "I'll see you later, Danella."

When Jade returned to the hallway, the men were there with several bags of assorted sizes, and Danella, a grizzling baby on her shoulder, was fishing in one of them for a bottle. "That's it," she said. "You can take the rest upstairs while I warm this. We're in the room next to yours, I suppose, Magnus?"

"You're in your old room this time," he replied.

"Oh—but we've always had that room, since we got married!"

Magnus said firmly, "Sorry. We're using it."

"Who is?" Danella demanded. As Jade paused at the foot of the stairs, Danella's gaze lighted on her and then returned to Magnus.

A glint appeared in Magnus's eyes. "I am," he said.

"What on earth for?"

"I snore," Magnus lied blandly, "and Jade isn't used to it any more."

As excuses went, it would hardly hold water. Jade had become accustomed to sleeping with much more disturbing sounds than the odd snore going on around her.

But Glen said quickly, "We'll be okay. Rose-Lee doesn't take up much room." He made for the stairs, followed by Magnus, who gave Jade an unreadable look as they passed her.

Jade hastily followed them. She didn't want to be left in the hall with a glowering Danella. But as a high wail sounded below, she heard Danella say, "*Hush*, for heaven's sake! It's on its way." And the rapid tattoo of her feet heading for the kitchen.

While the men went on along the upstairs passageway, she slipped into her room. She'd had no time to tidy the bathroom, and the towel she'd used to dry herself after swimming was a damp heap in one corner. She cleaned up and returned to the bedroom in time to hear a quiet rapping at her door.

"Come in," she called.

Magnus stepped in and closed the door behind him. "Are you okay?"

"You asked me that before. The answer's still the same."

His gaze searched her face. "That's good." He thrust his hands into his pockets, hesitating as though searching for something more to say.

"Glen's nice," she offered, trying to fill the silence.

"He seems to have been good for Danella," Magnus admitted.

Jade was aware that neither he nor his mother had been happy about the marriage, but Danella had simply gone ahead with a registry office wedding, and although technically she ought to have had parental permission, Magnus had persuaded his mother it was best to accept the *fait accompli* rather than risk losing Danella altogether.

She said, "The baby seems very healthy."

"Thank God, yes. It's ironic, isn't it—" He paused abruptly there, and made an exasperated, apologetic gesture with one hand.

Jade said, "Yes, it is ironic. I told your mother there's still time—for us to have a child," she explained, as he threw her a frowning glance.

Magnus swallowed, and his mouth clamped. "You think that would be a good idea?"

Jade's chin lifted. "Depressive psychosis isn't hereditary. Didn't they tell you that?"

He said harshly, "That isn't what I meant."

"So what did you mean?"

He walked closer to her, slowly. "Just that . . . we have a marriage to rebuild before we embark on rearing a family."

Of course he was right. "You do want to rebuild it?"

"Didn't I make that clear?"

He was standing two feet away from her, close enough for her to see the tiny, slightly raised scar just under his lower lip that he'd told her was the legacy of an encounter with another boy's boot in a childhood football match. Faintly, the scent of him came to her nostrils—pine soap and another insidious aroma that was male and yet uniquely his. Warm and musky, the way his skin used to smell when they made love.

"You said so." Her voice was husky, her eyes still on the scar, remembering how it used to feel under her lips. She raised her eyes to his, her head tipped to one side. Allowing her lashes to fall slowly, she peeked from under them and moistened her lips with the tip of her tongue. "But you know, actions speak louder than words."

She knew she'd got to him by the way his eyes narrowed, a sudden glitter in them, and a line of colour ran along his cheekbones. For a moment it seemed they'd both stopped breathing, the stillness in the room palpable. Then he stepped forward and his hands closed about her arms so tightly that she gasped.

Her eyes widened, and then instinctively closed against the peculiar rage in his taut face as he shifted his grip to pin her against him, and bent his head, his mouth meeting hers in what was less a kiss than a collision.

It was cataclysmic—a wild, furious possession of her mouth, her senses, with nothing in it of gentleness or pity, a storm of male passion that overrode her instinctive physical protest, that allowed her no quarter, his mouth driving hers open beneath it, his arms and hands locking her body to his so that his heart beat heavily against her breast. She could feel his belt buckle hard against her midriff, and her pelvis was pressed snugly to his so that she couldn't avoid knowledge of what the kiss was doing for him.

An answering heat stirred deep inside her, warring with shock that was like fear. Magnus shifted his stance, parting his legs, and both his hands came down to bring her even closer. He lifted his head slightly, making a small groaning sound of pleasure, his eyes still half-closed.

"Don't," Jade gasped, pushing her hands against his chest. "Magnus—"

"It's what you wanted," he said, his voice low and slurred. "What you were asking for."

"How dare you, Magnus!" Her voice an icy lash, she closed her fist and brought it down against his unyielding chest.

He laughed, and she raised her hand again, this time aiming for his face.

Magnus moved as quick as a snake, grabbing her wrist in a grip that made her veins throb, his other arm shifting again to her waist so that she couldn't escape him. "You were trying to turn me on, Jade. Don't blame me if you got more than you bargained for."

"I wasn't trying to turn you into an animal!" she said furiously. "A bloody *predator!*" She couldn't believe that Magnus, always so civilised, so considerate, had kissed her that way—as though she counted for nothing, as though all that mattered was the satisfaction he'd got. And she could see that he had got some, not from mutual sexual need, but from overpowering her with blind, selfish lust.

He was still on a high from it, she realised. His eyes were brilliant and hard as diamonds, his lips cruelly curved in a grin that looked barely human, and there was a dark colour in his face. She wouldn't have been surprised if he'd purred like a panther. "You've learned some language since you've been away," he said. "I don't remember ever hearing you swear before."

"You've never seen me this angry before!" She made another futile effort at escape.

He looked at her consideringly. "Yes," he said. "Why? What did you expect after years of celibacy? A teddy bear?"

He released her suddenly, and took a step backwards. "Well?"

Her lips parted uncertainly. They were stinging, and moist. She touched her tongue to them. Perhaps she'd been unfair, even mistaken. "Years?"

His brows drew together. "You know damn well how long it's been."

"You mean you haven't... there hasn't been anyone else?"

His breath exploded. "No," he snarled at her. "I thought we'd already covered this. Do I need to spell it out? There hasn't been anyone else. Not for me. I've spent two long, loveless years waiting for you—waiting to get our lives back. And now—" He swung away from her, going to the window and thudding a hand against the wooden frame at the side.

"I'm sorry." Jade's voice was hushed. After so long exercising restraint, it was no wonder he'd temporarily lost control. "I thought you didn't care about my feelings—that you wanted somehow to—punish me for something. I should have understood—"

He spun round to face her, his eyes sombre, the colour having receded from his face, leaving his cheeks sallow. "What the hell are you apologising for?" he asked her roughly. "You understood, all right. Why do you think I've been reluctant to make love to you? Make no mistake, Jade. You're damn right to be afraid of me."

He strode past her as she stood there, too stunned to stop him or to ask what he meant. He wrenched the door open and slammed it shut behind him, so that the floor under her feet vibrated. A baby's wail came thinly and distantly through the wood, and she heard Magnus give a muffled curse before he moved away.

She found that her legs were trembling. She touched a hand to her forehead and shambled over to the bed, sitting on its edge.

What on earth had that been about? Magnus was angry with her, deep-down furious. He hadn't dared make love to her in case he lost his fierce control over that inexplicable rage.

Jade shivered. "It's not my fault!" she whispered aloud. And then, louder, "I was *sick!*"

Her voice echoed in the big room. He *couldn't* be blaming her for that, could he? It wasn't *like* Magnus to hold anyone responsible for something they couldn't help. He had almost no prejudices. He'd practically forced his mother to open her home to Annie—Annie, whose unstable mental condition had kept her in hospitals on and off for half of her life.

She wished Annie was here. Annie would have injected some sanity into the proceedings, she thought, and then caught herself thinking it, and giggled. The giggle turned into a sob, and she felt stinging tears rise in her eyes, spill onto her cheeks. She drew up her knees and hugged them with her arms, laying her head on them.

She missed Annie. She'd never met anyone quite like her before—irreverent, loud, untidy. And fiercely loyal, with an unexpected quality of empathy for someone going through a bad patch. Annie knew all about bad patches herself. Jade had done her best to be there for her, as Annie was when Jade wanted only to retreat from the world and everything in it, huddling small into a corner and rocking back and forth, crooning to herself, refusing to speak or listen.

Turning yourself into a little ball, then? Annie had scoffed. "You know what happens to balls, don't you? They get kicked. You gonna let everybody kick you around? Okay? Okay, if that's what you want, I'll leave you to it."

The toe of her slipper had hardly been lethal, though it had connected quite painfully with the fleshy curve of Jade's behind as Annie turned away. But it was the contempt in her voice rather than the kick itself that had brought Jade to her feet, flushed with anger. "Hey!" she said indignantly.

A nurse had already scurried up, saying sharply, "Annie! You know we don't stand for that kind of behaviour. Are you hurt, Jade?"

Jade saw the rude sign that Annie made behind the nurse's back, the gleeful glint in Annie's blue eyes before she said meekly, "Yes, nurse. Sorry, nurse," and folded her hands.

Jade had realised then, with astonishment, that she wanted to laugh. And that she'd just experienced two emotions in the space of two minutes—amusement, and anger. She, whose emotions had been dead for months, who had felt nothing except, sometimes, a sweating, screaming, inexplicable fear.

"It's all right, nurse," she'd said then. "Annie and I were just fooling around."

"Yeah," Annie said immediately, grinning at Jade. "I think I'm Pelé and she thinks she's a football. We're both happy. Two nutters in perfect harmony." She gave a deliberately goofy grin, and Jade laughed aloud.

Turning yourself into a little ball, then?

It was as though she saw herself, scrunched up on the bed, her knees next to her tear-stained face. Annie would have been disgusted.

She jackknifed herself out of it, stumbling off the bed, scrubbing at her wet cheeks.

"No!" This wasn't the way to deal with it. *"No,"* she repeated, fiercely shaking her head.

The mirror showed her red-eyed and tousled. She picked up a brush and used it until her hair shone and her scalp tingled. Then she went into the bathroom to splash her face, holding a soaked cloth to her eyes for several minutes.

After changing into one of her new dresses, she occupied the time until dinner by carefully, meticulously, applying makeup to her face.

She descended the stairs looking cool and serene and, she hoped, confident. Unfortunately there was no one to watch her, but when she reached the hallway Magnus came out of the big front lounge.

"We're having drinks in here," he said. Then, staring a little, "You look very... lovely."

"Thank you." She smiled and met his eyes, finding them dark and with a faintly baffled expression in them. "I'd like a dry white wine, please," she said, sailing towards him with her chin high. Nobody, she had decided, was going to kick her around. This evening, she had set her mind to giving every appearance of not caring a damn.

It was really quite easy, she discovered, after two glasses of wine. By then she didn't care that Mrs. Riordan was regarding her with an expression of near-disdain, that Magnus watched her lynx-eyed. Or that Danella, joining them after putting Rose-Lee down to sleep, seemed more than a little put out when she found her husband sitting at Jade's side on the sofa, laughing loudly at her recounting of parts of Annie's letter.

Danella marched across the room to stand in front of them.

"Hello, honey," Glen greeted her, still grinning. "Rosie settled all right?"

"I thought we'd agreed not to shorten her name," Danella said. "I could do with a drink, please."

"Oh, sure."

But Magnus had already poured one, which he placed in his sister's hand. "Here, vodka and lemon, right?"

"Thank you, big brother," she said sweetly. "Boy, do I need this!" She sank into an armchair. "You don't know how lucky you are, not having any kids."

Magnus looked down at her thoughtfully. "I'm sure you don't mean that."

"That's what you think! Although it's not the same for you men, is it?" She looked pointedly at her husband.

Glen said, "Feeling a bit tired, love?" He got up and went to perch on the arm of her chair, his hand on her shoulder. "It was a long trip. Never mind—I'm on the night shift, remember?"

"She'll probably sleep right through, after today," Danella predicted peevishly.

"Yeah, maybe." Glen stroked her hair.

Magnus dropped into the vacant seat beside Jade as Glen was saying, "Tell you what, why don't I take her over for the whole weekend? Give you a proper break and let you spend time with your family, go and see your old friends if you like?"

Danella's face was transformed as she raised it to him. "Oh, Glen, would you?" She nuzzled her face against him. "I'm a bitch, and I don't deserve you."

"Yeah, I know." Glen grinned and dropped a kiss on the top of her head. "You'll want to get to know your sister-in-law again, too."

Danella didn't answer, or look at Jade at all. Magnus, who had been watching the by-play with a bemused air, turned to Jade, his expression resigned, perhaps apologetic.

Jade smiled back at him. Nothing could hurt her tonight. She was armoured. "Where's Ginette?" she asked him.

"It's her weekend off. She and Mrs. Gaines take turns. She left this afternoon."

Mrs. Gaines appeared in the doorway. "Dinner's on the table."

"Right." Magnus went to help his mother, who had dispensed with the wheelchair tonight. In the dining-room Mrs. Gaines had set a straight chair for her at the foot of the table, and she presided over the meal like a queen, her eyes brighter than usual, her cheeks showing a high colour.

"It's a pity Laurence and Andrew can't be with us," she said.

"Laurence will be in another year or so," Magnus told her. "Provided he passes his finals, of course."

Jade said, "He will, won't he?" Laurence had been a bright boy, and she didn't think he would have had any problems completing his degree in agriculture.

"I certainly hope so!" Magnus said.

Surprised at his vehemence, she gave him an enquiring look, but he had turned away from her to refill Danella's wineglass.

After dinner they returned to the lounge, but Mrs. Riordan wanted to go to bed quite early. Magnus got up and said, "I'll take you to your room and call Mrs. Gaines to help you."

"I can help if you like," Jade offered. Catching a slightly hostile look from Danella, she added hastily, "Unless Danella wants to. . . ."

But Danella's expression changed from hostile to irritable. "Mrs. Gaines knows what to do," she said. "I'm sure she doesn't need any interference—from anyone."

Jade flushed. Magnus, gathering his mother's sticks up, shot a glance at his sister and said, "It's kind of you to offer, Jade, but not necessary, thank you."

There was a tense silence as Magnus and his mother left the room. Glen looked uncomfortable, and Danella, her mouth clamped tightly shut, was swinging one of her shoes on her toes, her eyes firmly fixed on it.

Jade said, "I'm sorry, Danella."

Danella's eyes rose suspiciously to hers. Glen, his voice a little too hearty, said, "What for? You only offered to help."

His wife cast him a look full of scorn. "She was trying to show me up."

"No," Jade said wearily. From past experience, she knew it was futile arguing with Danella.

Glen looked startled. "I'm sure that wasn't what Jade—"

"That's right," Danella said resentfully. "Take her side!"

"I'm not—"

"How do you do it?" Danella asked Jade accusingly.

"I'm not sure what you mean." Jade stood up. "I think I'll—"

"Twist men around your little finger the way you do! You're not *that* good-looking—"

Glen said, "Hey, steady on, Danella!"

"I think I'll go up to bed," Jade finished. Her limbs trembling, she turned away from them, but Danella's voice followed her to the door.

"He's only taken you back out of pity, hasn't he—my brother? He's not fool enough to let you pull the wool over his eyes again."

"Danella!" Glen's voice unexpectedly rang with authority.

Jade glanced back from the doorway. Glen was glaring at his wife, while she'd turned to stare defiantly back at him. "It's true!" she said. "Why do you think they sleep in separate rooms?"

"It's none of our business." Glen cast an apologetic look at Jade.

"Magnus is my brother!"

"And he wouldn't thank you for discussing this," Jade said. Not for the first time, she sorely wanted to shake her sister-in-law. "Good night."

She walked towards the stairs, deliberately shutting out the sound of Danella's shrill voice saying, "Oh, go on, tell him, then! You always ran to him with tales!" followed by Glen's protesting murmur.

Magnus was coming out of his mother's room. He looked at the open door of the lounge, and then his gaze slid enquiringly to Jade. "Trouble?"

Jade shook her head. "I'm tired. I thought I'd go up to bed. Danella's—a little excited."

"Excited?" He frowned, cocking an ear, but Danella's voice had sunk to a muted note of complaint, and no words were audible. "What did she say to you?"

"Nothing," Jade insisted. "She's talking with Glen."

"Arguing?"

Jade shrugged. "It's none of our business, is it?" she said, quoting Glen.

"No, thank heaven. Glen seems to manage her moods better than I ever did."

"Or me," Jade said ruefully. "I failed you there, I'm afraid."

Magnus shook his head. "You did what you could. No one could fault you in that direction, Jade. You showed a great deal of patience with her. Maybe too much."

Magnus had said before he married her, "There's such a big gap between me and my younger brothers and sister, I feel more like an uncle, sometimes. And now my father's dead, even more so. You're nearer her age, and Danella needs a friend just now. I can't seem to get through to her."

But Jade hadn't got through to Danella, either, despite her best intentions. "It didn't do much good, did it?" she said now. "She still doesn't like me. But she seems very protective of you."

"Protective?" His gaze sharpened.

Jade bit her tongue. "Fond of you," she amended. "It's... nice."

"I'm fond of her, too. It doesn't stop me finding her damned exasperating on occasion. What *did* she say?" His gaze swung towards the lounge door, and he stiffened as though about to march in there.

"Never mind." Jade put a hand on his arm. "Girl talk," she said lightly.

"Girl talk!" His lip curled in disbelief. "You and Danella?"

"Please, Magnus." She dropped her hand. "I'd like to be friends with her some day. Let us work it out in our own way, will you?"

His eyes searched hers. "If that's what you want. Lord knows, anything I say will probably make things worse."

"Yes." It had before, when Danella had been almost rabid with adolescent jealousy of her older brother's bride. "We should have realised," Jade said, wearily, "that the last thing she wanted was a big sister." As the only girl, Danella had frankly been spoiled by a father who adored her and an older brother who treated her with casual indulgence. When her father died, she'd found Magnus less indulgent as, conscious of his new responsibilities, he'd tried to impose some discipline on a wilful young woman. "She must have felt that she'd lost her father *and* her big brother. It wasn't really surprising that she blamed me." And that any time Magnus had intervened on Jade's behalf, Danella had only disliked her more.

"Maybe," Magnus conceded. "It's easier to see these things in hindsight. But she's not a schoolgirl now."

"No, but my relationship with her has been on hold for a long time. Just as—"

"Just as ours has," Magnus finished for her. He gave her a curious, searching look. "You must feel like Rip van Winkle."

"A bit," she agreed, with a pale smile.

He stepped back. The voices in the lounge had died to a murmur. "I'll see you tomorrow," Magnus said.

Jade's smile turned ironic, but she said nothing. Trying to make love while Danella, with her husband and child, slept just across the way was hardly her idea of bliss. She gave Magnus a small nod of acknowledgement, and went on up the stairs.

Chapter Seven

When Jade went down for breakfast, Magnus was buttering toast, and Glen was there with his daughter cooing on his knee. "Danella's still sleeping," he said. "She was more tired last night than she realised—the journey did her in."

Jade smiled at the oblique apology. "It's a long way, and it must have been a strain, with the baby."

Rose-Lee had grabbed a spoon from the table and was examining it with interest. She looked up at the sound of Jade's voice, smiled and dropped the spoon on the floor. Jade bent to pick it up and the child stretched out her hand for it, gave it a cursory glance and dropped it again, regarding Jade with a demanding, owlish gaze.

Magnus said, "She'll have you doing it all morning if you pick it up again."

"It's the latest game," Glen explained, as Jade did so. He took the spoon himself this time and placed it out of Rose-Lee's reach. Offended, the baby strained unsuccessfully towards it, and settled for investigating her father's plate of sausages and eggs instead, covering her small fist in egg yolk.

"Oh, hell!" Glen picked up a napkin and wiped his daughter's fingers.

Jade laughed. "I'll hold her for you until you've finished eating, if you like."

"What about your breakfast?"

"I can wait a few minutes." She held out her hands and the baby happily lifted her arms. "Did she sleep through the night? I didn't hear her cry."

"Nearly. We had to give her a bottle at five. The joys of parenthood."

Jade sat down with the baby, shifting her chair away from the table. Rose-Lee looked at her with solemn concentration, and patted her face with a slightly sticky hand. "Hi," Jade said softly. "Remember me?"

Magnus put down his knife and fork with a small clatter and pushed away his plate. "Coffee, Glen?"

Glen nodded, his mouth full of sausage and ruined egg. Magnus turned to Jade. "Some for you?"

"Later. I wouldn't want to spill hot coffee on Rose-Lee."

He poured some for Glen and himself, and sat watching her with the baby. Jade looked up and caught his eyes. Something wordless passed between them, and she recalled telling him what she'd said to his mother—that it wasn't too late for them to have a child of their own. Deliberately, she smiled at him, and saw his eyes turn wary before he looked away and began to talk with Glen.

Glen was just finishing his coffee when Danella appeared in the doorway. Her eyes found Jade and the baby first, and her mouth parted and then closed tightly before she turned her gaze to her husband.

Jade said, "I'm just holding Rose-Lee while Glen finishes his breakfast."

Danella came round the table and her hand clamped on the back of the chair next to Jade.

Jade stirred, shifting her grip on the baby. "Do you want to take her?"

Danella looked across the table at Glen, then back to Jade. She pulled out the chair and stiffly sat down. "She looks happy enough where she is."

Considerably surprised, Jade said, "I'm enjoying it, too."

Glen smiled at Danella and put down his cup. Pushing back his chair, he said, "I'll take the baby now, Jade. You need breakfast, too."

Over his coffee cup, Magnus raised an eyebrow at Jade as she relinquished Rose-Lee to her father.

Danella took a piece of toast from the pile on the table. "Glen, are you sure you don't mind if I go off to visit my friends and leave Rose-Lee with you?"

"I don't mind, honest. You go and enjoy yourself. I'll take her down to the beach and introduce her to the water. It's much warmer now than last time we came."

"You're an angel, and I love you!" Danella said fervently.

Glen grinned back at her.

Danella ate quickly and skipped coffee. Magnus was still lingering over his, and Jade was pouring her first cup when the others left the room. "You're right," she said. "Glen does know how to handle Danella. They seem very happy."

Magnus put down his cup. "I'm just glad she's not my responsibility any longer."

"You take your responsibilities very seriously."

"Is that a criticism?"

Jade looked at him, finding a slightly bitter little curve on his mouth. "What makes you say that?"

His eyes searched hers. "Things might have been a lot easier for you if I hadn't been so engrossed in my responsibilities to my family."

"But if you hadn't been the sort of person you are, I wouldn't have...married you." *Fallen in love with you,* she'd been going to say, but a new shyness with him held her back.

"Security? Is that what you were looking for? I wasn't such a good bet, then, was I?"

She opened her mouth to deny both suggestions, but perhaps there was some small element of truth in the first, at least. Wryly, she said, "Maybe I fancied the idea of having a family again. A mother, brothers, a sister...and a real home."

Magnus gave a crack of laughter. "Sarcasm. That's new, from you." He regarded her thoughtfully. "You've changed," he said with a kind of respect. "Grown some kind of shell."

"You mean I'm harder?" It might be true. She'd had to fight to regain her health, and it hadn't been easy. She felt battle-scarred. And determined not to let anything or anyone send her spiralling again into a pit of despair and illusion.

"Harder?" Magnus considered. "Less...accessible, perhaps."

Jade said involuntarily, "You're the one who's running away."

"Running away?" His shoulders stiffened, a frown in his eyes.

She hadn't meant to say that, but now that the words were out, she wasn't going to retract them. "You moved out of our room, suggested we wait—"

She broke off as Mrs. Gaines entered the room. Magnus cast an impatient glance at the woman and shoved his chair back, standing up. "We'll finish this discussion some other time."

Jade stood up, too. "When?"

The housekeeper hesitated inside the doorway, her expression flustered. "I didn't realise you were still here. I'll come back later—"

Magnus shook his head. "It's all right, Mrs. Gaines," he assured her. "We were leaving now, anyway."

Jade followed him to the door, so that he was obliged to step back and let her through. In the hallway, she turned to face him. "When?" she repeated.

His eyes flickered. He glanced back through the doorway, and grasped her arm, propelling her along the passageway to his office. There he closed the door on them and dropped her arm. "What are you trying to do, Jade?"

"I'm trying to—" she groped for the right word—save? renew? resurrect? "—get back our marriage," she finished. "If you won't sleep with me, and you won't talk to me—"

"I didn't say I wouldn't talk," he interrupted. "I said we'd discuss it some other time. You surely don't expect me to spill my guts in front of Mrs. Gaines?"

"You know I don't!"

"So stop trying to goad me," he said. "Unless you want a repeat of what happened last night."

Jade's head snapped up. "Is that a threat?"

She thought the expression in his eyes was surprise, but they quickly narrowed so that she couldn't be sure. He said softly, "It's a warning. Back off, Jade."

Her heart pounding, Jade swallowed, but she wouldn't let her gaze drop from his. "I *wasn't* trying to goad you," she said steadily. "But I won't be intimidated by you, Magnus. You said we'd talk."

He gave a sharp sigh. "I know." One hand jammed into his pocket, he thrust the other over his hair. "Look, it wasn't my idea to have Danella and her family here this weekend. But you can see that it's hardly the time for the kind of discussion we need."

If they'd been sharing a room, she thought, things might be different. But she conceded his point. She could hear the baby's distant wail, and Danella's voice calling something to Glen. A rattle of dishes and a succession of brisk footfalls denoted Mrs. Gaines's progress towards the kitchen.

"I'm trying to clear myself some space," Magnus said. "I thought we might take a week, get away from here, spend some time together and sort ourselves out, you and I."

"That sounds like a very good idea." Surely once they were alone their problems would resolve themselves. She was heartened that Magnus was willing to make time for her, for them. It had never been easy for him to put his business, or the farm, aside. And of course his family commitments had complicated matters still further.

"Let's just get through this weekend, first," Magnus suggested. "Then we'll decide where you'd like to go."

Jade quelled the thought that his promise was a kind of sop, something to keep her quiet meantime. "All right," she agreed. If Danella continued to be as amenable as she had been at breakfast, maybe the rest of the weekend wouldn't be too difficult. Particularly if Danella was to spend most of it visiting her friends instead of remaining about the house.

Magnus looked at his watch. "I have to see the farm manager before lunch," he said. "Do you want to come along and meet Dave and his wife?"

Surprised at the offer, Jade agreed, overcoming her instinctive cringing from meeting strangers who must know something of her history. It was nothing to be ashamed of, she reminded herself. "I'd like to," she said. "When do you want to go?"

"If we walk, it should be soon. But I can take the car if you don't feel up to that."

"I can walk easily. It's only about a mile."

"Good. I'll let my mother know. Glen may like to come with us, as he's left literally holding the baby. You wouldn't mind?"

Some of her pleasure in the prospect dimmed, but she said brightly, "Of course not. Rose-Lee will probably enjoy it."

Of the four of them, Rose-Lee seemed to enjoy the outing the most. She was passed from her father to Jade as they walked along the sand towards the headland. Then Magnus took her while they climbed a steep path bounded by blue-tinged, sword-leaved flax and wind-driven marram grass.

A seagull angled its wings above them, swooped to the cliff face and rode the wind up again, and Rose-Lee, squinting against the stiff, salty breeze, followed its flight and cooed approval. The gull opened its beak and quarked. Rose-Lee, her arms waving, emitted a similar cry, setting the three adults laughing.

Watching Magnus with the child in his arms, his eyes warm with humour, Jade felt the laughter catch in her throat, turning to tears. Abruptly she brushed her eyes in a pretence at fighting the wind that dragged her hair across her face.

At the top of the path a stile over the wire fence led them to sheep-shorn, uneven grassland, and they could see the farmhouse on a small rise about half a mile further on, red-roofed and with a grove of trees protecting it from the sea winds.

Glen said, "Here, I'll take Rose-Lee now. You wouldn't think a baby could be that heavy, would you?"

Jade heard Magnus say, "Coming?"

Glen had gone ahead. Magnus waited for her in the shade of a shaggy, silver-leaved pohutukawa with tightly closed buds, and as she drew level with him he caught her arm. "Sure you're all right?"

"I'm fine." She threw him a smile, not looking directly at him, and pulled her arm from his light grip as she passed him. Hurrying, she caught up with Glen and chatted with him and Rose-Lee the rest of the way to the farmhouse.

The manager's wife, a sturdy, fair-haired woman in her thirties, gave them tea and biscuits on the wide veranda while her husband and Magnus talked. If she was curious about Jade she didn't show it. Magnus must have prepared them for her homecoming, Jade realised. He had, in his way, done everything he could to make it easier for her.

They walked back along the road, arriving a little hot and dusty in time for lunch. Danella, Mrs. Gaines told Glen, had phoned to say she was invited to eat with her friends. Jade felt a distinct relief, followed by a twinge of conscience.

Glen fed the baby and put her down for a nap before joining them at the table. "I'll just stick around and read a book until Rose-Lee wakes up," he answered Magnus's enquiry as to his plans for the afternoon. "Later I might take her down to the beach and see how she likes the water."

"You'll excuse me if I go and do some work in my office, then?" Magnus asked. After the barest hesitation, he added, "Jade, could I impose on you to type a few more letters?"

"Of course," she said instantly. "No problem."

It didn't take long, and his manner was so impersonal that she found herself being the brisk, capable secretary, the face she'd presented to him when she'd first worked for him. It had been a conscious thing then, an eagerness to impress him with her skills, her business acumen, her ability.

From the first she'd been aware that she was attracted to her new boss, but wary of betraying it, knowing how messy office affairs could be, and how one gone wrong could damage her future prospects. She'd had a casual boyfriend when she began to work for Magnus, and for a while had gone on seeing him despite her waning interest, using him as a sort of buffer.

It had helped, of course, that Magnus had not made any moves in her direction, although occasionally she'd thought his gaze lingered on her when she wasn't looking. She'd feel a faint prickle of awareness, and perhaps look up to find his eyes on her, but always he either looked away, his face quite expressionless, as though he'd been dwelling absentmindedly on a pot plant or a piece of furniture, or he'd ask her to bring him a file or a cup of tea, or note something down.

Only a week before his father died, Magnus had taken her to dinner after asking her to work late one evening. Fearful of jumping to unwarranted conclusions, she'd been careful to act as though it were nothing more than a business meeting. Towards the end of the meal Magnus had asked about her parents, and she'd told him briefly about the accident that had taken both them and her sister when she was barely sixteen.

"It must have been rough for you," Magnus had said with appalled sympathy, "losing your family at that age. Did you have any other relations?"

"Only in England. Mum and Dad had emigrated before I was born. My mother's parents were dead before then. My other grandparents suggested I should come to them, but I'd never met them. Everyone I knew was here in New Zealand, and besides, my parents had come here because they wanted their children to be New Zealanders." And she couldn't bear the thought of leaving the three graves on one side of the world while she lived on the other.

"So what did you do?"

"I boarded with a friend's family for a while, finished my schooling, and used some insurance money for secretarial training."

"Are you in touch with your grandparents?"

"I write to them, let them know how I'm getting on."

"And . . . are you living with anyone at the moment?"

"Yes," Jade said briefly.

"Female?"

"Lida Farrell, from the office." She was so anxious not to read any personal meaning into that question that he obviously misunderstood the crisp brevity of her reply.

He said, "It's none of my business, of course."

"It's all right—"

But before she could think of anything more to add, to soften what he'd obviously regarded as a snub, he'd steered the conversation back to some innocuous subject, and it remained on that plane for the remainder of the evening. Then he'd got her a taxi and given the driver some money to get her home.

The next day she'd made a point of thanking him again for the dinner, but he'd just given her a searching look and she wondered if she'd overdone it, made him think that she was hinting at a repeat performance that he had no intention of providing. She reverted smartly to her office manner, and Magnus remained aloof and businesslike.

"You terrified me," Magnus had teased her, after they were married. "For a minute or two I thought I'd got through the efficient-secretary armour to the warm, real woman underneath. And then, when I tried to find out if there was a man in your life, you froze me out."

"I didn't want you to think I was a designing female, angling to hook the boss," Jade had confessed. They were in bed, and she was leaning on his shoulder, smiling down at him with her fingers idly playing over his bare torso, while his toyed with the strap of her nightgown.

"Well, you did, didn't you?" Magnus raised his brows and grinned at her. "You had me panting after your body from day one—"

"I *what?*" Outraged, Jade pulled away.

Magnus hooked a lazy arm about her and hauled her against him. "Are you offended? The first time you walked into my office I thought how attractive you were—" He stopped with a small laugh. "No, it wasn't ever that luke-warm. I lusted for you, but I told myself it was only a per-verted—"

"Perverted?" Jade raised her head.

"Perverted—" Magnus repeated "—attraction to a mind like a steel filing cabinet, combined with the body of a houri—not to mention a face that was all my adolescent dreams come true."

"You dreamed about a *face* when you were an adoles-cent?"

He laughed. "I was very innocent."

"Hmm." Her expression was sceptical, and he laughed again.

"I'd never have known," Jade told him. "If you felt like that, you hid it awfully well."

"I didn't want to frighten you off. I forced myself to give it three months, to convince you that I wasn't the sort of man who habitually made a play for his employees—"

"Lull me into a false sense of security, you mean?"

Magnus grinned. "Something like that. Then I took the plunge and asked you out to dinner and you accepted as though I'd asked you to take a letter—"

"You said it was only because you'd kept me working past dinner time."

"Part of the plan," he explained. "The next time, I was going to suggest we did it properly."

Jade widened her eyes. "Wouldn't that have been a bit premature?"

He tugged at her hair, his chest shaking with laughter. "You know what I mean—do *dinner* properly. A date. And then..."

"Your father died," she said soberly.

"Yes." His hold on her tightened, his hand stroking her hair as she laid her cheek against his shoulder. "All my plans went overboard. I just knew that I needed you—your quiet strength, your sympathy, your love."

"You already had that."

"You'd never let me see it until then. And I was selfish enough to take advantage of it when you did."

"It wasn't selfish. I was longing to help you, to comfort you."

"You were so utterly generous," he said. "When I asked you to have dinner with me again, on my first day back at the office, I didn't dare hope that—well, that what happened would happen."

It had been a subdued dinner, but he'd talked a little, haltingly, about his father. "I don't think he ever felt really at ease with children. We got on much better after I grew up. Andrew looked to me rather than Dad, even though I'm living in Auckland now. And I don't think Dad has—*had* any understanding of Danella at all. Laurence was the closest to him. He's the one who's interested in farming. Dad can—could relate to that."

At the end of the dinner he'd paid the bill and walked her out to his car, and when they got in he turned to her and blurted out as though he couldn't help it, "Jade—I don't want to be alone tonight."

She'd let hardly a second elapse before she said, lifting a hand to his cheek, "You don't need to be, Magnus. I'll come home with you."

She'd gone home with him that night and other nights, shared his bed and brought him, she hoped, a measure of comfort, of forgetfulness, of happiness. "It wasn't selfish," she insisted. "I wanted it as much as you did."

"I should have waited—at least before asking you to marry me. I rushed you into it, without even a proper wedding. Took advantage of your... compassion."

"It wasn't just compassion, Magnus. I've never been so happy in my life as I am now."

"Is that true?"

"It's true." She turned a little and kissed his cheek.

"Well," he said, sliding down the strap he'd been playing with, "let's see if I can make you still happier."

He turned her in the bed, his fingers stroking down her arm, his eyes on the curve of her breast where he'd bared it. Then he bent his head and kissed her there, his lips lingering. Jade gave a sigh of content, and he lifted his head, replacing his lips with his hand, his mouth capturing hers.

"Jade?"

She found herself staring into space, her fingers idle on the keyboard, her body tingling and her cheeks flushed with remembered desire. Magnus was standing in front of her.

"Yes, Magnus." She raised her eyes languorously, and saw his pupils darken in response before his gaze narrowed.

"You've finished?" he asked, his voice grating.

"Oh—yes. Just this last envelope." Flustered, she rapidly typed the address, found that she'd made two mistakes, and said, "Sorry, I'll do it again."

He waited until she'd done it, then said, "Are you tired?"

Jade shook her head. "A bit out of practice." She wished he'd stop standing there. Her body was still warm, and her fingers not quite steady as she straightened the stack of letters and envelopes. "You can sign them now." She picked them up to hand them to him, but he'd come around the desk to stand beside her chair, taking a pen from the container by the typewriter. His shoulder brushed hers as he bent to skim the work and put his signature at the bottom of each sheet.

He was very close. His cheek showed a faint shadow where he'd shaved, and his neck was tanned. She fought the urge to put out her hand and brush away the hair from his eyes as it fell forward, to make him turn his head and look at her again.

He did it anyway as he straightened. His hand, replacing the pen, missed the container, and the pen rolled.

Jade automatically made a grab for it, and so did Magnus. As her fingers came down on the pen, his hand closed over hers.

He didn't lift it, and she felt its weight, and the tensile strength of his fingers. She could hear him breathing, and her chair moved very slightly as he put his other hand on the back of it, steadying himself. She was looking at their hands, at his fingers curving about hers.

She thought he said, "Hell!" And then he lifted her hand within his, and closed his other hand about her upper arm, drawing her from the chair.

Jade's eyes met his, half-afraid, because his touch was not quite gentle. And he swore again, and said, "Don't look like that." His face was taut and angry, and for a moment before he lowered his head she thought that what she read in his eyes was some kind of contempt. But then his mouth touched hers with fierce control, moving lightly, almost teasingly at first, gradually becoming more demanding, an expert, carefully constrained seduction of the senses. She hardly knew when he'd persuaded her lips apart for him, and even then he didn't take advantage of it straight away, although his arm about her waist tightened, and he leaned back on the desk, parting his legs and urging her forward to stand between his warm, hard thighs.

He still held her hand, and as she instinctively clutched at his shoulder with the other, he moved their linked hands so that her arm was bent behind her, his free hand sliding down over the rounded curves, touching her thighs, intruding under her skirt.

She felt her mouth open as he urged her closer to him, her back arched and her pelvis snug against his.

And then he was kissing her deeply, freely, completely overwhelming her senses, so that the blood raced along her veins and beat in her ears, and her limbs felt fluid with pleasure.

He dragged his mouth away, and she opened her eyes and saw that his were brilliant with passion, his cheekbones darkly flushed. He turned, so that it was she who was pressed up against the edge of the desk, and his voice rasped when he said, "Do you know when you first came to work for me, I used to fantasise about making love to you on your desk—or mine?"

"No." Her voice felt raw. He'd never told her that, even after they were married.

The hand that had been caressing her beneath her skirt was on her breast now, moving over the fabric of her blouse while he watched, apparently fascinated. She knew he could see her arousal even through the blouse and the thin, seamless stretch satin of her bra, could feel it under his palm. He raised his eyes to hers and gave her a tight, glittering smile. "No, you didn't? Or no, you don't want to?"

"I never...knew," she managed to say, her eyelids growing heavy with desire as his hand went on stroking, kneading, discovering.

"*Do* you want to?" he asked her. He released her briefly, only to drag both his hands into her hair, tipping back her head so that she had to look at him.

"N-now?" Her voice faltered.

"Have I shocked you?" His mouth came back to hers, in a kiss that was wild and hot and abandoned. She felt dizzy when he finally lifted his head and said, "We can't, though, unfortunately. Mrs. Gaines is going to bring in afternoon tea any minute now."

That shocked her. She stiffened, coming upright, clutching at his sleeve to steady herself.

Magnus stepped back, laughing. "Don't panic. We've got a few minutes. Anyway, she knows that we're married, and that we've been apart for a long time. I don't suppose she'd be surprised."

"She'd be embarrassed," Jade said, smoothing her hair, making sure her blouse was tucked in. "And so would we."

"You might be. How do you know I'm not a secret exhibitionist?"

"You're the one who mentioned we might be... interrupted," Jade pointed out. "Anyway, after twelve months of marriage, I'd have known."

A strange expression crossed his face. "Are you sure? There seems to have been quite a lot I didn't know about *you*, after twelve months of marriage."

"It...wasn't very long," she said, not quite sure what he meant. "Oh! The letters!" she remembered, and turned, wondering if in the heat of passion they'd crushed them. But the pages were away from the edge of the desk, and untouched.

A discreet tap came at the door before Mrs. Gaines opened it and carried in a tray bearing two cups. Magnus cast Jade an ironic look and casually moved back to his own desk.

When they had drunk the tea, Jade asked, "Is there anything more I can do for you?"

She flushed at the way he raised his brows, his eyes making an explicit unspoken comment as they ran over her, but he said only, "No, I don't need your *secretarial* services any more. You could take the tray out of my way, if you don't mind."

She picked it up and walked away from him, but as she reached the door his voice stopped her. "The sooner we take that week away together, the better," he said. "Have you given any thought to where you'd like to go?"

She half turned, but kept her eyes on the tray in her hands. "I don't mind," she said. "Somewhere quiet. I'm happy to leave it to you."

"I'll see what I can rustle up."

She felt tense and restless, and decided a swim would help settle her body, if not her emotions. Arriving at the beach she found Glen and the baby sitting on the sand, Glen in swim shorts and Rose-Lee wearing a diminutive frilled yellow bikini with red polka dots, and a matching sun-hat.

·Jade laughed, and Glen looked up at her with a grin. "Ridiculous, isn't it?" he said cheerfully. "My sister gave it to her. At least the hat's practical." It shaded Rose-Lee's face so that Jade could see only a fat baby cheek and tiny pointed chin.

"How do you like the beach, Rose-Lee?" Jade asked, making the baby look up with curiosity at the sound of her name, squinting in the sun.

"She's not too impressed with the water, but she's enjoying the fresh air." Glen made a grab for the baby's fist just before it reached her mouth, with the remains of a handful of sand in it. "Going in?"

"Yes," Jade said. Seeing his shorts were dry, she said, "I can watch her for a while if you want a dip."

"Thanks, but you go first." He picked up a plastic rattle and handed it to Rose-Lee. "Here, if you must eat something, try that."

When Jade came out and sank down on a towel, Glen ran into the water. Rose-Lee, bored with the rattle, was inspecting a piece of dried seaweed now, and Jade removed it twice from her mouth, finally sitting the baby in front of her on the towel and gently replacing the seaweed with a piece of smooth, whitened driftwood, saying, "I hope it hasn't got too many germs on it."

Danella's voice said, "She tries to eat everything in sight at the moment, and she's never been sick for a day."

Dressed in a high-cut one-piece white suit, she dropped a towel on the sand and sat down beside Jade and the baby. Rose-Lee blew some bubbles and waved plump arms at her mother. Danella picked her up, made a face at her, and grinned. "Blub-blub to you, too."

"Did you enjoy your day with your friends?" Jade asked politely.

"Yes, thanks. Where's Magnus?"

"Working. I worked with him for a while, but he didn't need me any more, and I came down for a swim and found Glen here with the baby."

Danella threw a glance at her, and then stared over Rose-Lee's head at the water. "You don't have to explain. I trust Glen." She paused, chewing on a thumbnail. "He says I owe you an apology."

"I don't expect one," Jade told her coolly, "and certainly not if *you* don't think it's owed."

Another look slid her way, and Danella said shamefacedly, "No, he's right. I shouldn't have said all those things. The thing is, I have this possessive streak."

"I know." Jade smiled dryly.

Danella picked up the piece of driftwood that Rose-Lee had been playing with earlier and began absently digging in the sand. "I don't really blame you for telling Magnus about the drugs. I hated you at the time, of course."

"You were only sixteen. I couldn't let you ruin your life. You needed help."

"Yeah, I know I did. And Magnus tried to give it to me, only I wouldn't listen."

She'd run away instead, and Magnus had been frantic, trying to locate her, worrying about what sort of life she might be leading, or if she was alive at all. For weeks he had scarcely come home, spending all his spare time hunting the streets of Auckland, then further afield as rumour and guesswork led him fruitlessly to other cities.

So, do you think your illness is a bid to gain your husband's attention? The voice intruded in her head—she recalled a woman in a white coat facing her. *No!* she heard her own voice giving its emphatic reply, and then the brief flash of memory abruptly faded.

Eventually, after months of worry, Danella had telephoned from Sydney in Australia, hysterical and broke, and Magnus, dropping everything, had flown over to fetch her home. She'd been alternately remorseful and defensive, her mood swings a trial to live with as she battled to break her addiction, or gave up and disappeared again for days on end.

Magnus had pulled strings to get her a job in his office where he could keep an eye on her, and she'd vacillated between gratitude for his help and resentment that he insisted on keeping her under his wing. He'd been remarkably patient with his sister, but occasionally the strain he was under showed, and he'd snapped at other people—his wife included.

Rose-Lee reached for a passing grey-blue butterfly, and almost toppled. Danella lifted her closer and submitted to having her hair grabbed in a relentless fist. "I suppose if Magnus has taken you back, it's not up to me to throw stones," she said gruffly, casting a half shamed, half defiant glance at Jade. "You must have resented the time he spent on all of us, when you were just newly married, after all. I know I would've. And if I helped to send you off the rails," she added hurriedly, as though wanting to get it over with, "I'm sorry." Untwining the baby's hand from her hair, she added with relief, "Look, Rose-Lee, here comes your daddy."

Glen had left the water and was running towards them. "Hello, love," he said, bending to kiss his wife. "The water's great. Want to go in?"

Jade rose, picking up her towel. "See you later," she said. She didn't want to spoil her new, tentative rapport with her rather prickly sister-in-law by sticking around with Glen while Danella was in the water. Danella's possessive streak had caused enough problems already.

Chapter Eight

Glen suggested they all go out for dinner at a nearby tourist hotel. "My shout," he told Magnus. "Mrs. Gaines offered to babysit instead of cooking tonight, and your mother said she'd enjoy an evening out."

Magnus looked slightly surprised at that. "Thank you," he said. "I'm sure we'll enjoy it, too, won't we, Jade?"

Inwardly doubtful, she had no choice but to agree.

Jade felt locked in to a number of uneasy truces. Danella, perhaps mellowed and relaxed by a day freed of the stress of caring for a baby, was making an effort at being, if not friendly, at least normally courteous. Mrs. Riordan treated Jade with chilly graciousness. And Magnus was giving a careful performance, she decided, as the considerate husband, although he seemed reluctant to touch her. It was as though that torrid interlude in the study had never happened.

For herself, she was abnormally conscious of the masculine grace of his every movement, of the faint scent of pine aftershave that teased her nostrils as he opened the car door for her, and the warmth emanating from his body while he drove, his arm inches from hers. Mrs. Riordan had elected to go with her daughter and son-in-law in their car, following behind.

"You and Danella seem to be getting along," Magnus said.

"Fairly well," Jade agreed. "I think that having a day with her friends helped. She needed some time off."

"From being a mother? She still seems too young for it."

"Perhaps she'll always seem young, to an older brother." Jade paused. "I imagine motherhood is like marriage—no matter how well prepared you think you are, the reality is different from your expectations."

"Is that how marriage was, for you?" He looked at her.

"Wasn't it, for you?" Jade countered.

"In the end, yes. I suppose you're right."

When they arrived at the hotel they sat in a shaded courtyard for a pre-dinner drink. They must, Jade thought, look like a normal family party on a night out. Did other families have similar strains and tensions? Perhaps they did. Maybe most of them put up some kind of façade in public.

At the other side of the table Glen was talking to Mrs. Riordan and Danella. He seemed eager to get on with his wife's relatives, Jade reflected. Mrs. Riordan was looking reluctantly interested, leaning forward slightly in her chair, her sticks hooked over its arm.

Magnus leaned over and brushed away a moth that whirred close to Jade's glass as she set it on the wrought-iron table. "I could get a cottage on the shore of the Hokianga

Harbour for a week," he murmured. "It's fairly remote, but quite comfortable. You did say you'd like a quiet place."

A cottage where they could be alone. Her heart quickened at the thought. "It sounds fine," she said.

"We can have it for a week, anytime in the next month or so."

"Longer than our honeymoon," Jade said. They'd snatched three days then, a long weekend at a luxury hotel in Taupo.

It had rained most of the time, but the rain hadn't mattered. They'd been discovering each other in every way, delighting in finding that they both enjoyed cryptic crosswords and walking in the rain, hated tomato sauce, opera and the colour mauve. Delighting, too, in the more intimate discoveries that they made in the wide bed where they spent the three precious nights.

Magnus said, breaking into her thoughts, "You haven't finished your drink. Do you want to bring it in to dinner?" He was on his feet, and Glen and Danella were helping Mrs. Riordan up, arranging her walking sticks.

Jade picked up her glass and emptied it. "I'm ready."

The dining-room was discreetly lit and the table set with a red linen cloth and gleaming silver. Magnus, studying the menu, said, "I suppose you'd like the avocado and shrimp starter, Jade?"

Glen smiled at her. "You like avocados?"

"Love them."

That was another of the things she and Magnus had found out on their brief honeymoon—Jade was passionately fond of avocados, which Magnus heartily disliked, while she turned up her nose at the chocolate ice-cream sundaes that he found irresistible.

She ordered the avocado followed by a lamb dish, and perhaps it was the bottle of wine they shared, or the effect of the surroundings and the novelty of dining out, but by the time the waiter presented the dessert menu, Mrs. Riordan seemed almost mellow, Danella was sparkling, and when they left the restaurant after lingering over coffee and liqueurs, Jade was feeling both stimulated and relaxed.

On the way home, as Magnus followed the red tail-lights of Glen's car, she found herself humming some half-remembered tune.

Magnus turned briefly. "You sound happy."

"I'd almost forgotten what it was like."

Magnus said soberly, "Me too."

"Oh, Magnus!" Impulsively she stretched out her hand and touched his on the steering wheel. "I promise I'll make it up to you!"

He turned his hand and gripped hers, and his foot trod on the brake, bringing the car to a sliding halt at the side of the road. "If you mean that—" he said.

"I mean it."

His fingers were cool and hard, curled about hers. "You should be careful about your promises," he said strangely, "in case you can't deliver on them."

Jade's voice was husky, unsure. "I want to!"

"And I want you to," he said. "Heaven help me."

"Magnus—?" The intensity of his gaze, even in the near-dark of the interior of the car, almost frightened her. She wasn't sure what he was getting at. He couldn't mean that he didn't want her any more. This morning had dispelled any thought of that. Instinctively she leaned towards him, her face lifting.

Magnus made a low sound like a groan. One hand thrust into her hair, tilting her head as he lowered his mouth to hers, kissing her without inhibition, without mercy. She felt an anger in him, and a driving need that she tried to meet, letting him delve into her open mouth, arching her body to his when his arm dragged her closer. Her taut-stretched throat began to ache under the onslaught of his kiss, and the hold he still retained on her hand moved to her wrist and became painfully tight, but even as her hand throbbed she didn't protest, partly because she didn't think that this hard-edged, headlong passion would acknowledge protests, and partly because despite those small discomforts, her blood was racing, and a slow heat was unfolding in the pit of her stomach, melting hotly through her limbs.

Magnus broke off the kiss so abruptly that she gasped, shivering in his suddenly slackened hold. He released her hand, and shifted back into his seat as she automatically rubbed at her wrist to restore the circulation. He said unevenly, "Did I hurt you?"

"You didn't intend to."

"You're very confident."

She stared at him, a faint unease stirring. "Of course."

"*My God,* but you take a lot for granted!" he said.

Unease turned to fear. She squashed it quickly, deliberately. "I'm sorry," she said, "but...I'm not sure what you mean."

"Don't you?" He sounded almost accusing. "Never mind," he said, and gave a short, harsh laugh as he turned from her and restarted the car. "The others will think we've broken down if they don't see our headlights."

Frustrated, Jade sat back in her seat, watching the leaping shadows of the trees pass by, the shivering ladders of ferns momentarily lit by the glare as the lights swept the curving banks lining the road.

They arrived at the gates of Waititapu only yards behind the others, and at the garage Magnus excused himself to go and help his mother out of Glen's car.

Inside, Mrs. Gaines reported that the baby was soundly sleeping, and came forward to help Mrs. Riordan to bed. The hallway seemed full, and it wasn't until she was at the top of the stairs, on her way to her room, that Jade realised Magnus hadn't followed, although Glen and Danella, their arms about each other, were right behind her.

It was hours before he came up, and then she heard him dimly in the next room, through the mist of exhausted sleep.

Danella and Glen and the baby left after lunch the following day. Jade, standing on the terrace beside Magnus to wave them goodbye, felt herself relax slightly as the car swept down the drive. She hadn't realised until then that she'd been so tense during the visit. But things could have been worse.

She said, as she turned to go inside, "Danella's very lucky."

"Because of the baby?"

"And because she has a kind and considerate husband."

"Glen has a capacity for getting people to like him. Especially women."

"He's not a womaniser."

"I didn't say that."

Struck by his curt tone, she asked him, "Are you jealous?"

Magnus shook his head. "Envious, perhaps, of his ability to get on with almost anyone. It's a rare gift."

"You have other gifts," Jade said.

He looked startled. "I won't ask you to name them."

"I will if you like."

Magnus laughed and shook his head, standing back to allow her to precede him inside.

"Do you want me?" she asked him as he joined her, the house seeming dim after the brightness outside.

He stared down at her. "Want you?" he repeated softly, his brows lifting.

"If you're going to work," she said, "shall I help?"

"Actually, I thought I'd go for a swim." After the slightest of pauses he added, "Would you care to join me?"

It was a peculiarly formal invitation, but Jade leapt at it. "I'll go and get changed."

She tucked a towel about her waist, over the one-piece swimsuit, and padded barefoot down the stairs. Magnus was waiting for her in the hall, wearing dark briefs and with a towel slung about his neck. He had broad shoulders and long, muscular, tanned legs. She thought that he didn't look like an accountant. Of course, part of his time was spent on the farm rather than in the office.

He watched her coming down to him, his eyes unreadable. When she reached him he didn't touch her but asked, "Did you bring sunscreen? It's quite hot."

"I've already put some on," she said. "It's waterproof."

He put out his hand and touched a finger to her skin, trailing it from the edge of her jaw down the side of her neck to her shoulder, and examining the faint greasy film left on the tip. "Right," he said, "let's go."

Stilling the sudden beating of her pulse, Jade took a quick breath and followed him to the door as he opened it for her.

When they had reached the sand he asked, "Straight in, or sunbathe first?"

She felt hot and sticky and with a residue of tension from preserving the tentative truce between herself and Danella. "Straight in," she said, "for me."

He actually smiled, briefly. "Come on, then." He held out his hand and she put hers into it and went racing with him into the water's cool embrace.

Once they reached a swimmable depth, he released her hand but stayed near, watching for breakers and riding over the unbroken crests to deeper, calm water.

Jade turned onto her back, keeping herself afloat with tiny movements of hands and feet. The sky was an intense, throbbing blue, wispy white clouds drifting across it. Nearby, Magnus was treading water, his hair sleeked close to his head. He caught her gaze and then shook his head and dived like a seal, with a swift, economical and almost silent movement.

Jade closed her eyes. After a moment she was aware that Magnus had swum away from her. She was too good a swimmer for him to imagine she'd try to drown herself.

Once he'd taken her out from the hospital, driven her into the city for a visit to the art gallery. It must have been a difficult afternoon for him, because she'd been unable to muster any interest in the exhibition, and the crowds had made her nervous. They'd only stayed for half an hour, and although Magnus had tried to conceal his exasperated disappointment, she'd felt it as they left the crowded gallery and waited to cross the road to where he'd parked. Cars and a large yellow bus streamed downhill, and on a blind impulse, she'd suddenly lunged forward, pulling herself from his surprised grasp, into the path of the bus.

She remembered the hoarse sound of his wordless shout, the high, anguished screech of the brakes as the bus driver slammed them on, the sickening crunch of the car behind crashing into the back of the bus.

Something had thumped into her back and she went sprawling, and then amid the cacophony of hoots and angry obscenities she'd been hauled up and dragged to the footpath by a whitefaced, flint-eyed Magnus whose hands were hard and angry as he held her arms, turning to fling apologies, explanations and promises of compensation at two outraged and badly frightened drivers.

When they'd gone at last, he'd turned to her and his face was still pale, still furious. *"What in the name of hell did you think you were doing?"* He gave her a fierce little shake.

"You should have let me," she whispered. "It would be all over, now."

"It wouldn't be all over for me!" he rasped. "Or for the poor sod who ran over you! How do you think he'd feel? Try to think of someone else for a change, will you, instead of wallowing in self-pity!"

She'd stared back at him and felt the hopeless tears well in her eyes, hot and heavy.

Then suddenly Magnus changed his grip, his arms coming around her, holding her tightly. "Oh, Jade, Jade," he murmured. "Please, *please* get better."

It had been a long time after that before he'd taken her out again. And then, he'd accepted with something like relief her request that they take Annie, too. She thought that he hadn't been all that anxious to be alone with her.

"Jade—*Jade!*"

She opened her eyes. Magnus's voice said, "You're drifting. I think it's time we went back to shore."

Jade turned over, her arms moving as she looked towards the beach, further away than she'd realised. "All right," she said, and began swimming in a leisurely crawl.

When they emerged from the water and flopped onto towels, she found she was panting. Out of condition, she thought, burying her head in her arms and trying to make her breathing slow. The sun was warm on her back. A gull screamed overhead.

Magnus's hand smoothed the wet hair back from her cheek. "That tired you."

"Don't fuss, Magnus." Her voice was muffled against her arm. "I have to get used to swimming again. Real swimming, in the sea." She turned and sat up, squeezing water from her hair. "That was good."

Magnus was reclining on one elbow. Jade lay back on the towel, her knees raised, her breasts still rising and falling rather rapidly. Her skin tingled, pleasantly stimulated by the salty water that was fast drying on her body.

She turned her head and found Magnus examining her, from her sand-dusted feet to the shallow valley between her breasts where droplets of water still lay. His gaze seemed to linger there before it travelled slowly to the line of her throat, touched on her mouth and finally met her questioning eyes.

His mouth twisted. "You're as beautiful as ever," he said.

Why did that seem to anger him? Jade's lips parted, and she moistened them with her tongue, tasting salt. "Magnus?" she whispered.

Something leapt in his eyes. "Don't look like that!" he said harshly.

Jade blinked, and dragged her eyes away from him. How had she looked? Apprehensive? Bewildered? Aroused? She was all of those at this moment. She knew he wanted her, too. But there was a new and disturbing quality in his kisses, in the way he touched her and looked at her, that had never been there before. It was almost as though he didn't dare to touch her for fear of igniting something within himself that he might not be able to control.

When she looked at him again she found that he was sitting up, his forearms laid across his knees, his frowning gaze on the glittering horizon. The hand she could see was tightly clenched. He had the look of a man fighting some private, internal battle.

She wanted to reach out to him, run her hands over the taut curve of his spine, feel the texture of his skin, the strength of his fingers twining into hers. But his aloof, impenetrable posture was a deliberate attempt, she felt, to shut her out.

"Magnus," she asked him, "how soon can we go to this cottage on the Hokianga?"

At first she thought he wasn't going to answer. Then he briefly turned his head, but without looking at her. "As a matter of fact," he said, "I'm not sure it's such a good idea."

Her stomach went hollow with disappointment. Then an alien, white-hot emotion took her over, and she sat up abruptly. "Why?" she demanded, her voice hard. "You have something more *urgent* to do, I suppose! What is it this time?"

He turned to her. "Jade—"

But she was beyond listening. "Whatever it is, obviously it's more important than me, more important than our marriage. When are you going to have time for that, Magnus? And how long do you think I'll wait?" She jumped up, scooping the towel into her hands and giving it a vigorous little shake, uncaring if Magnus was showered with sand.

He stood up, too, glaring at her, his voice full of raw impatience. "You don't understand."

"Understand?" Jade gave a bitter little laugh. "No, I don't. Why don't you explain it to me, Magnus?"

"All right," he said, his eyes glittering. "I will." He hauled a breath into his chest. "I *know* that I was partly to blame—if I'd taken more notice of your needs, if I'd not expected so much of you, if I'd given you half the attention that I gave to my family—I can provide excuses till the cows come home. But if the two of us are alone, I can't promise to behave like a civilised human being."

At first bewildered, she rapidly sorted out an explanation. Subconsciously he was angry with her for withdrawing from life, from their marriage, into a world of her own. He had enough insight to analyse his own feelings and recognise them for an unfair and unreasonable reaction, but one that he couldn't entirely control.

But Magnus was no sadist, and he wasn't a bully, either. "I'm willing to take the risk," she told him huskily. If they were ever to get their relationship back on track, she didn't see them doing it easily at Waititapu, with the constant demands made on him by his business and his family, the lack of real privacy, and not least the memories of the past that hung about it. "I'm not made of glass, Magnus," she said.

His eyes went very dark suddenly, and his cheeks blanched. "What are you saying?" he demanded hoarsely.

"Saying?" Jade took a step backwards, her feet sinking into the warm sand. "I suppose," she said slowly, "that I'm saying I know you're angry with me, but I'm strong enough now to take it."

Her chin lifted. "But I'm angry, too, Magnus. I hadn't realised it until now." It was true, she hadn't recognised her tightly reined-in rage for what it really was. But it was there, smouldering beneath the surface. He *was* being unfair, and unreasonable, and his self-accusation held more than a grain of truth. She wouldn't have been human if she'd failed to resent his preoccupation with everything, everyone, except her, in the time they'd spent together. She said, her eyes defiantly holding his, "It's one of the things we need to... resolve."

The colour gradually returning to his face, he deliberately looked away for a moment before returning his steady gaze to hers. "I don't want to be responsible," he said sombrely, "for making you ill again."

Jade shook her head. "No chance. We need this... holiday, Magnus. To clear the air between us. So, when do we leave?"

"Tomorrow," he said, finally. "As early as you wish."

The last part of the trip was made on a car ferry from the little town of Rawene. Here the harbour was broad and tranquil, and a faint breeze ruffled Jade's hair and made Magnus's shirt cling to his body when they got out of the car to lean over the low side and gaze at the water.

The bushy hills were a soft, shadowed green, and lazy mists lay in some of the hollows. The harbour, a long, fretted waterway from the unseen ocean, reaching deeply inland, had once been a source of timber and spars for the British navy. By the end of the nineteenth century the vast forests of mighty kauri trees had been cut down, and now only remnants were left for tourists to admire.

The ferry glided to a halt, and the metal ramp clanged down. A large, battered truck began revving its engine, and Magnus touched Jade's arm. "Come on, we'd better not hold everyone up." They returned to their car.

In Rawene they'd had lunch and bought boxes of groceries that now sat in the back. Slowing at another small settlement, Magnus said, "Any last-minute thing you need?"

Jade shook her head. "No, I've brought everything, I think."

He drove a little further and slowed again at a yellow signpost, then turned off the main road, eventually arriving at a wooden gate barring access to a winding drive.

"I'll get it." Jade got out and swung the gate wide, closing it when Magnus had driven through. The drive was cut through rough scrub, and when she got back in beside him, she asked, "Are you sure there really is a house here?"

He slanted her a tight smile. "I've been here before, with the owner. You'll be surprised."

She was, when they finally arrived at a long, low cottage built on a slope that commanded a breathtaking view of hills graduating in a series of lowering humps to the wide sweep of the Hokianga, now ablaze with the midday sun, a shining sheet of breathing silver.

Magnus unlocked the door and led her into a large open living area furnished with cane loungers and big Indian cushions. "The kitchen's over there," he said with a nod. A high counter separated it from the rest, and a round table was set near a bay window overlooking the sea. "The bedroom's here."

He shouldered open a door, and Jade saw a large room, with a broad dais on which a king-size mattress had been laid, covered with a heavy cotton quilt. One wall featured a built-in dressing table and a wardrobe with a mirrored door. "And the bathroom's through here." Magnus had put down the cases he was carrying and opened another door. "And the spa room, off it. There's a toilet and shower near the laundry, too."

"One bedroom?" Jade queried.

"There is a guest room downstairs."

"I . . . didn't realise there were two levels."

"Being on the slope, there's room for a basement. You don't notice it from the drive." He pushed his hands into his pockets, lounging against the doorway to the bathroom. "Are you having second thoughts about sharing a room with me?"

"We're married, aren't we?" She faced him, looking into his eyes. It was silly to be suddenly shy of the idea. She'd been eager enough to resume sharing their room at Waititapu, but so much seemed to have taken place in the last few days, she was nervous at the thought of spending the night in this king-size bed with Magnus.

He straightened, strolling across the room to stand in front of her, his eyes alert and challenging. "Yes, we are," he said. "And I don't intend you'll ever forget it again."

Jade winced visibly. There had been times, during her illness, when she scarcely remembered her own name. But she supposed it must have hurt Magnus if he thought she could have forgotten the intimacy that they'd shared. "Magnus—" she said, putting out a hand to place it on his shirt front, her eyes pleading. "I'm so sorry!"

He raised his own hand and held hers in a crushing grip, his eyes glinting down at her. "Yes," he said, "I believe you are. And so am I. The trouble is, I'm also bloody furious, and no matter how hard I try, I can't seem to overcome that."

"It's all right," she said. "You can't help it . . . I understand."

"Do you?" He shook his head. "I wish I could say the same." His eyes went narrow, and he lifted his other hand and traced the line of her lips.

Jade frowned, puzzled. "You can't?"

"I can't," he confirmed. "Believe me, I'm trying. Logic says it was understandable but my heart won't listen to logic. My heart—feels betrayed."

As if he felt he'd said too much, he abruptly released her and turned away. "I have to turn on a generator and water pump," he said, "so that we can have our home comforts. When the water's heated, which should be in a couple of hours, how about a spa bath?"

"Together?"

"The whole idea of this week is to do things together, isn't it?"

He sounded grim rather than teasing, but Jade swallowed and said, "Yes, if that's what you'd like."

"No," he said, "if it's what *you'd* like."

"Then—I think I'd prefer it after dinner. I thought I'd cook something special for us."

"Okay," he agreed.

She did feel hot and sticky, though. It had been a long journey. "I suppose I could have a cold shower. We're quite a long way from the harbour, aren't we?"

"Yes, but there's a water-hole we could walk to. It's not like the sea, of course. But refreshing. And very private."

"I'll put on my swimsuit while you do things with pumps and generators," she said.

He looked amused in a sardonic way, but said nothing as she turned away from him to open her bag.

The route to the water-hole was through a couple of hundred yards of twiggy manuka and shady tree ferns. She could hear the rushing of swift water before the path ended in a small, grassy space. A narrow, fast-moving stream foamed over scattered boulders into a deep pool between ferns and creepers and hanging branches. The water was clear all the way to the pebbled bottom, and overflowed into a miniature foam-edged waterfall before breaking up again and tumbling downhill to disappear at a bend hidden by overhanging bush.

"Oh, you didn't tell me!" Jade exclaimed. "It's lovely!"

Magnus smiled. "I thought you'd like it."

She walked onto the rock slab that overhung part of the pool, and looked back at him. He was bare-chested, having stripped off his shirt before leaving the house. His hand was on the fastening of his jeans.

Jade wore a light pair of cotton trousers and a T-shirt, and she dropped the towel she carried and pulled the shirt off quickly, revealing the top of a scanty apricot bikini, then hesitated as she realised that Magnus hadn't moved but was watching her with a peculiarly analytical expression on his face.

Deliberately, she turned to face him, and slipped off the trousers.

Magnus grinned rather wolfishly and pulled down the zip of his jeans.

Jade didn't wait to see if he wore anything underneath, but stepped to the edge of a flat, sun-warmed rock, pausing there to survey the depth and nature of the pool, assessing if it was safe to dive.

Then a strong, bare arm came about her waist, and Magnus said in her ear, "Take a breath."

Instinctively she obeyed as they plunged in feet first, his arm still locked about her, and the clear water closed over her. The world was cold, quiet, her eyes closed and her hair drifting about her head. She found she was clutching his shoulder, could feel the powerful movements of his naked thighs against hers as he brought her back to the surface.

"Breathe," he said, and when she'd filled her lungs his cool mouth found hers, and they sank again into a world where sound and sight didn't exist, where there was only sensation—the coldness of the water contrasted with the warmth of their mingled breath, the hard planes and muscled surfaces of his body moving against hers in a muted, weightless, erotic dance.

When they surfaced again and he abruptly released her, she was gasping. She moved her arms, kicked herself away from him, drinking in gulps of air. Magnus stayed where he was, but watched her, his eyes hungry and heavy-lidded. His body was lightly tanned, and a dark-coloured pair of tight-fitting swim briefs sat on his hips.

Jade wrenched her gaze away and contemplated the trees and ferns around her. A tui called throatily somewhere nearby, but she couldn't see the bird. Against the sky, leaves lazily stirred in a faint breeze. The water burbled into the pool, eddied around the edges and spilled over the rocky lower lip. It was cold on her skin, almost cold enough to hurt. She closed her eyes, floating near the bank, holding onto a branch that swept the water, her legs moving gently.

After a while she opened her eyes and found that Magnus was stretched out on the flat rock beside their discarded clothes, face down with his head in his arms.

The sun played over his nearly nude body, and her eyes involuntarily followed the line of it from his feet along the length of his legs to the taut curve of his behind sheathed in the skimpy garment, and the shallow depression of his back to the powerful shoulders and arms. He was beautiful like that, a perfectly sculpted masculine form, but with the warmth of real flesh, the dampness making it gleam in the sunlight. His face was hidden from her, but as if he'd sensed her scrutiny he raised his head and looked at her, then shifted his upper torso a little, propping himself up with one arm on the rock, his cheek resting against his hand.

His gaze remained on her face, not her body, with a strange, brooding look, nothing sexual in it at all. She was suddenly conscious of the chilliness of the water, and goosepimples arose on her skin. She moved, turning to swim back to the rock and haul herself out.

He directed that strangely impersonal look at her and didn't alter his lounging position. Jade grabbed a towel and, turning her back on him, wrapped it about her like a sarong, then sat on the edge of the rock, her toes just touching the water.

Her hair dripped unheeded on her shoulders. Her body tingled all over. She felt more alive than she had for a long time, every sense and nerve end excruciatingly sensitive. She heard the infinitesimal sound of a dried leaf drifting onto the rock beside her, the trees moving above, the faint flutter of wings as a fantail flashed from branch to branch. She was acutely, pleasurably aware of every tiny, separate droplet of water that ran over her skin, and knew when a fleeting, insubstantial cloud momentarily dimmed the sun. She felt the warm, slightly gritty smoothness of the rock under her palms, and heard Magnus's even breathing behind her. And time stood still.

When he moved, she knew by the change in his breathing, the small sounds he made. She held her own breath in anticipation, then heard him gather up his jeans, the swift slide of the material over his legs, the rasp of the zip.

"You look cold," he said. "You stayed in too long. Let's go."

Chapter Nine

It was more of a shock than the plunge into the cold pool had been. Jade felt her spine stiffen, then she got to her feet and turned to face him.

He had her clothes in his hands, holding them out to her. "Do you want to dress first?"

She snatched them from him. "Do you want me to?" she challenged him. Her cheeks burned, her eyes, too—they felt hot and bright.

Something flickered in the depths of his. In a voice like oiled silk, he said softly, "Is that an invitation?"

Her forehead pounded tightly. Something that had been simmering inside her was welling up, coming to the boil. "It's a *question!*" she said. "This was your idea, Magnus. I thought—"

As she paused, he said, "What did you think?"

That he'd hoped the swim might turn into a romantic interlude, of course. That they'd recapture some of the spontaneous joy of their long-ago lovemaking.

Why else had he given her that amused look when she said she'd put on a swimsuit, as though to suggest she didn't really need it? Why else engage her in that provocative underwater embrace? Why else, for heaven's sake, put himself on display the way he had? He must have been well aware of the signals he was sending out.

Refusing to back down, she said, "You know perfectly well. What are you trying to do to me, Magnus?"

"What *have* I done to you?" he enquired, his eyes glinting. He stretched out a hand suddenly and with one finger loosened the towel tucked under her arms so that it slipped down to her waist, exposing her barely covered breasts in the damply clinging bikini bra to his lowered gaze. She might as well have been naked.

His mouth moved in something like a smile, and his eyes slowly returned to hers. "Ah," he murmured. "I see. That's very flattering, darling—but here?" His disparaging glance passed over the rock they stood on. "Or on the grass, perhaps? A bit less spartan, I'll grant you. Actually, I'd planned to return to the house and the comfort of a proper bed—I thought maybe you'd prefer that. But you're not good at waiting, are you? If you're that impatient, I'll be happy enough to accommodate you—"

Humiliated, confused, angered, Jade felt her temper give way. She raised a hand and slapped him with her open hand, hard. His head jerked momentarily to one side, and she swept past him wordlessly, one swift glance showing her the red mark of her hand on his cheek, and a look in his eyes that couldn't possibly be *relief*.

Then she was on the path, her palm fiercely stinging, like her eyes, and her hands hauling the towel up again as she went, clumsily because of the clothes she still held and also because her fingers were unsteady.

She was halfway to the house before she realised that her feet were being hurt, on the rough pathway. She'd neglected to put on the thongs she'd been wearing, must have left them back at the pool.

At the house she flung the towel onto the bed, stripped off the bikini and rummaged in her bag for clean undies and the first garment that came to hand. Everything she'd brought with her was either extremely casual or extremely sexy. She hauled on the green silk wrap that would at least cover her up, tied it tightly at her waist, and went into the bathroom to rinse her feet under the cold tap of the bath.

The water was stained pink, and she examined the underside of her foot, finding a small cut welling blood.

Cursing under her breath, she swung herself away from the bath and started investigating the bathroom cupboards. There was soap, toilet paper, towels and even a couple of toothbrushes still in their wrappings, but there didn't seem to be any medical gear. She took a clean facecloth and pressed it to her foot, still cursing. The bath had a wide lip, and she sat on the corner, cradling the foot up on her other thigh.

Then she heard Magnus calling sharply, "Jade?"

He called again, from the bedroom, before she answered, "In the bathroom."

He threw open the door and stood on the threshold, looking oddly gaunt and sallow. His gaze raked over her. "There's blood on the floor out here."

"Sorry, I didn't notice until I started to wash my feet. I'll clean it up."

He held her thonged sandals in one hand. "You make a habit of forgetting your shoes, don't you?" he said, and dropped them on the floor of the bedroom, before coming towards her. "Let me see."

Jade shook her head. "The pressure may stop it bleeding, I don't want to let go yet. It's quite a small cut. I can't find any plasters or disinfectant."

"I'll have a look." He investigated the cupboards and then moved out into the other room. She heard him in the kitchen and a few minutes later he came back with a plastic container marked with a red cross.

He took a box of plasters out and said, "How big?"

"Very small, really," Jade said. "I told you." She gingerly removed the cloth. "It's almost stopped."

He poured disinfectant onto a cotton wool swab and crouched in front of her. "This will sting."

It did, but she didn't complain. Magnus carefully wiped the wound with another piece of cotton wool and pressed a plaster firmly onto her foot.

"Thank you." Jade prepared to stand up, but his strong fingers curved about her foot where it lay across her thigh, preventing her from moving. He hadn't looked up, apparently still inspecting his first aid. She could see the way his hair grew back from his temples, and the slant of his eyebrows, and the hard planes of his cheek and jaw.

"Jade."

She stiffened. "What?"

"I didn't mean to say those things. Probably I deserved that slap."

Jade took a deep, hasty breath. "*I* thought so," she said. Then, "Why did you say them?"

He raised his eyes. They told her nothing. He seemed to have deliberately made them blank, cold, expressionless. "You don't know?"

Jade shook her head.

"I tried to warn you," he said.

About being alone with him. Better words than blows, she supposed. But words had the power to hurt, too—to cripple.

"And I told *you*," she reminded him, "that you're not the only one to be angry."

A glimmer of a smile touched his mouth. "I believe it. You pack quite a punch. My head's still ringing."

Her voice heavy with irony, she enquired, "Am I supposed to say I'm sorry?"

Magnus's mouth was rueful. He shook his head. "No." Releasing her foot, he stood up and drew her upright with him, his hands on her upper arms. "One thing I did mean," he said seriously. "I had planned to take you to bed—and I do mean bed—at some stage this week, but not in haste or on some uncontrollable impulse. When I make love to you again, I want everything to be as nearly perfect as I can make it."

She could understand that. Hadn't she carefully packed her sexiest nighties, her most frivolous underwear, and bought herself a range of bath oils and body spray and perfume, with exactly the same thought in mind?

"So," Magnus went on, "maybe it's just as well we got rid of some of our. . . aggression this afternoon."

Jade hated conflict, but she had to admit that now she felt rather less tense. She'd put it down to the energetic, hurried climb back to the house, and to the gentleness with which he'd tended her wound. Still, perhaps he had a point. Bottled up anger and frustration couldn't be good for a relationship. She said, "You didn't hit me back."

Magnus looked thoughtful. "No. I hope you're not intending to capitalise on the fact."

"Did you want to?" Her eyes held his.

After a moment he shook his head. "What I wanted to do was—just exactly what I suggested—get you down on the ground right there and then, and do something equally violent."

Jade felt herself shiver, and her eyes widen. "You... wouldn't," she whispered.

"*God,* I hope I wouldn't!" His hands had tightened on her. "Until I married you, I'd always thought of myself as a very civilised animal."

She'd thought she was, too, until Magnus and their mutual passion had taught her otherwise. If they had made love this afternoon by the pool—or even in it—that wouldn't have been the first time they'd done so outdoors, or without the benefit of a bed. He might never have fulfilled his fantasy of doing so on one of their desks, but she recalled not only midnights on the beach, but midday in a secluded corner of a hay paddock, with the swaying, sweet-smelling grasses hiding them from view, a couple of hours spent on a blanket spread under concealing trees overlooking the sea, and more than one interlude in the dim, cool recesses of the hay barn, when afterwards, laughing, they'd had to pick bits of dried grass and clover from each other's clothes and hair.

There had been times when, with only half an hour between Magnus's return from the city office and the serving of the evening meal, they'd barely made it to the dinner table, with clothes hastily donned and hair quickly combed, and Jade had found herself blushing under Mrs. Riordan's astute and scornful eyes.

In fact, their bedroom had been the place where Jade felt most inhibited, least likely to enjoy more adventurous forms of lovemaking. Magnus had teased her about it, and she'd laughed at his teasing, but she was unable to shake the knowledge that the bedrooms of his brothers and sister were not far away, or her morbid certainty that his mother was lying awake, staring at the ceiling and listening for the slightest creak or distant moan of pleasure.

"Jade?" Magnus was staring at her, still holding her shoulders, his eyes questioning, almost suspicious. "How about a truce?" he suggested. "At least until after dinner."

"I don't want to fight," she said. "If you can be... civilised, I can."

A smile touched his hard mouth. "I promise I'll try." He looked at her a moment longer, then bent his head slowly and kissed her mouth, with extreme precision and gentleness.

She stood quiet in his hold, not moving at all, her lips unresponsive but quiescent.

He stopped kissing her and looked at her gravely, then his hands slid down and he swung her off her feet, cradling her in his arms.

Startled, Jade stiffened. But he only carried her through into the bedroom and, going down on one knee, deposited her on the wide, low bed. "You'd better stay there for a while," he said, standing up. "I'll clean up the blood spots and start dinner."

Jade sat up. "There's no need! I can walk."

"You don't want to start it bleeding again, and making more mess. I'll tell you when you have to get up. Want a book or anything? There are some books and magazines in the living-room."

"Actually," Jade confessed, "I wouldn't mind a nap." The mattress was firm and very comfortable. And lying on it made her want to curl up against the piled pillows.

"Have one," Magnus suggested.

"I was going to make dinner."

"I can do it." At her surprised look, he added, "I guess you know I'm no gourmet chef, but I've done some cooking over the last few years, and with all the supplies we bought, I'd have to be fairly helpless not to be able to turn out a decent meal."

She watched him walk out, her mind somewhat bemused. She wasn't used to the new, mercurial Magnus, who changed moods as easily as he changed his socks, and more frequently. She found it difficult to reconcile this concerned, considerate man—the Magnus she'd always known—with the hard, insulting stranger at the pool. She had the feeling that some kind of deadly serious game was going on between them, only she didn't know the moves, and no one had told her what the rules were.

She closed her eyes, grateful that at least for now hostilities had been suspended. She didn't believe in solving problems with violence, and she knew Magnus didn't, either, but perhaps the fact that he'd driven her to that had shocked them both back into a less hostile frame of mind.

Nothing had been resolved, she reminded herself. But maybe they were in the process of working out ways in which they could reconcile their hurt and anger with each other, turn them into something more constructive.

She woke to find him sitting on the end of the bed, watching her.

"How long have you been there?" she asked.

"A few minutes. You look dead sexy, asleep." He stretched out a hand and fingered the green silk of her robe. "I remember this." The room had dimmed, and his eyes gleamed, colourless.

"You bought it for me."

"I know. I hoped you'd wear it just for me."

"I did," she said, wondering at the oddly questioning note in his voice. "I have."

A corner of his mouth twisted. "Good. I've been thinking."

He seemed to hesitate then, and Jade prompted, "Yes?"

"I had some idea of having things out," he said slowly, "before we went any further. But digging over past mistakes—at this point, anyway—is a fruitless exercise. We've both made our apologies, inadequate though words are for some forms of betrayal. Recriminations aren't going to help either of us. Better to make this week the start of something new and enduring. It's what you've wanted all along, isn't it?"

"I suppose so." Certainly she had wanted nothing more than to return to the loving, trusting and passionate relationship they'd once had.

Magnus stood up. "Dinner's ready. Are you going to eat like that?" His eyes lingered on her lying there, one arm across her waist, her legs bared almost to the top where the satin robe had parted in her sleep. "Not that I have any objections."

He'd changed into a pair of dark trousers and a white shirt. She said, "I'll put something on." She got up, too. "Can you give me ten minutes?"

"I'll open the wine." He sauntered out.

Jade went straight to the bathroom to freshen up and brush her teeth. She knew what dress she was going to wear—the one that Magnus had chosen for her.

She put it on, and a dash of fuchsia lipstick to match, blotting it so that it only hinted at an echo of the colour. She made up her eyes carefully, and dabbed perfume on every pulse spot. Yesterday she'd washed her hair, and the fresh water of the water-hole had left it soft and a little wayward. She brushed it into shape.

Lastly, she slipped her feet into a pair of high-heeled sandals that flattered her ankles, and went to join her husband.

The table had been covered with a cream cloth, and a single red candle in a crystal holder sat in its centre. One glass bowl held a lettuce salad, another sliced tomato and cucumber, and on a large serving plate Magnus had arranged cold ham, stuffed pork, and chicken liver paté. He'd found white china and stainless-steel cutlery, and two tall fluted glasses were filled with pale amber liquid, alive with tiny bubbles.

"I was about to call you," Magnus said. "I don't want the champagne going flat."

She paused at the table and he took her arm and gently turned her to face him, letting his gaze take in her appearance. "You look lovely, Jade. And smell nice, too. Thank you for dressing up for me."

He leaned forward and kissed her cheek. "Sit down," he invited, and pulled back a chair for her.

Her hand closed around the stem of her glass as he seated himself opposite her. The candle was a still, cold flame between them. Magnus lifted his glass to her and held her eyes until she picked up hers. "To our future," he said, and added, almost as though he was making an effort to mouth the words, "and to forgetting the past."

"Not all of it," Jade replied steadily. "We share some good memories, Magnus."

"Yes," he said after a moment. "To the good memories, too."

They sipped the wine, and Jade said, "It's nice. Real champagne?"

"Not officially," he told her. "It's a New Zealand wine, so we aren't allowed to call it that, although the process is the same."

She sipped again, then put down the glass and helped herself to salad. Surprisingly, she found she was hungry.

After the main course, Magnus got up and served cheese and fresh fruit. "I don't run to pudding, I'm afraid."

"This is fine. It's all I want, just now. You've excelled yourself, Magnus." He poured her more wine, and she lifted her glass to him, smiling.

"Thank you. There was no real cooking involved, though." He seated himself again, and looked at her across the table as she cut herself a piece of cheese riddled with small round holes. "You love that stuff, don't you?"

"I do?" She looked up at him in surprise, then back at the piece of cheese. "What is it? I don't recall picking it out today."

There was a tiny silence before he replied, and she looked up at him, suddenly flustered. Then he said evenly, "No, I chose it with you in mind. Locally made Swiss-style. You used to buy it regularly at the supermarket in Warkworth."

"I see." She stared at it, willing herself to remember. Nothing. She might never have seen the stuff in her life. She tried to recall the packet, casting her mind back to the little shop they'd bought it in, Magnus saying casually, "We'll have a couple of cheeses, shall we?" She'd agreed, thought he was buying what he fancied for himself, hadn't really looked. At the time she'd been weighing the merits of the various pâtés on display.

"Well," he said, "you'd better see if you still like it."

Nothing to get upset about. She tried to smile, put a piece in her mouth and said, "It's delicious."

The moment passed, but she knew that she wasn't the only one who'd experienced a renewal of tension. Magnus's eyes had gone peculiarly opaque for a few seconds, and his hands, peeling a hard red apple, had temporarily stilled. Now he was concentrating on quartering the apple, stabbing the knife into the pieces one by one and lifting them to his mouth.

"Coffee?" he asked her. "Or we could go and have that spa and finish off the champagne there. I've got the water ready."

It sounded deliciously wicked, Jade thought. "Should we?" she asked him. "Directly after eating?"

"Alternatively," he suggested, "we could finish up the bottle outside, and open another to take to the spa room."

Even more decadent. She smiled at him. "Let's do that."

They put away the remains of the food and cleaned up, then Magnus dragged some of the big floor cushions to the terrace that was built out over the bush-covered hillside, and poured the last of the sparkling wine.

"I can't see the harbour," Jade said. "There's no moon." It was fully dark now, and the sky was gradually filling with stars.

"Look again," Magnus advised, and she peered into the blackness and said softly, "Oh...."

Where the stars ended must be the black line of the hills on the opposite shore, and below that, now and then came a fugitive gleam of silver. As her eyes became accustomed to the night, she could pick out the ragged edges of the bush, and discern the limits of the harbour, its quiet waters never completely still, the stars lighting a ripple here, a restless wavelet there, that glimmered for a moment and disappeared.

A cricket began singing, and a large huhu beetle whirred close to the window behind them and flicked for a few minutes up and down the pane, then blundered off into the night. Small moths silently flitted in and out of the faint light cast by the candle still burning on the dining table.

She sat on one of the cushions, her knees hunched in front of her, sipping the wine's fresh, flowery flavour. Magnus lounged on two more cushions just behind and to one side of her. The night air was quite warm, a quiet breeze bringing the woody scent of manuka and, more faintly, something that might have been honeysuckle, on its gentle breath.

She heard the small sound of Magnus putting down his glass. A finger, cooled and moistened by the chilled wineglass, traced her spine from her nape to her waist, and he said reflectively, "I can't decide whether I like the back of this dress most, or the front."

Jade felt herself shiver with anticipation. She sat very still, her fingers clutching her glass. "Your finger's cold," she said.

He gave an almost soundless laugh, and shifted on the cushions so that he was sitting almost behind her. His shoulder was against hers, and the cool finger ran down the side of her neck and along her collarbone to the edge of the dress. "Are you going to finish that drink?"

"Maybe." She took another sip. The glass was still half-full. As she lowered it, his fingers closed about hers, and he lifted the glass to his own mouth. Now it was three-quarters empty. "Greedy," Jade said.

"Don't complain," he admonished her. "There's plenty more."

Then she felt his breath at her nape, followed by the warmth of his lips drifting down the path his finger had followed. She closed her eyes, her skin accepting the sensation, the prickling, melting delight. He moved again, his hand going about her waist as he urged her back against his chest. He was squatting on the cushions, his thighs cradling her. She gulped the rest of her wine, her hand closing convulsively on the stem of the glass as his fingers wandered across the skin of her back, and his teeth nibbled at her ear.

"What about that spa?" he whispered.

Jade swallowed. She felt boneless. Tiny thrills of pleasure were chasing over her body. "All right."

He took the glass from her slackened grasp and helped her up. She was glad that it was dark. He gathered up the glasses in one hand, collected another chilled bottle from the kitchen, and led her through the dimness inside to the glassed area next to the bathroom. There, he flicked a switch and outside a concealed light came on, silhouetting dense ferns and shrubs that screened the room. The air was humid and the glass had misted, giving an ethereal quality to the greenery on the other side. The water in the blue-lined spa tub bubbled quietly.

Magnus said, "It's only warm, not hot."

He hadn't switched on the centre light, and Jade was grateful for that. The outside light was enough, reflecting softly into the room. There were tiles on the floor and on the one wall that wasn't glass, and several large folded towels sat on a chrome shelf.

Magnus said, "Do you want me to look away while you undress?"

Jade shook her head and, lifting her hands to the front of his shirt, she very deliberately began unbuttoning it.

He took a breath that lifted his chest, and stood rock-still while she finished the task. Then he moved, and flipped open the buttons of his cuffs, while she unbuckled his belt.

He shucked off the shirt, but when she fumbled for his zip, he said, "My turn." And he reached around behind her and opened the short zip of her dress, then ran his hands slowly up her back and eased the dress off her shoulders, so that it slipped down over her arms and into a heap on the floor.

He undid his own zip and pulled off the pants, revealing a pair of underpants that barely covered his hips. Eyeing the equally brief lace-and-satin panties that Jade wore, he smiled tightly and said, "I will if you will."

She stepped out of her sandals, kicking them aside, and took off the panties. In the soft, dim light she didn't feel exposed, and the air was warm.

Magnus had climbed down into the pool and turned to help her, but she was already sliding in, subsiding on the moulded bench beside him. He poured more sparkling wine and handed her a glass, and sat back, sipping at his.

The warmed water played over them, and she closed her eyes, enjoying the soothing, relaxing feeling. She sipped at her glass and let her mind float, trying to empty it of thought, of tension. When Magnus offered more wine, she shook her head and turned to place the glass on the tiled surround before closing her eyes again, resting her head against the side of the pool.

"Are you asleep?" Magnus asked, sounding faintly amused.

Without opening her eyes, she shook her head, barely moving it.

He said, "If we stay here much longer we'll come out all shrivelled up."

"Don't care," Jade murmured.

He laughed. "I'd forgotten your ability to immerse yourself in the pleasure of the moment."

"Seems a suitable verb for this," she said. Dimly she recalled him saying something of the sort a long time ago...in a sunlit field, while he trailed a finger along the line of her thigh after they'd made love.

He said now, his breath feathering her cheek, "And for this?"

Perhaps he remembered, too, for his hand was taking the same path again, and then his mouth was on hers, warm and tender and searching.

It seemed so utterly right—her mouth flowered beneath his, and his hand stroked her gently, gliding up over her hip, her ribcage, and settling softly on her breast, but only briefly, as though he didn't want to hurry. A finger touched the tip, and moved to its mate, and she knew he must have recognised her immediate response. Then his hand was travelling upwards again, caressing her throat, curving about her chin as he lifted his mouth from hers and looked down at her, his eyes dark and questing. "Can I persuade you," he asked her, "to go to bed?"

She needed no persuasion. She smiled into his eyes and got up, her back proud and straight as he watched her leave the pool, and without haste she pulled one of the towels from the shelf and draped it loosely round her body, turning to face him. "Come on, then," she said.

He erupted from the pool in a wet, splashing vision of glorious manhood, and grabbed another towel, tucking it swiftly round his waist. Jade was already preceding him through the door, and when he got to the bedroom she was standing by the bed saying, "We'll make the sheets wet."

"No," he said. "I'll dry you."

He bent to tug the covers back first, then stood up and took the towel she was holding round herself, and dried her face, her shoulders, her breasts, and the rest of her body, using slow, sensuous movements.

Then he stepped back, and she knew by the glitter in his eyes that he was aroused almost beyond bearing. His chest rose with a deep, shuddering breath. "I think I need a cold shower," he muttered, swiping at his own face and body with the towel he'd used on her, his eyes devouring her, as if he couldn't drag them away. "For God's sake," he groaned, "get into bed, Jade!"

She said, "If you come with me." And stepped forward, deftly removing the towel he'd fastened around his waist.

He grabbed her hands, but too late. His teeth clenched, he said, "This isn't . . . the way it's supposed to be. I want—"

"I know what you want," Jade told him. "I can see it. I know—" she placed her hand over his mouth as he started to speak again, his face contorted almost as if in pain "—you meant it to be slow and sweet and romantic, every moment savoured. But I can't wait, either, Magnus. I want you inside me, now! Please—I need it as much as you do."

He looked at her as though he couldn't believe what she was saying, his face taut and his eyes burning.

She freed her hands and brought her body deliberately closer to him, her eyes half closing as she made contact with his, and he drew in a sharp, unsteady breath. *"All right!"* he said, his voice harsh as moving gravel. "You asked for it."

He pushed her down to the mattress so that she was lying sideways across the turned-down cover, her legs only half on the bed, and he took her there, without preliminary and without mercy, in an out-of-control, mindless fury of dammed-up passion.

Chapter Ten

Jade gasped, her body momentarily rigid against that first deep, hard thrust, and then it softened about him, and she wrapped her arms round his neck, brought her knees up to cradle his thighs within hers, and answered the hot, hurried rhythm of his headlong invasion.

Within seconds she felt an intense rush of pleasure beating at her senses, engulfing her from head to toe, radiating from that centre where Magnus had become a part of her, filling her with himself, making her whole again. She heard him cry out hoarsely, his voice agonised, animal. And her own voice echoing the cry, mingling with his, their mouths clashing as they instinctively, blindly searched for each other, for a way to share this ultimate experience in every way. She opened her mouth to him and took his tongue inside, felt his hands stroke and touch her all over, exciting her beyond bearing. Her body stiffened, and shuddered, and shuddered again, as his did the same, and her hands grappled at him, wanting him still closer, closer, inside her, around her, everywhere...

Minutes later she opened her eyes, and the room slowly swam into focus—the dark outlines of furniture, and the starlit window, and the white turned-down sheet that her head lay on. Magnus still sprawled on top of her, breathing unevenly as though he'd been running, his weight heavy now, his cheek against hers slicked with a film of sweat.

Jade moved her head a little, trying to see his face.

"Oh, God!" he muttered. "I didn't mean—"

"Shh!" Jade lifted a hand and placed her fingers over his mouth again. "It's all right. We both wanted it."

For a moment longer he was still, then he rolled off her and sat up, his shoulders hunched. "You *enjoyed* it?"

"I thought you'd have noticed," Jade said. "It's been a long time for me, too, you know."

He took an unsteady breath, momentarily dropping his head into his spread hands. Then he lifted it and said, "Can I get anything for you?"

"Some tissues."

He brought them to her, and she crawled under the covers and moved over to make room for him. But he stood by the bed, saying with sudden urgency, "Jade!"

"What is it?"

"I didn't—I didn't think to use anything. Had you taken care of it—I know you visited a chemist?"

"No," she said. "No, I don't want to, Magnus."

For several seconds he was silent. Then he came down onto the bed, half sitting, his hand resting on the mattress on her other side so that he could dimly see her face. "You want a baby?"

"I know you said that you don't." Her voice held doubt, uncertainty.

Slowly he replied, "I didn't say that. I said we should wait."

"How long do we wait this time, Magnus? You said we have a marriage to rebuild, but don't we need to show some faith in it? It's not conditional, not on my part, anyway—"

"Nor mine." His eyes were piercing, searching hers. He said slowly, "Do you feel ready to have my child?"

"Yes! Yes—I want it, Magnus—very much!"

"Medically, there's no reason you shouldn't—"

Jade shook her head. "None."

"Well. . . ." His hand touched her face, his fingers outlining her lips, then trailing down to her shoulder. He caressed her arm that was holding the sheet over her breasts. "If it's what you want. . . ."

His hand wandered, encountering the sheet and exploring beneath it. Her eyelids fluttered, her lips parting as he touched her, and he bent to put his mouth to hers. The sheet slipped as she raised her hand, touching him in turn, her fingers gliding over his shoulders, stroking the once-familiar softness of his hair.

He lifted his mouth from hers, shifting to slide under the sheets beside her, and she nestled close to him and sighed.

"What is it?" he asked.

"Nothing." She raised a hand to stroke it over his chest, and around his shoulders. "This is . . . so nice. Being together again, like this."

"I'll try to make it that way," he promised. His hand shaped her hip, found her thigh and returned to her waist, her midriff, the yielding firmness of her breasts.

This time he deliberately made the pace slow, languorous, paying attention to every part of her body in turn, keeping his kisses light at first, only allowing them to deepen gradually, attuned to her quickened breathing, the small, gasping sounds that she made, the way her lips parted in invitation, and her body moved under his ministrations.

She knew he was holding back—holding her back, too—determined to make this time different, an unhurried building of exquisite sensation, a progression of delight from one plane to another, and to another.

Perhaps it didn't last quite as long as he'd intended, because there came a point when their mutual impatience overcame every intention, and they melded together in an equally blinding, intense and eventually shattering climax.

The aftermath this time was even more enervating, and when they had reluctantly parted, Jade simply turned her head against his shoulder, laid her hand on his warm chest, and fell asleep.

She woke feeling cold, and discovered that Magnus had turned in his sleep and taken the blanket with him, leaving her with barely half the sheet. She shivered, and smiled at his oblivious back, carefully retrieved some of the blanket and moved close to him, fitting her body against the contours of his. Softly, she danced small kisses along the line of his shoulder, and insinuated her arm about his waist, her fingers floating against his skin.

She knew by the change in his breathing that he'd awakened, but when he turned suddenly, his arms going about her, he had his eyes closed. He lay still for a few moments, and then said, "Tell me I'm not dreaming."

"You're not dreaming," she said, and gently bit his earlobe.

"Dreams lie," he said strangely, his voice husky and slurred, and Jade thought that he was, after all, half-asleep.

"I'm not a dream," she assured him. "And I'm not lying."

She kissed his closed eyelids, and they didn't open. She touched his mouth with her hand, loving the masculine contours of it, and then pressed her lips to his, coaxing them open.

He turned on his back, bringing her with him, still kissing. His hand came up to massage her nape, tugging a little at her hair. She shifted her legs, straddling one of his, and he ran a hand over her from shoulder to knee and then up to hold her more firmly against him, setting her blood pounding.

He turned further, so that they lay on their sides, and their mouths broke apart, and she saw his eyes open at last, his gaze locked to hers. Then he moved again and she was on her back, looking up at him as he lay poised over her. He lowered his head to her mouth, and just before their lips met he said something else, under his breath. It sounded like, "You're a liar, but not a dream."

She couldn't have heard right, or else he was still not fully awake. Although his body was telling her that it needed no more arousing. Aroused herself by the unmistakable evidence of his virility, she made an inviting movement against him with her hips, and he surfaced from the kiss, gasping.

"If you do that again," he said, his eyes brilliant and dark, "I won't be answerable for the consequences."

"Oh?" She directed a distinctly brazen look at him, and very deliberately did it again.

A harsh sound escaped his throat. "Jade—"

"Magnus?" She stared boldly into his eyes.

"You want me again?" he demanded. "So quickly?"

"I want you," she confirmed. "Again. Quickly. Now."

He took a great, audible breath, adjusted his legs between hers and obliged, surely and deeply.

Jade's head went back on the pillow, her lips parted in a sigh of relief and pleasure. *"Thank you,* Magnus. I love you."

His eyes were blazing. Their bodies were moving in unison, singing ancient songs of joy. *"I love you!"* He sounded as though the words were torn from him. *"Nothing else matters!"*

They got up late and lingered over breakfast, Jade wearing only her green robe over a pair of panties, Magnus dressed in a casual shirt and trousers.

Jade nibbled dreamily at fruit and toast, watching Magnus eat bacon and eggs washed down with coffee. She'd got up to cook them for him while he showered.

She loved the sure movements of his hands, the way his throat rose from the collar of his shirt, the dark crescent of his lashes lying on his cheek as he lifted his cup and finished off the coffee.

"I'll pour you some more," she offered, getting up.

"No." He retained his hold on the cup as he placed it on the table. "I've had enough." He was looking at her in a way that made her uneasy, as if she were a puzzle he was trying to solve.

"What's the matter?" she asked him.

Magnus shook his head. "What could be the matter," he said, "after last night? And this morning."

Perhaps she imagined the note of irony in his tone. He held her eyes for a moment, a strangely set smile on his face, and then got up, packing his dishes together. "What would you like to do today?"

"I feel lazy. I'd like to read, admire the view, maybe visit the water-hole again later, when it gets hot. Unless you have other plans?"

He didn't rise to the bait. "Sounds fine to me," he said easily. "Leave the dishes," he added as she made to start washing. "I'll do them, if you want to get dressed."

She went back to the bedroom, smiling ruefully as she surveyed the state of the bed, which had a well-used look. After she'd showered she would change the sheets and make it decent again.

Later in the day they went to the water-hole, and this time neither of them bothered with swimsuits. Magnus didn't pull her down on the hard grey rock afterwards, but he spread their towels on the grass in the shade of the trees and made leisurely, delicious love to her, completely wiping out the disturbing memory of the strange, bitter little contretemps of the previous day.

And in bed that night they made love again, a lingering, tender journey of rediscovery.

Only twice in that week did they take the car from the garage—to have a look at some historic battle sites of the nineteenth-century wars between Maori warriors and Queen Victoria's army, and to replenish their supplies.

They walked along bush tracks and the lonely country road, and watched the ever-changing view of harbour and bush and sky. Talked, but not of Jade's illness or Magnus's family. Read quite a lot, lying side by side on the deck or in the bed, sharing quotes from their respective books, as they'd sometimes done a long time ago—but they'd never had such long stretches of time before.

They swam, used the spa and made love. Sometimes it was fierce and explosive, although never as wildly turbulent as on that first evening, and sometimes it was tender and lazily erotic.

Magnus seemed determined to make up for the physical deprivation they'd both suffered not only in quantity but quality. He was inventive and adventurous, and so bent on giving Jade pleasure in every way imaginable that once, when they were still in bed at nearly midday, she teased him about wanting to make her a slave of love.

He didn't smile. He lifted his head, momentarily distracted from his total concentration on what he was doing to her body, and his eyes gleamed at her so that for an instant she was reminded of some untamed animal, as he said quite seriously, "If that's what it takes to bind you to me."

"Magnus!" she said, half-shocked, yet unable to stifle a thrill of primitive satisfaction. "There's more to loving than sex."

"So?" he murmured, holding her eyes and touching her in a new way. "Tell me about it."

"Magnus!" It was part protest, part plea. She writhed in his hold, biting her lip to stop a cry of sheer ecstasy. "You can't—"

"Can't what?" His voice asked in her ear, as her eyes closed and her mouth parted, gasping. "Do this to you? But you like it, don't you, darling? You want more?"

"I—no! *Yes!*" Her head turned frantically towards him. She felt as though she were on the brink of a mountain, about to fly straight up to the sky. And only he could take her there, and guide her safely back to earth.

"Yes?" he said. She heard the deep, rasping note in his voice and knew that he was near the brink, too.

"Yes," she breathed, *"yes, please yes!"* And her hand raked into his hair, her mouth frenziedly searching for his. "Kiss me, Magnus, please—"

He did, as she drowned in sensation, released from the sweet, raging torment at last. And she surfaced drowsily minutes later, her body glistening with a fine sheen, her limbs lethargic and pleasantly aching, her eyes heavy.

"Sometimes," she said tiredly, "I think it's too much."

Magnus gave a small, breathy laugh. "Are you saying you don't like it?"

She could hardly claim that, when she'd just been sobbing with sheer rapture in his arms. She shook her head. How could she explain that despite that, deep down was a small, ineradicable core of unease?

Maybe she had some unacknowledged guilt feelings about sex? She didn't think she was a prude, but her experience had hardly been extensive. Perhaps she secretly resented Magnus's apparent familiarity with the refinements of lovemaking. She said, "Where did you learn to—do things like that?"

He laughed. "Imagination is a great teacher."

"You haven't done them all with other women?"

He was quiet, the hand idly stroking her hip still for a few seconds. "No," he said finally. His eyes had turned dark and brooding, and he opened his lips as though about to ask her something, but then he moved suddenly, rolling away from her to leave the bed and gather up his discarded clothes before making for the bathroom.

On their final morning Magnus brought her breakfast in bed, and after clearing away the dishes took her in his arms and made love to her one more time, with exquisite thoroughness.

While he packed their bags into the car later, Jade wandered out to the terrace, to take a last, regretful look at the view. In the daytime the harbour glinted in the sunlight, and whispers of white cloud skimmed the distant hilltops.

She heard Magnus come quietly out behind her, and then his arms slid about her waist, drawing her against him. She sighed. "I wish we didn't have to go back."

"You've enjoyed it?"

"Yes, of course, but—"

"But?" His breath feathered her ear.

"It's been almost a dream world, up here. Now we have to face up to reality."

"And you're not very good at that, are you?"

Jade stiffened in his arms. She felt as though he'd drenched her in icy water, the cruelty of it taking her breath. She pulled away and turned to face him, shock and hurt showing on her face.

Magnus frowned, and cursed quietly. "I didn't mean that!" he said forcefully. "Not the way you think. Jade, I'm *sorry.*"

Her lips felt stiff. "What . . . did you mean?"

He looked at her tight-lipped, and then shook his head. "This isn't the time," he said. And then, almost under his breath, he added, "Maybe there isn't one."

"For what?" She didn't understand what he was talking about, or why he was looking at her so strangely. And yet it wasn't a new look—she'd caught glimpses of it before—a baffled, wary scrutiny, as though he was unsure of something about her.

He said, "There are still things you don't remember, aren't there?"

"You know there are. Little things, mostly. It's annoying, but not important."

"You haven't forgotten any of the important things?"

"I don't think so." She smiled. "But then, how can I know something's important if I've forgotten it?"

Magnus didn't seem to think that was funny. "Do you remember the . . . accident?"

Her smile faded. "No. But that's normal, they said. Quite common." Her car, they'd told her, had gone over a cliff, smashing onto rocks in the water below.

"If that young couple hadn't come by," he said, "if they hadn't gone to the rescue so fast, you'd never have got out of the car alive." His face looked drawn suddenly, the skin over his cheekbones taut and pale. "I've wondered if it *was* an accident. What were you doing on that cliff, anyway? Miles from home?"

She turned from him, her hands clutching the wooden railing about the deck. "I don't know. I can't remember—"

"You knew you were pregnant." He sounded almost accusing.

The pregnancy must have been unplanned, inconvenient. It had been tacitly understood between them when they married that it would be some time before they could think about a family.

She turned to face him again. "You were very angry about that, weren't you?" she asked him.

His head jerked up as if he'd received a shock. "Who told you that?"

"I could feel it. I thought, when you first visited me in the hospital, that you wanted to kill me, or kill the baby. That's why I screamed when you came near." In that terrifying world where she couldn't distinguish between reality and the distorted images that filled her mind, she'd had strange fantasies.

Without moving from his stance a few feet away, Magnus seemed to withdraw from her, become more remote, his eyes sinking back in his skull. "You'd *lost* the baby."

"I know. In the accident. But sometimes I thought she—"

"She?" Magnus queried sharply.

"I've always thought of it as she. A little girl, black-haired, with dark grey eyes. She had a little dimple in her chin, and long, curling eyelashes—"

Magnus was staring at her. She tried to explain. "For a long time she was very real to me. More real than what was going on around me. I think I resisted getting better because as long as I was sick I had my daughter, my baby, safely with me. Deep down I must have known that once I was cured, I'd have to let her go—admit that she was dead." Her voice sank to a whisper of pain.

"You cried for days," Magnus said hoarsely, "when you were under that latest treatment. I thought it was making you worse."

Jade admitted, "I hadn't allowed myself to mourn her before. Instead, I'd imagined her alive, and growing into a little girl, as she ought to have. I don't remember how the crash happened, but it wasn't deliberate, Magnus. I would never have taken my baby's life."

"And now you want to replace her?"

"I suppose that's part of it. I do miss her."

She hoped he wasn't going to say she couldn't miss someone who had never been a real, living person. Even though she knew that, the child who had been her shadowy companion was a sweet and tangible memory.

He didn't. Instead, his eyes dark and brooding, he said with a peculiar violence, "*I hope you're pregnant now, Jade.* I hope I've planted my child—*our* child—in you this week."

"So do I," she whispered, but the harshness of his face, his voice, stirred again that familiar apprehension that for days had been almost—though never quite—smothered by his determined concentration on the more enjoyable aspects of their relationship. Not just the sexual dimension, but other shared activities like reading and crosswords and walking. And talking, although this was the first time they'd talked about anything so personal, so important.

Magnus's mouth twisted in a strange kind of smile. "Perhaps it's what we both need to wipe out the past."

Mrs. Riordan greeted Magnus with cool affection, and Jade with her usual distant courtesy. Jade thought that the older woman had never got over the humiliation of those early months after her stroke, when she had been forced to accept the most intimate services from her daughter-in-law. The loss of her dignity, for such an imperious person, must have been mortifying, and Jade's renewed presence in the household was, she supposed, a continual and unwelcome reminder.

Ginette was unable to hide the bright curiosity behind her cheerful smile. "You both look more relaxed," she said over dinner. "Your second honeymoon has done you good."

Mrs. Riordan looked at her with faint distaste and asked her to pass the pepper.

Magnus slanted a lightning-fast glance at Jade, but she pretended to be only interested in her meal.

When they'd come home, he'd unpacked in their room and without comment replaced his clothes in the previously empty wardrobe.

Tonight he didn't retire to his office after dinner, but stayed in the lounge watching television and catching up on some of the newspapers they hadn't had the opportunity to read that week. And when Jade rose and said good-night, it wasn't very long before he joined her in the bedroom.

She'd showered and put on a satin nightgown, its sea colour enhancing her eyes, and applied perfume to her skin. She hadn't heard Magnus come in, and when she emerged from the bathroom he was standing in the middle of the room.

"Déjà vu," he said softly, his eyes wandering from her hair, damp at the ends and a little untidy, over the low-necked, figure-skimming gown to her bare feet.

He walked over to her, and warm, hard fingers lifted her chin. His kiss lingered lightly on her lips. When he raised his head, his eyes were still closed. "You even smell the same," he murmured, before he opened them and looked at her again. His glance was suddenly searching. "Did you used to—"

"Used to what?"

Magnus shook his head, stepping back from her. "Never mind. It—isn't important." His eyes passed over her again, and this time she thought there was a bitterness in them, mingled with unmistakable desire. "I'll be with you shortly," he said, and walked past her, closing the door of the bathroom behind him.

Jade quickly brushed her hair and got into bed, picking up a book that she'd brought with her from downstairs. It was silly to be nervous, she told herself. For the past week she'd been sharing a bed—as well as several more unconventional venues—with Magnus. Just because this was the first time since her homecoming they'd been together in this bed—the one they'd slept in and loved each other in for scarcely a year—there was no reason for her to be feeling like a new bride again.

Even then, her bridal jitters had been faintly ridiculous. It wasn't as though they'd never slept together before. Jade had been sharing a flat then with Lida Farrell, but Magnus lived alone. After she'd spent the night at his place several times Lida had guessed, of course, that there was a man involved, but to her chagrin Jade had refused to satisfy her curiosity as to who he was.

Then had come the shock of Mrs. Riordan's stroke and her emergency admission to hospital. Magnus had rushed to the hospital, then home to Waititapu and his younger brothers and sister. When he returned to the office he said to Jade, "I'm going to have to move to Waititapu for a while."

"Your business—"

"I'll commute. I can't leave the youngsters to cope entirely on their own. I can at least be there at nights and weekends. I don't know yet how bad my mother's condition is, whether she'll be able to return home. If she does, she'll probably need nursing care for some time, if not forever—and my father's will is still awaiting probate. The lawyers are dragging their feet. I suppose the farm accounts need sorting out. Dad was never good at the paperwork, and he was too proud and stubborn to let me help. Until that's finalised I can't make any arrangements about the farms, or anything else." He passed a harried hand over his hair, closing his eyes for a moment.

Instinctively, Jade had moved closer to him, slipping her arms about him. "I'm sorry, Magnus. You know I'll do anything I can—"

"Thank you. I must go back to the hospital this afternoon, and hope the doctors can tell me something more specific. Once I've cleared some of this backlog, can you hold the fort a bit longer?"

Of course she could, and she had.

The patterns of Magnus's life shifted. Each evening he left the office at five and made the long drive to Waititapu. There were no more leisurely dinners followed by a nightcap at his flat and the inevitable slow, sweet lovemaking afterwards. One day he looked up from his desk as Jade came in carrying a pile of folders, and said, "I can't stand this. Will you come home with me at lunch-time, Jade—to the flat?"

They left the office together at twelve, drove to his place and tumbled straight into bed. Afterwards they had to scramble into their clothes and hurry back, and she was sure that the receptionist was smirking behind her desk as they entered the building again, knew that the flush of passion hadn't yet had time to fade from her cheeks, the soft lustre of fulfilled desire from her eyes.

She'd been distracted for the rest of the day, unable to concentrate, fumbling with her work.

At five, Magnus had thrown some papers into his brief-case and stood up, grabbed his jacket from its hook behind the door, and then turned to look at her.

She looked back at him, and something in his face changed. He came over to her desk, and put down the briefcase, dropping his jacket on top of it. "I'm sorry," he said. "I'm a selfish, unthinking swine. I shouldn't have asked you to do that, at lunch-time."

"You know I wanted you, too."

"Oh, sure, you . . . enjoyed it, in a way. But it felt wrong, didn't it? A bit sordid, in fact."

Jade looked down at her electronic typewriter. He was right. She did feel as though something wonderful and shining had become slightly soiled. "It can't be helped," she muttered. "I know you don't have time for me, with your family and . . . everything. There isn't much we can do about that."

"There is something," Magnus said. "You could marry me, and come to live at Waititapu with me. We'll be to-gether at night, as well as during the day. When my father's will is probated and we know what the prognosis is with my mother—and I've sorted out what to do about the farms, the children and everything—we'll be able to move back to Auckland. But right now I don't know when that will be, and ... I need you, Jade! You're too good for a hole-and-corner office affair. I want you to be my wife."

Of course she'd said yes, and they'd been quickly and quietly married with only his business partners, his brothers and Danella, and Jade's erstwhile flatmate and another friend as witnesses.

She'd bought herself a special frock for the occasion, and indulged in a trousseau of lovely undies and nightwear. That was before Magnus had discovered that his father's business affairs were not only in a muddle, but that somehow he had managed to run the family farms into debt. Before the hospital discharged his mother, still needing a good deal of physical care. Before Magnus had returned grim-faced from a visit to the lawyers and said to Jade, "I can't see getting Waititapu back on its feet in under four or five years. The only alternative is to sell up."

It would have been another major blow for Mrs. Riordan, and an upheaval for Andrew and the older children, coming right after their father's death and the shock of their mother's stroke. It was Jade who had suggested that if Magnus hired another secretary, she could look after Mrs. Riordan, take care of the house and supervise the twins and twelve-year-old Andrew, while Magnus continued to commute to Auckland.

"I can't ask you—" he'd protested. But she saw the faint light of hope in his eyes.

"You haven't asked me," she'd told him. "I volunteered. It's the sensible solution."

"It's only for a while," he'd said, giving in. "And Jade—I'm really grateful."

Magnus came out of the bathroom, interrupting her memories. She looked over at him, his hair damp and tousled, his chest bare above a towel wrapped about his waist.

He didn't smile at her, his eyes lingering on her with a disturbingly remote expression in them.

For some reason Jade recalled Mrs. Riordan's words. *He married you because he needed someone to give him practical help...*

For a moment she contemplated asking him if it was true. But of course it wasn't! He hadn't known until after the wedding that there wasn't any money to provide nursing for Mrs. Riordan, or hire household help. Had he?

Needing physical contact to disperse her thoughts, she held out her hand to him and murmured his name. He hesitated for a second, then crossed to the bed. "What do you want, Jade?" he asked, his fingers enclosing hers.

She tried to smile, feeling the blood rise in her cheeks. "You know what I want," she said.

He was looking at her now with a dark, brooding intensity. His gaze slipped from her face to the thin nightgown that barely covered her shoulders, and dipped low between her breasts. "I think I can guess."

He leaned forward and touched his lips to the tender swell above the neckline of the nightdress. "This?" he murmured, and raised his head to look into her eyes. "Or—this?" His lips grazed her cheek, settled on her mouth, then wandered down her throat, and his hands caressed her. "This?" His voice was deep, his hands growing bolder. Her breathing quickened, her eyelashes flickering over her eyes.

He settled on the bed beside her and pulled her closer to him. "Tell me, Jade," he commanded. "Tell me what you want."

A long time later he finally parted from her, rolling onto his back in the darkness, his breathing gradually steadying.

Jade, her body bathed in a warm, pleasurable lethargy, turned to him, nuzzling her cheek against his shoulder.

"Now," she said quietly, "I really feel as though we're married again."

"Again?"

"I mean—being on holiday isn't the same, is it? It was like a second honeymoon, as Ginette said. Here—back in our own room, our own bed—this is reality."

"A letdown?"

"*No!* Not a letdown at all. It was wonderful."

He turned his head, his eyes gleaming in the darkness. "I'm glad," he said, "that I give satisfaction."

She gave a small laugh. "You always did."

Magnus made a sudden movement, surprising her so that she lifted her head. "Then why—?"

"Why—what?" she queried.

"Nothing. Never mind." But he shifted away from her a little, raising an arm to prop his head.

She thought she knew. Surely he must realise that when they were first wed, lovemaking, however satisfactory, hadn't been enough to release the various tensions that had assailed her, trying to fit into his family and care for all their disparate and sometimes conflicting needs? "I felt—isolated," she said. "Especially when you weren't here. You were away a lot."

"Danella—"

"I know. You had to find her. In a way it should have been easier without her here—when she first left I'd have been relieved not to have to deal with her hostility any more, if I hadn't been so worried and felt so guilty."

"About Danella? You had no cause—"

"I had told you I'd look after the children. I never succeeded with her. She just hated me." And had been savvy enough, after a clash or two with Magnus over her bad manners, to hide much of her antagonism when he was home. Jade had felt quite unable to carry tales about her to

Magnus, who in any case had enough worries without being asked continually to mediate between his wife and his sister.

He said, "I don't think she hated you."

Jade gave a small laugh. "She thought she did. I thought so, too. And the fact that Laurence tended to stick up for me only made it worse. It must have been hard for her—even her twin seemed to be deserting her, emotionally."

"He did have a bit of a crush on you. At the time I thought it was rather funny."

"Not to Danella." In many ways Laurence, the only member of the family who had reacted positively to her presence, had made everything even more difficult. Jade dared not encourage him, for Danella's sake and his own, and yet she didn't want to hurt his youthful feelings, either. It had been akin to walking on eggshells.

"She is rather possessive," Magnus said.

"Yes, she admitted as much to me, during this last visit."

"Something that runs in the family, I'm afraid." His voice sounded clipped. "So be warned."

"Warned?" A shiver of apprehension ran up her spine.

"We agreed to bury the past, to go on with our marriage, looking forward instead of back. That's what last week was all about. This time, I don't expect to be leaving you to care for my family while I'm off somewhere—at work or hunting for my sister. And I expect you to keep to your side of the bargain. I need to know I can trust you, Jade. That I have your absolute fidelity."

"Of course you can trust me!" Jade said. "There's no *question* about that!"

"Isn't there?" He snaked out a hand suddenly and snagged it into her hair, bringing her closer. "None?" he queried softly.

"None!" She was indignant, and hurt that he could think otherwise. "You're my husband, Magnus—the only man I've ever loved."

His hand tightened, tugging at the roots of her hair until they hurt. He said harshly, "I'm not asking you to lie to me!"

"I'm not lying—you know I'm not!" He hadn't been unaware, the first time they made love, of her virginity. The inevitable discovery had even shocked him a little.

"Sometimes I think I don't know anything about you." He searched her face, his eyes stone-hard, even in the semi-darkness. "You're not trying to tell me that *Patrick* is one of the things you've forgotten?"

"Patrick?" She was lost, bewildered.

"Patrick," he said, as though the name left a bad taste in his mouth. And then, the words seemingly forced from him almost against his will, he added, *"Your lover!"*

Chapter Eleven

He let her go as though he suddenly couldn't bear to touch her, but Jade stayed as she was, staring down at him where he was propped on the pillow, her mind in turmoil. "My... lover?" she repeated stupidly.

He went on, "It's no good. I find I just can't pretend it never happened. I need to get it out in the open, even if you prefer to sweep it under the carpet."

Finding her voice at last, Jade said, "It *didn't* happen! Magnus, I've never had a lover—except you!"

Magnus leaned over and switched on the bedside light, making her blink. He turned and eyed her narrowly. "You never slept with Patrick?"

"I don't even know who he is!" Even as she said it her voice faltered, for in her mind's eye a man's face floated momentarily into view. Quite good-looking, with gold-rimmed glasses, and brown hair falling over his forehead, blue eyes looking into hers with an alert, sympathetic gaze.

Then it was gone, replaced by Magnus's darker, accusing eyes, his shadowed, gaunt-boned face. "It's a bit late to deny it now," he said. "This isn't really the first time since you came back that the subject has come up, is it?"

"I don't... understand. I don't recall discussing anything like this before." She swallowed a moment's panic. Could they have had conversations that she'd forgotten? Was she still sick after all? Was *this* unbelievable discussion a delusion? She put out a hand to touch Magnus, to reassure herself that he was real, solid—and *here*.

He was there, his skin warm and taut over bone and muscle. Automatically she ran her hand down his arm, and felt him flinch. Her hand dropped.

He said with weary cynicism, "Oh, we've avoided naming names, skirted round it all very carefully—being civilised. Pretending we weren't really mentioning it at all."

"We weren't!" Jade cried. "*I* wasn't! Whatever you've been doing—Magnus, *I don't know what you're talking about!*"

He made an impatient gesture, then went very still, staring at her suspiciously. Slowly, almost unwillingly, he said, "There were times when I wondered if you'd genuinely forgotten, when you seemed to act as though nothing had happened."

"*Nothing had!* Not the sort of thing you're suggesting." She willed him to believe her. "Whatever you think we've been discussing, it wasn't that!" Although, she realised, it explained some of the puzzling aspects of his behaviour that she'd put down to other things. His occasional cruel remarks, the barely suppressed ferocity that had disturbed her, that had even sometimes been latent in his lovemaking. "I knew you were deep-down angry," she conceded. "I thought it was an instinctive reaction to my being ill for so long, and maybe to your own guilt because you felt partly responsible.''

''I am *not* angry with you for getting *sick!*''

''Perhaps not consciously, but—''

''That isn't the issue here!'' He denied it violently. ''Are you really saying that you didn't realise I knew about Patrick?''

Growing angry herself, she raised her voice, trying to get through to him. ''*No,* that's not what I'm saying! I'm saying *I* don't know anything *about* any such person, so I could hardly have known that *you* did, could I?''

Magnus made an exasperated sound, and threw back the covers, getting out of the bed. He pulled a robe around himself, belting it with swift, almost vicious movements, then strode to the window and turned, a powerful silhouette against the night sky, a hand thrusting through his hair. ''Why do you think I offered you a divorce?'' he demanded. ''Oh, I know he left you, and that was what finally sent you over the brink—quite literally—''

''He—left me?'' Dazedly, she put a hand to her head. ''Magnus, none of this is making any sense. I thought *you* wanted a divorce—''

''I made it clear it was your choice,'' he reminded her.

''I thought you were being gallant—''

''*Gallant?*''

''You knew I'd been unhappy here. I thought you were hoping that I'd want to be free of Waititapu—even of you. You didn't want to callously reject me outright. So you gave me the choice, hoping I'd take it. Even though you said there wasn't anyone else, I couldn't help wondering if you had someone in mind, or you . . . just didn't want to be tied to someone like me.''

''Someone like you?''

''Someone who's had a mental breakdown.''

"For God's sake, what do you think I am?"

She dropped her hand and looked at him again. "What do you think *I* am?" she said. "That's rather more to the point, isn't it? Is this what you meant when you talked about my failures? And—" her eyes widened "—forgiveness?"

He shrugged. "What else?"

"Magnus, I felt I'd failed you in so many ways—your sister loathed me and I hadn't been able to prevent her going on drugs, and then running away. Laurence liked me a little too much, and that only complicated things. Your mother barely tolerated me. Andrew didn't seem to need me except to feed him, although as the youngest he probably felt the loss of his father the most—"

"He coped in his own way. You did as much as you could—for all of us. I know that."

"—I never seemed able to keep the house the way your mother was accustomed to—"

"No one expected you to, on top of everything else!"

"She did." Mrs. Riordan had never really complained, only made it clear that she was fretting about her standards not being adhered to, although allowing that she knew Jade was doing her best. . . .

"If you'd told me—"

"You had enough on your plate without a complaining wife adding to it."

"So you complained to Patrick instead," he said flatly.

They were back to that. Jade fell silent, totally baffled. "Whoever he is," she said carefully, "he was not my lover. I swear to you, Magnus—"

"You say you don't remember him!"

"I don't remember anyone called Patrick." Another flicker of memory came and went in a flash. Herself walking into a room, a man rising from a chair. The name, *Patrick,* hung in the air.

"You're lying," Magnus accused her. "I can see it in your face."

"I'm not lying! I just—for a moment the name rang a bell, that's all. Faintly."

"If you don't remember the man, how can you swear to me that you never had an affair with him?"

"I'd know!" she declared. "Don't you think I'd *know?*"

"Maybe," he said slowly, taking a few steps away from the window into the pool of light. "Or maybe that's what you were trying to blot out of your mind when it went haywire on you. The fact that you loved him, and he'd left you. Left you carrying his child."

Jade felt all the blood drain out of her face. She whispered, "*His* child?"

Magnus's face might have been carved in stone. His mouth was a hard, ungiving line.

Shaking her head, she said, "It was *your* child! She *looked* like you!"

It was, she realised immediately, a mad thing to say. She'd never seen the prematurely born baby, had not even known what sex it really was. The little girl who had been her companion for two years wasn't real, only a figment of her then abnormal imagination. "I mean," she stammered, "she—it—" why did that feel like a betrayal? "—it was yours. It couldn't have been anyone else's."

"Couldn't?"

Her mind had gone off on a tangent. She said, "*That's* why you frightened me so when you came to see me at the hospital. You tried to hide it, but I knew that you wanted to hurt me—that you hated the baby."

"You didn't have any baby by then."

"I know, but I was right, wasn't I?"

"*Yes!*" he admitted at last. "I wouldn't have laid a finger on you, but if you're talking about gut feelings, baser instincts, yes. I *felt* like killing you, and if you hadn't already lost the child—I suppose I'd have felt the same way about...her, although obviously the child was totally innocent. I hoped—I tried—to get over those reactions, to be reasonable about the whole thing. It wasn't surprising you'd turned to someone else for the emotional support that I'd failed to give you, and as for the baby—I'm sorry I didn't hide my emotions better. It can't have helped."

"You're still angry, aren't you? That's why you've been afraid of hurting me."

He breathed deeply, fighting for control. He wouldn't look at her, apparently talking to the wall opposite. "For so long I'd concentrated on helping you get well, telling myself that nothing else mattered as much as that. I didn't realise that the anger was still there, that I'd only succeeded in hiding it, not conquering it." He paused. "I spelled it out for you before we went to the Hokianga. You said you'd take the risk."

Hushed, staring at him, she said, "If you've bottled it up for all that time, no wonder you were afraid you'd not be able to contain it. But I knew I was in no danger from you. You're not violent."

"If I'd ever got hold of your bloody Patrick, I'd have wrung his damned neck!"

"He's not my Patrick," she protested, without hope. Then, as the words penetrated, "You don't know where he is?"

"I don't even know *who* he is. All I have to go on is a first name."

She blinked at him. "Then how can you accuse me of sleeping with him? Where did you *get* this story?"

He looked at her. "From you."

It was like a blow in the stomach. "Me? What did I say? Magnus—you know I was hallucinating! I really am not responsible for half of what I said and did. Surely you understand that?''

"You didn't *say* anything at all about him," Magnus said, "even to the doctors—as far as I know. It was what you wrote in your diary that gave you away."

"I don't keep a diary!"

He cast her another penetrating, sceptical look. "You did, for a while. I suppose it was more of a journal—a very secret journal. Not so much a day-to-day diary as random jottings, although you did record the dates of the entries. It covered the last couple of months before you drove your car over the cliff."

"And you read it?"

"For that," he said, his voice suddenly clipped, "I apologise. But you'd just nearly killed yourself, you'd been moved to the psychiatric wing for assessment, and I was desperate. I thought—it might throw some light on what was happening. Well...." His mouth twisted. "...It did that all right."

"You've got it all wrong!" she said passionately. "Show it to me! I'll *prove* that you've got it wrong."

He shook his head. "I can't. I... burnt it."

Jade stared at him. *"Burnt my journal?"*

He frowned. "I know I had no right—either to read it, or burn it. But it's done, now."

"Then," she said, her lips feeling stiff, "you've left me no way to defend myself."

"It would hardly have helped," he said sardonically. Coming closer to the bed, he seemed to loom threateningly over her. "Do you want me to quote you some passages from it? The last entry is burned on my brain. 'I don't know how I'm going to survive. Patrick, how could you walk away when you know how much I need you? I can feel myself slipping into a black abyss, it's swallowing me up. Oh,

Patrick, please. Please don't go away. I can't manage alone. Without you, I'll die.' Do you want to hear more?''

Jade swallowed hard. ''I—can't have written that,'' she said. ''I couldn't have.''

''I do know your handwriting—even if I hadn't found the journal hidden under the nightwear in your drawer. And you'd written about me, too.''

''You?''

''I don't figure as largely as the beloved *Patrick*,'' he said with extreme sarcasm, ''but there were obviously times when you remembered that you had an inconvenient husband. 'I can't keep it secret from Magnus much longer. Patrick says I'll have to tell him. But I'm afraid.' With good reason. If I'd known what was going on—''

''Did you read it all?''

''No. It sickened me too much. And besides, I—couldn't help but realise that I was never meant to see it. The reason I burnt it was to remove the morbid temptation to read and reread every word.''

''But you're taking bits out of context—''

''I read enough to realise that you'd been seeing this— man on a regular basis. Enough to know that you became utterly dependent on him. You wrote that you told him things about yourself that you'd never told anyone before, that your—relationship—was more intimate than marriage.'' Ignoring her small sound of shock, Magnus went on, ''And his threat to leave you was enough to sink you into total despair. Was it because you refused to tell me about him, to ask for your freedom, that he left?''

''No!'' Jade pressed a hand to her temples, dropped it again and shook her head. ''I don't know! It makes no sense.''

''No? Not even, 'I need to talk to Patrick about the baby. He has to help me. I don't know what to do.' What did you do, Jade? I found out about your pregnancy only because the doctors told me you'd miscarried after the 'accident.' Do you know what a fool I felt, accepting their commiserations for the loss of a baby I hadn't even known about? If you wanted to get rid of it there were easier ways, less dangerous for yourself. Or had you already done something before you drove off that cliff? Was that why you decided to take your own life, too?"

"Magnus, don't! I told you, I didn't drive over the cliff on purpose!"

"You just said you don't even remember it. You're beginning to get your stories muddled, Jade."

"*It's not true!* I would never have done a thing like that—"

"You were desperate enough to do anything, it seems. Even to ending your own life along with the one you carried. Pregnant by a lover who'd deserted you, and afraid to tell your husband—"

Jade bit her lip. "I just can't accept it," she said, starting to shiver. "Why are you doing this to me, Magnus?"

"You think I'm making it up?"

She was silent. Of course he wouldn't do that. "No," she admitted. "I think you really believe it. But the whole thing is fantastic, and—what proof do you have? You destroyed the—evidence. If I could see it, I might remember—be able to explain." A thought struck her. "Maybe Patrick was an imaginary confidant. Someone I could pour out all my private thoughts and fears to, but not a real person at all. A sort of 'Dear Diary' figure personified."

Magnus gave a short, scornful laugh. "I considered that. Nearly had myself convinced, too, for a while. But it won't wash. He was real enough."

"How do you know? Our—my daughter was real to me, too. For a long while. But she never really existed, not in the way I knew her."

"For one thing, you were not that sick at the time. It was after you lost the baby that things went seriously wrong."

"How would you know how sick I was? I was still hiding it quite well, but maybe I was already having delusions. You were away a lot. I was under stress, which you didn't seem to notice." He winced slightly, and she knew she was being unfair. She'd made heroic efforts to hide her stress from him, determined to be the strong, rocklike helpmeet that he needed. He'd told her often how much he relied on that strength, how grateful he was for it. And she'd been proud of her ability to conceal the toll it took—with the pride that goeth before a fall, she realised in retrospect. "Maybe," she suggested, "I needed some imaginary—friend."

"Friend?"

"All right, then, *lover!*" she snapped. "If you insist that's what he was. Don't you think it's a little ridiculous to be jealous of someone who only ever existed in my mind?"

"If that's so," Magnus drawled, "why did you have to ask Lida to lie to me about where you really were?"

"Lida?"

"Have you conveniently forgotten her, too? Lida, your ex-flatmate. Who covered for you when you were going to an assignation with your lover."

"I know who she is!" Jade muttered. This was growing more bizarre by the moment. Lida had turned up at their wedding looking exceedingly glamorous, and Graeme Upton, the junior partner, had kept staring as though he didn't pass by her desk every morning and had never seen her before. Three months afterwards they got married, too, Lida giving up her job with the greatest relief to "stay home and breed babies," she'd cheerfully told Jade, accepting her congratulations. Without a blink she added, "The first is already on the way. You might as well know. Everyone will, pretty soon."

"Lida," Jade repeated now.

Impatiently Magnus told her, "You used to meet Patrick when you took my mother to Auckland for physiotherapy, pretending you were visiting Lida. I asked you to have lunch with me on one of those days, when I knew you would be in town. You said Lida was expecting you. I phoned her at lunch-time, hoping to speak to you, and she seemed very vague, then eventually said you'd left early to do some shopping before picking up my mother from the physio's. I thought nothing of it at the time, but later I realised the truth."

"What truth?" Jade made her voice as withering as she could. She was certain that whatever evidence he thought he had, it was purely circumstantial. In her bones she knew she would never have been unfaithful to Magnus. "You're jumping to conclusions!"

"Lida knew about Patrick. She said I'd only myself to blame. The way I'd treated you, it was no wonder you'd gone out and got yourself another feller, was how she put it."

Jade closed her eyes. "Lida said that?"

"I expect she was right, but having her tell me so didn't help me feel less murderous."

Jade sighed. Lida had at first not realised what Jade's decision to leave her job entailed. "Good for you," she'd said. "No more slaving over a hot typewriter. Let Magnus keep you in the style to which I'd like to be accustomed."

Jade hadn't explained that it was because Magnus now couldn't afford to keep anyone in the style Lida was thinking of that she was leaving. The one occasion when Lida visited Waititapu, some time after her own wedding, and quite visibly pregnant, it had turned out to be the worst time she could have chosen. Mrs. Riordan had suffered a physical setback, resulting in wet sheets that Jade was washing when Lida arrived. Mortified, Mrs. Riordan had been displaying an even more haughty manner than usual, so that at one stage Lida had whispered to Jade, "Why do you put up with it?"

"It's not usually this bad, she's just compensating."

Lida snorted. "If you ask me, she's an ungrateful old witch. Does Magnus let her treat you like that?"

With a wintry smile, Jade said, "Magnus is hardly ever here, these days. She can't help it, you know. The stroke has made her very bad-tempered."

"You mean she was a sweet old thing before?" Lida asked sceptically. "I must admit, I'd never have picked it."

Jade had laughed a little. She'd met Mrs. Riordan a few times prior to her illness, as Lida must have, and it had never been her impression that Magnus's mother was sweet. Forceful, more like, and occasionally gracious in a regal sort of way. "She wasn't so unreasonable or so demanding. It's hard for her, being almost helpless like this."

"As hard as it is for you?" Lida demanded. "Can't Magnus afford to get proper nursing help for her? Or send her to a rest-home?"

"She won't hear of a rest-home, and neither will Magnus," Jade explained, leaving the other question unanswered. She knew Magnus wouldn't have thanked her for spreading news about the family's financial crisis.

"When did Lida tell you I'd been . . . having an affair?" Jade asked, trying to make some kind of sense out of what Magnus had told her.

His smile was more of a grimace. "At the office Christmas party. I gather she and Graeme had been having an argument on the way. Lida had a bit too much to drink, over Graeme's protests, and in the course of the evening decided to hold forth on the evils of marriage and men in general. After she'd finished embarrassing her husband she decided to start on me. That's when she said she'd agreed to cover for you when you were meeting Patrick.''

Jade gasped. ''She said that in front of the whole staff?''

''A good proportion of it, anyway. Including my partners—and my sister.''

''Danella?'' Of course, the girl had been working in his office then. No wonder Danella still didn't like her. And no doubt she'd told her mother the story, too. Possibly even her brothers, unless Magnus had managed to stop her. ''You believed all this?'' she asked Magnus. ''If Lida was drunk, and angry, I don't suppose she knew what she was saying.''

''She knew well enough. She enjoyed off-loading a few home truths she'd obviously been storing up. Anyway, added to the entries in the diary—journal—it seems pretty conclusive to me.''

Her heart sinking like a stone, Jade had to admit it sounded damning to her. ''But if this—Patrick was so important, how could I have forgotten all about him?''

''Perhaps,'' Magnus suggested sombrely, ''because he was so important that you couldn't bear the thought of not seeing him again. You couldn't take that, so your mind conveniently expunged all memory of him.''

But I love you! her mind cried silently. She opened her lips, but the expression on his face was so forbidding, so full of some kind of grim distaste, that the words died before she could utter them. ''No,'' she murmured, dropping her head into her hands. ''No, you're wrong. You're wrong about all of this!''

''I wish that were so.''

Her mind cast about feverishly for an explanation. "Maybe he was a doctor! I was pregnant—"

Magnus shook his head. "Your G.P.'s name is Leon, remember?"

"A gynaecologist, then—"

"Leon would have known if you'd been seeing a specialist. I checked that out with him. He said you'd seen him a couple of times and the pregnancy had seemed perfectly normal. Of course, he thought I knew all about it. He's another who offered me sympathy for my supposed loss."

Defeated, Jade fell silent.

Then Magnus said, with an odd formality, "I'm sorry if all this is news to you, now—it's obviously upset you. But do you really think denial is going to help our relationship?"

With a fierce uprush of anger, Jade lifted her head. "I don't care how much 'evidence' you have. I feel...*betrayed* that you believe it against my word."

"I don't have a lot of choice."

"Yes, you do! I'm your wife—the woman you're supposed to love, and...and trust—" Her voice broke and she turned away from him, biting her lip hard, hoping the pain would stop her tears.

It didn't work, and she couldn't stop the sob that escaped, either.

She felt his weight depress the bed. He put his hand on her shoulder. "Jade—"

"Don't touch me!" she said hoarsely, pulling away. Her voice rose. "I'm surprised you can even bring yourself to!"

"Don't get yourself worked up," he said with careful calm. "Please."

She turned on him. "Don't you think I'm entitled, when you've just accused me of cheating on my marriage? It *is* a bit of a shock, you know!"

He stood up. "Where are those tranquillisers?"

Her anger went white-hot, but she swallowed it with a superhuman effort. "I don't need a tranquilliser," she said, gritting her teeth. "I'm not going to fall to pieces over this, I promise you. I just—" she swallowed and went on steadily "—would like to be left alone, if you don't mind."

She thought he was going to argue. Then he shrugged and said, "If that's how you feel. I'll sleep in the other room, then. Let me know if there's anything you want."

"I may never want anything from you again!" she said as he made to go.

He turned back, and she thought he was going to come over to the bed, touch her again. In anger or an attempt to soothe, she didn't know. But every nerve ending prickled at the thought. If he came near she would, she knew, erupt into some kind of physical violence.

But he stayed where he was, immobile, perhaps sensing her mood. After a while he said, "Perhaps in the morning you'll see things more clearly."

"I see perfectly clearly now, thank you," she said. "You don't trust me, you don't believe in me—you took me back on sufferance when I came out of the hospital—" She was almost choking on her rage and hurt. "Was it because you were *sorry* for me?"

"It was because you're my wife!" he said.

She closed her eyes, gulping in a painful breath. Not because he loved her, but because, as he'd told her on her first night home when they'd been walking on the beach, he took his marriage vows seriously—for better or worse. She hadn't realised then that he thought she'd taken hers lightly. Recalling his mother's views again, she asked, "Did you marry me because it was . . . convenient to have a free housekeeper and nurse?"

Glacially, he said, "I don't think that deserves an answer, do you? I understand you wanting to hit back, Jade, but take care. I'm not in the best of moods, myself."

"What will you do?" she taunted him. "Hit me? It's what you've wanted to do all along, isn't it?"

He stepped back. "Don't tempt me," he said, and swung away, closing the bathroom door with a decisive snap. A moment later she heard the door to the adjoining room bang shut, too.

Slowly, she lay back against the pillows. The tears had dried on her cheeks, checked by anger. Deliberately, she held on to that, the anger. Because as long as she had that, the hurt behind it remained muted.

It was monstrous that Magnus should think what he did. Without reason.

No, logic intervened. Not without reason. He'd had what he thought was evidence, incontrovertible evidence.

Still, couldn't he have had some faith in her? He knew her, *knew* she loved him. How could he have imagined—

Patrick—again a face came to mind. A voice—restful, soothing. Concerned blue eyes behind glasses. A feeling of—comfort, relief, release from a burden. Gratitude.

She closed her eyes, but the memory fled. Memory, or imagination?

All right, suppose it had been a memory? Suppose she had, once, known someone called Patrick? By itself, that didn't mean a thing.

The journal, then. Her eyes opened, went to the dressing table. She supposed Magnus had been looking for some nightwear for her to use at the hospital. And found nothing suitable, so he'd rummaged right to the bottom, and found...

She got up as though mesmerized and approached the dressing table, knelt to open the second drawer. Plunged her hand in, pushing aside lace, silk, diaphanous nylon, to the back left-hand corner. That's where it should have been. A small book with a plain navy-blue leather cover.

There was no book, but her fingers touched something cool and hard and cylindrical that rolled under them. Her heart stopped. She scrabbled for it, caught it, and lifted out the pen, staring at its familiar shape, her hand automatically adjusting to hold it in the writing position.

She leapt to her feet as if it had burnt her, dropping it with a faint, metallic ring on the dressing-table, backing away while her eyes remained on the pen with an awful fascination. "No!" she whispered.

The light from the bedside lamp gleamed faintly along the pen's length. Almost fearfully, Jade reached out her hand and picked it up in trembling fingers. She turned back to the bed, pulled open a drawer under the bedside table and took out a writing pad.

Seating herself on the bed, she opened the pad, and poised the pen over it, breathing in deeply. Then she began to write, trying to remember the words exactly.

I don't know how I'm going to survive. Patrick, how could you walk away when you know how much I need you? I can feel myself slipping into a black abyss. It's swallowing me up. Oh, Patrick please. Please don't go away. I can't manage alone. I'm frightened. Without you, I'll die.

She stopped and stared at the words, and began to tremble all over. Dimly she recalled a terrible despair, a feeling of being abandoned, forsaken, betrayed. The words danced before her eyes, filled with a horrible familiarity. "Patrick—" The name left her lips involuntarily, a heartbroken whisper. "How could you—?"

Shaking, she deposited pad and pen on the bedside table. The pen rolled off and landed with a soft little thud on the carpet. She shrank back against the pillows, her knees raised, legs pulled up before her so that she could wrap her arms around them, rest her head on them, her eyes tightly closed. Even so, the room seemed to whirl about her.

Was Magnus right after all in his fantastic assumptions? But how? How could the unthinkable be the truth?

Chapter Twelve

Jade slept badly. She decided not to join Magnus for breakfast and lay in bed, hoping that by the time she went down he'd be away in his office.

Instead, he tapped on her door, and she sat up, tempted to tell him to go away. But he tapped again, and then opened the door and came into the room. He was dressed in fawn trousers and a cream shirt, and her heart ached because he looked so handsome, and so desirable, and she felt as though a thousand miles lay between them instead of a few feet. As she sat up, he took several steps across the carpet and then stopped. "Are you all right?"

"Yes," she said. "Thank you for asking." She wasn't able to keep the note of bitterness from her voice.

"If you want to talk some more—"

"I think we've done enough talking for now," she said. "I don't think I can take any more."

"All right. If you're sure you're okay...." For once he seemed uncertain, a frown between his brows, his shoulders less straight than usual. "If there's anything I can do for you...."

Her mouth tight, Jade shook her head. "You've done quite enough. Just...go away. Please."

He hesitated a moment longer, then turned to leave. "I'll be in my office downstairs." With his hand on the doorknob he looked back at her. "We'll work it out, Jade," he promised. "We've come this far, and I'm not giving up."

The door closed gently after him, and Jade hauled a pillow from behind her and hurled it at the unyielding panels.

Well, she wasn't giving up, either. She snatched coffee and toast in the dining-room and then waylaid Ginette as the nurse-aide came out of Mrs. Riordan's sitting-room with a tray in her hands. "Ginette—can I ask a favour? Are you using your car today?"

Ginette shook her head. "It's not really mine. Mrs. Riordan's feeling tired, she says. I don't think we'll be going anywhere."

"Could I borrow your keys, then?" Jade asked, trying to sound casual.

"Oh, sure. I'll fetch them for you when I've put this tray in the kitchen."

"I'll take it. You go and get them." Jade smiled at her.

Five minutes later she had the keys in her hand. "Thanks. I don't like to disturb Magnus," she said. "If he asks, will you tell him I'll be back for dinner?"

She hoped that Lida was going to be home. She could have phoned first, but that would have given Lida a chance to put her off, and this wasn't something that would wait, she'd decided. She wanted it sorted out today.

It was strange driving again, but she didn't grate the gears or bunny hop as she left the garage and steered slowly down the drive. She negotiated the winding stony road carefully, extra cautious on the numerous corrugated curves, and once having to pull into the side to make room for a small truck laden with bales of hay to pass. After she reached the highway, with its tar-seal and marked double lanes, the smooth stretch of road looked easy.

She was nervous of entering Auckland, but the increase in the amount of traffic happened so gradually that she was over the bridge and into the city almost before she realised it. She took one wrong turning when she'd left the motorway, but although it was some time before she sorted herself out and found the correct route, it was no great disaster.

Eventually she drew up outside the house in Remuera and pulled on the brake. Only then did she allow herself to sit for a while, drawing deep breaths of relief.

As she stood on the front porch and pressed the bell, she realised she hadn't checked that Lida and Graeme still lived here. Then the door was opened by a young woman with close-cropped black hair, holding a small child while another clung to her skirt.

For a moment Jade's heart sank. Then she saw the dismayed recognition dawning in the dark eyes, and said, "Hello, Lida. When did you have your hair cut like that?"

Lida didn't move, and Jade wondered if she ought to put a foot into the gap left by the scarcely open door. Then the other woman said stiffly, "Ages ago. It's easier, with the kids...." At last she stepped reluctantly back and said, "How are you, Jade? Come in."

It was some time before they were able to talk. The baby was cranky—"Teething," Lida explained—and the toddler was persistent in demanding his mother's attention. "He's always like this when I have a visitor," she said, trying to detach his clinging hands from her skirt after leading Jade into the kitchen. "You'd better stay for lunch. They'll both be going down for a nap about then, with any luck."

"Can I give you some help?" Jade asked, picking her way through a scattering of toys on the floor. A basket of clean washing occupied a chair, and breakfast dishes were stacked in the sink. At Lida's wary, doubtful look, she added gently, "It's all right—I didn't escape. I'm officially recovered, and quite capable of folding nappies or washing dishes, if you'd like."

Lida blushed. "I knew you were home—Graeme said. I meant to visit you in the hospital, but...well..." She looked at the children. "I don't know, I couldn't bring them, and I just never got organised."

"I understand," Jade assured her. "Well, which is it? Nappies, or dishes?"

For the first time, Lida smiled and seemed to relax a bit. She put the baby down on the floor, where it immediately made a grab for a plastic tractor and began enthusiastically chewing on it. "If you're insisting, you won't have to break my arm. You wash and I'll dry."

By the time the children had been put down for their nap and Jade had helped Lida lay the table and butter sandwiches for their own lunch, the atmosphere was less strained. "Thanks, Jade," Lida said as they sat down. "Sometimes they can get me down."

They were on to coffee before Jade felt able to broach the subject she'd come to talk about. "Lida," she said carefully, "what do you know about Patrick?"

Lida put down her cup so suddenly that coffee slopped into the saucer. "I thought that was all over. Graeme said you'd gone back to Waititapu with Magnus."

"I have. But..." Jade stared into her own cup. There was no way of avoiding this. "Magnus thinks I was having an affair with—this Patrick. And he says that you knew about it."

Lida had gone scarlet, her eyes stricken with guilt. "Oh, *hell!* He told you what I said at the party, didn't he? Graeme gave me heaps afterwards. Look, I'm *awfully* sorry. I've never gone overboard on the liquor since, believe me! And I haven't dared show my face at another office party. I can't tell you how ashamed I was, when I realised what I'd done, shooting my mouth off like that."

"You did tell Magnus I'd been having an affair?"

Lida shut her eyes. "Graeme says I did. To tell you the truth, I passed out on the way home and I don't really remember much—except Magnus's face." She shuddered. "I think I'll remember that to my dying day. Honestly, Jade, I can't apologise enough."

"Never mind the apologies. The thing is, I have a memory problem, too. I don't remember anything about anyone called Patrick."

Lida's eyes opened roundly. "Nothing?"

"A vague idea of a face. Who is he, Lida?"

"Well . . . he's your other man. The one you were meeting in secret. Your affair. You just said—"

"I said Magnus believes I was having an affair. He thinks you know all about it. So tell me what you know. Did you ever meet Patrick?"

Lida shook her head. "Never. You were very mysterious about him. The first I knew that something was up was when Magnus rang one day and seemed to assume you were here. It took me a minute to twig in that you'd told him so, and I got you off the hook. Then I called you at Waititapu the next day and asked you what was going on, and you said you couldn't tell me on the phone, but you came to see me a day or so later."

"So, what did I say when I saw you?"

"Not an awful lot. You apologised for using me without my knowledge. And I said okay, I was happy to help, but next time let me know so I could be more convincing." Lida paused. "You don't remember this?"

Jade shook her head. "Go on."

"Well, then you asked, in an embarrassed sort of way, if I'd mind if you told Magnus that you were visiting me while his mother was having her regular physio session. You said it would be convenient for you, and save a lot of bother."

"I didn't tell you where I'd be?"

"Not exactly. You gave me a phone number, though, so I could contact you there in an emergency."

Jade said quickly, "Do you still have it?"

"Sorry. Threw it out ages ago."

"And you thought I was seeing someone behind Magnus's back."

"I was sure of it, ducky. You were awfully anxious that he didn't know. Besides—"

"Besides, what?"

Lida leaned towards her, elbows on the table. "That time, I remember you looked frightfully tense and nervy. Even more so than the day I visited you at Waititapu and the old harridan was on your back all the time. But after you'd been with Patrick you always seemed more relaxed and normal. You used to call here occasionally on your way back to fetch Mrs. Riordan—just so you could truthfully say you'd been here, I guess—and the difference in you was amazing. Obviously Patrick was good for you."

"I told you his name?"

"Let it slip, more like. You were really cagey. I was sort of teasing you a bit, one day. I'd poured some sherry for us both—it was one of *those* days and I felt the need, but I never liked to drink alone—slippery slope and all that. So I persuaded you to join me. I said something like, 'So, is he married, too, your other man?' And you said, 'Patrick isn't—' But I couldn't get any more out of you. After that you just clammed up and refused to talk about him. It was just like when we were flatting and you wouldn't tell me who you were seeing then, either. Of course, that time it was Magnus."

"So, all you had was a first name and the fact that I was secretly meeting . . . someone?" Jade said slowly. "Weren't you just a little bit shocked?"

"What shocked me," Lida told her, dark eyes sparkling with indignation, "was Magnus thinking he could marry you and then shut you up in that great barn of a house, miles from anywhere, with his bossy old mother and his spoiled-rotten family, and expect you to slave away like some wretched Cinderella for the lot of them, when he could well afford—"

"No, he couldn't," Jade interrupted. "There was no money after his father died, except for what Magnus earned. If he hadn't poured it all into the estate, they'd have had to sell the farms and the house."

"Is that so?" Lida's voice rose. "But still, he had no right to sacrifice you for his family. And frankly, I think you were nuts to let him do it!" She gulped. "Oh, sorry!"

Jade waved that aside. "It was my idea, not his. I wanted to help."

Lida looked unconvinced. "Anyway, I reckon you deserved any happiness you could get, on the side. Pity it didn't last."

"How long?" Jade asked. "How long did I go on keeping these—appointments?"

"Oh. . . ." Lida thought. "Two or three months. Towards the end, though, you were looking haunted again. I figured things must be going wrong. Then I realised you were pregnant. So I thought maybe it was just that. Only I wondered..."

"Wondered?"

"If you knew whose baby it was," Lida confessed. "I mean, it must have been pretty awful if you didn't know. When I heard...what happened, I thought maybe that was why."

"I never told you?" Jade asked, her heart thumping uncomfortably.

"Never even told me you were expecting. I figured it out for myself. You didn't show much, but you had that look. And once, you threw up in my bathroom." Lida picked up a spoon and stirred her coffee, though it must have been lukewarm by now. "Are you trying to find him—Patrick? Do you want to see him again?"

"I just want to know...if I was really having an affair with him—with anyone," Jade said. "Do you truly think that's what it was?"

"Oh, come on, Jade! What else was I to think? What's anyone to think?" Lida shook her head, smiling at the naïvety of it.

Jade's shoulders slumped. "I see." What, indeed, was anyone to think? Was she tilting at windmills, refusing to acknowledge the incontrovertible evidence against her? The facts apparently spoke for themselves. And yet deep inside her some small, stubborn core of resistance refused to accept them.

Lida picked up her coffee cup and grimaced, but drained it all the same. "Graeme says Magnus has been devoted to you all the time you were in hospital. Full of admiration, Graeme is. I said," she added darkly, "that it was a pity he waited until then. You could have done with some devotion a bit earlier in the piece."

"You're being unfair to him," Jade said. "I never let him know what a strain it was. I rather prided myself, you know, on being some kind of Superwoman. He thought I was strong."

"Hmm. Is he looking after you now?"

"I'm scarcely allowed to raise a finger."

"Well, that's a change. Maybe he's learned his lesson. I'm having another cup of coffee. How about you?" Lida asked, getting up.

"No, thanks. I'll be going soon. There's someone else I want to see. May I use your phone?"

"Sure, help yourself."

Annie had left the hospital, the voice on the other end of the line told her briskly, for a halfway house in the city. No, she couldn't have the address, but after some demurring she was given a number to ring.

"*Jade!*" Annie shrieked when she heard who it was. "Yeah, of course you can come and see me! Now? That's great—of *course* I'll give you the address. Got a pen?"

Jade arrived back at Waititapu late in the afternoon, drove into the garage and had hardly released her safety belt before the driver's door was flung open and Magnus's voice, low but vibrant with suppressed anger, said, *"Where the hell have you been?"*

She stepped out of the car before answering him. "Auckland," she said calmly. "Didn't Ginette—?"

"Auckland! Ginette just said you'd be back before dinner. She had no idea where you'd gone to."

"I didn't think she needed to know."

"*I* needed to know," he grated, glaring at her. He hadn't moved back when she stood up, and she could see the blaze in his eyes, the faint creases beside them, feel the heat of his body. "You didn't think to tell *me* you were planning to drive to Auckland and back?"

"It isn't Timbuktu!" she said. "I have done it before."

"The last time you drove a car, you—"

"Crashed it into the sea," she finished for him. "Actually," she said, rather pleased with herself in retrospect, "that never even crossed my mind. I suppose there are some advantages to forgetting things like that."

"*You* may have forgotten," he said between shut teeth. "*I* haven't! I've been worried sick the whole day."

Realising the source of his white-faced fury, she felt her defensiveness melt away. "Magnus!" she said. "I'm sorry!"

He took her arm, moving her to one side, and slammed the door behind her, then took the other arm, so that she was trapped between him and the car. "So you bloody ought to be!" he said. "I could—"

His hands had tightened on her arms until they hurt, and his eyes flared with temper. She said, trying to wriggle from his hold, *"Magnus, don't!"*

A kind of shock replaced the temper, and he stepped back, releasing her, then swung away, thumping a hand against the garage wall, leaning on it with his back to her. His breathing was harsh, loud.

Jade said, "It was all right. I have to start living a normal life sometime, and I had—things to do. I didn't mean to worry you."

"Didn't you." His voice was muffled, his face still turned from her, his head bowed. Then he swung round, thrusting his hands into his pockets, his shoulder against the wall, almost as though he needed something to prop him up. "Well, you've done it. Very successfully. Next time I'll try to remember that you've made it home safely before." The temper had died, leaving his eyes curiously opaque. "Do you mind if I ask what *things* you had to do that were so important?''

Jade swallowed. "People to see."

He didn't move, but she had the impression that all his senses were alerted suddenly. "Oh?"

The question, *Who?* hung in the air. He said, "Patrick?"

Anger stirred in her. She said, "If I could, I would have gone to see Patrick—*yes!* Unfortunately I don't know where to find him."

His eyes had narrowed. He said softly, "But you've remembered something about him, haven't you? Who he is. What he . . . was to you."

Jade shook her head. "No. And Lida couldn't help."

"You've seen Lida."

"That's right. She doesn't know any more about him than you do. Less, in fact."

"Really."

"Yes, really!" she flared. "I hoped she could tell me something about him, since you seemed to think she knew so much. All she knows is that I mentioned his name once. And said that he wasn't—"

"Wasn't—what?" The words emerged as though bitten off.

"I . . . don't know," Jade admitted. "Wasn't married, or wasn't . . . my lover."

"Well, which?" Magnus asked, at last straightening away from the wall. "There is a difference, don't you think?"

"Of course there's a difference! I can't tell you any more. I told you, I don't know!"

"What you don't know would fill a book, wouldn't it?" he asked her derisively.

"Maybe it did!" she shot back. "But you burnt the book, didn't you?"

He took his hands out of his pockets and spread them. "True. So we're back to—page one, if you like."

She stared at him, her back stiff, a pulse hammering at her temple. "A new beginning? I'm not sure if that's possible, Magnus."

"Neither am I." His eyes had darkened, and his mouth was stern. He came towards her again, and without touching her, placed his hands on either side of her against the roof of the car, caging her between his arms. "But I should tell you now, Jade, that if you ever find Patrick, and if you want to go to him, I'll fight you—and him—every inch of the way."

"You can't hold me against my will." She met his eyes with defiance in hers.

"Maybe not," he said, "but there are other ways. I'll hold you, one way or another—or die in the attempt."

She couldn't drag her eyes away. He seemed to pin her with his brooding gaze, and for long seconds they were held by some invisible tension humming between them. Then it was broken by quick footsteps on the patio from the house, and Ginette's light, pretty voice.

"Everything all right, Jade?"

Without haste, Magnus removed his hands and stepped aside, turning as Ginette appeared in the garage doorway.

"Oh!" she said. "Sorry! I didn't realise you were both here. I heard the car, but you hadn't come in, so I wondered if you were having a problem. The key sticks sometimes when you turn off the ignition. I forgot to warn you."

"No problems," Jade assured her.

"You haven't mentioned that to me," Magnus was saying.

Ginette gave him an apologetic smile. "Well, gift horses and that, you know. It's only occasionally, and I didn't want to bother you."

Magnus said, "Give me the key, Jade, and I'll try it out now."

She handed it to him and walked towards the house. Ginette stayed behind, saying rather breathlessly, "It probably won't do it now, but it's just that I have to jiggle it a bit when—"

Jade went inside and shut the door. Mrs. Riordan called, "Ginette?"

Jade closed her eyes, contemplated calling Ginette, and decided against it. She moved towards the door of the small sitting-room. "It's Jade, Mother Riordan. Can I do something for you?"

The older woman was sitting on the sofa, a newspaper open across her knees. "I wanted Ginette."

"She's . . . busy."

"Busy?" Mrs. Riordan's head went up. "She's paid to attend to my needs."

"There's some trouble with the car. I think Magnus needs her to explain to him what it is. I'm sure she won't be long."

"I hope not. You've been away all day. Magnus was concerned."

"I know, he told me. I've apologised for worrying him."

"And Ginette had no right to let you have the car without consulting me."

"She thought you were feeling too tired to want to go anywhere. Are you better now?"

"I'm as well as I ever am, thank you. Where did you go?"

"To see some friends." As she saw the sceptical surprise in Mrs. Riordan's eyes, Jade said, "I do have some, still." She was tempted to see what her mother-in-law would say if she told her that she'd seen Annie, and asked her to come and stay. Firmly squelching the impulse, she offered instead, "Are you sure there's nothing you want me to do?"

Grumpily, Mrs. Riordan said, "Help me up and hand me my sticks, then. I need to visit the toilet, and heaven knows how long that girl will be."

Once on her feet, she insisted that she needed no further help. Watching her slow progress, Jade felt a rush of pity.

Contrary to instructions, she waited until the older woman returned, and helped settle her back on the sofa. When she went upstairs, Ginette and Magnus had still not re-entered the house.

Pleading tiredness after her day out, Jade went up to bed early. Once in her room, she realised that it was true she was tired. She took her green robe into the bathroom and had a shower, dried herself quickly and pulled on the robe before opening the bathroom door.

Magnus was standing by the bed, his hands thrust into his pockets. She stopped short in surprise.

"I didn't mean to startle you," he said. And then, "It is my room, too."

"I . . . just wasn't expecting you. I didn't hear you come in." And he never went to bed this early, himself. She advanced warily, then paused a few feet from him. Her nightgown was under the pillow, but she wasn't going to get into it in front of him. She stood nervously fingering the belt of the robe. "What do you want, Magnus?"

His eyes were wandering over her as though he couldn't help it. His mouth turned wry as his gaze returned to her face. "What do you think?"

Jade stiffened. "I told you, I'm tired."

"Yes. I wasn't sure if it was true, or just an excuse."

She said, "It wasn't meant to be an invitation!"

He shrugged slightly. "Too bad."

She glanced towards the bed, and Magnus said, "Go ahead. I won't insist on joining you, if you don't want me to."

He didn't seem to be intending to leave. She moved jerkily towards the bed and lifted back the covers. As she slid beneath them, he said, "Aren't you going to take off your robe?"

"Later."

His brows rose in mild surprise, and then his mouth curved. "You've got nothing under it? Why so shy, Jade? I've seen you naked before—many times."

She didn't answer, and he said softly, "Maybe you're right. I might find it difficult to exercise restraint." To her surprise, he sat down on the side of the bed, turned toward her. "You're *not* lying to me, are you—about not remembering Patrick?"

Jade shook her head. "I don't remember that he was my lover. I . . . I think I did know someone by that name."

His eyes were probing. "There doesn't seem to be much point in trying to find him, then."

"There does, to me."

He frowned down at her. "Why stir up something that brought you nothing but pain and unhappiness?"

"Lida says he made me feel good—better."

Of course she shouldn't have said it. She sat, biting her lip, looking away from the sudden coldness of his eyes, the bitter twist of his mouth. "I mean," she said hastily, "she told me I seemed more relaxed when I'd been with him."

The silence was electric. Then he spoke at last, his voice butter-smooth. "Did she? You're more relaxed when you've *been with* me, too. Lovemaking has that effect on you."

Jade's cheeks flamed, a pulse beating heavily in her throat. She started to say, "I don't think—" *that's what she meant,* but the final words died in her throat. It had, actually, been all too obviously exactly what Lida meant. She stopped, and said feebly, "There may have been other reasons."

"You think so?" Obviously he didn't. He stood up, looming over her. "Why keep on with this denial, Jade? I freely admit that I neglected you, that you had every reason to turn to someone else. We've agreed we'll put it behind us now. The fact is, if he still wanted you, he's presumably known where to find you—or at least could have found out easily enough. You'd do better to put him out of your mind now and concentrate on the future—our future."

"I apparently *had* put him out of my mind," Jade objected, "until you brought the subject up."

"Yes, well—my mistake. Perhaps it would have been better if I'd known for certain that you didn't remember anything of him."

"Perhaps. But now I do. And I want to know the truth."

"You know enough, surely?" His voice roughened. "What more do you need? You've had your chance, Jade. I gave you the option of a divorce when you first came home, and you chose to stay with me. We've come too far down the track to turn back now."

He was right, but she reminded him, "You talk as though you were giving me the choice between him and you. But I didn't know about Patrick then."

His eyes became narrow, glittering slits in a granitelike face. "And now that you do, you think he might have been a better option?"

It was a ridiculous suggestion, and the unfairness of it roused her to anger. "You're being quite unreasonable, Magnus! Surely you can understand that I—I *need* to fi—"

Find out the truth about him.

But Magnus gave her no chance to finish the sentence. He swooped so suddenly that she broke off in alarm and gasped as his hands fastened on her shoulders, dragging her towards him, one of his knees on the bed as he drew her level with him, giving her a small, hard shake. His eyes were blazing. "I understand that you're bent on finding the man you were sleeping with behind my back! The man who made you pregnant and deserted you! Who had you so screwed up that when he left, you tried to kill yourself!" Ignoring her instinctive murmur of denial, he gave her another little shake. "Don't tell me to be reasonable about that! And don't tell me it's what you need! I'd see you in hell before I'd let you go back to him. Do *you* understand that?" he snarled.

"For God's sake, Magnus—" Jade stared back at him, mesmerized by the scarcely tempered savagery in his face, his voice, the unyielding grip of his hands through the flimsy green silk. "I just need to—"

He stopped her this time in a more devastating manner. His mouth on hers was an assault, an invasion, bearing her back on the pillows behind her, and when she pushed against him in protest he released her shoulders only to grasp her wrists, holding them down on either side of her head. He shifted so that he lay over her, his legs preventing her from kicking off the bedclothes, from any chance of escape or real resistance. His mouth was hot, and hard, and merciless until she made a small sound of protest in her throat. Then he removed it briefly and looked down into her shocked eyes, his own still glowing darkly with temper and with desire.

"This is what you need, Jade," he told her, his voice low and rasping. "What we both need." And as she started to argue, he captured her parted lips again under his, but with an erotic tenderness that took her by surprise. This time he coaxed and caressed her mouth with his lips, touching softly, then firmly, withdrawing to nibble gently at her upper lip, then her lower one, until he'd persuaded her to open her mouth to him. But, content not to take advantage of it straight away, he went on teasing, tasting, experimenting with lips and tongue and teeth, until her stiff, resisting body imperceptibly relaxed beneath him, her breath sighing into his mouth, her skin beginning to burn as hot little shivers ran across it.

Then he kissed her properly, deep and long, until the spiralling circles of need that arose from the pit of her stomach encircled her entire body, quickened her breathing and heated her blood.

At last he raised his head again, and kissed her jawline, her throat, nudged aside the edges of the robe to find the smooth, swelling curves of her breasts. "Tell me your needs now," he whispered against her skin. "Tell me what you need, lovely Jade."

Her eyes half closed against the sensations he was arousing with his mouth as it moved lower, she choked out, "Please—let go my hands, Magnus."

He looked up at her for a moment, his gaze brilliant, his mouth taut, and released her wrists, using his own freed hands to open the robe completely, staring down at her. Then his eyes met hers again as one hand floated light as thistledown across her breasts, scarcely touching and yet effecting an instantaneous response that she couldn't hide. He felt it, and smiled, then glanced down to confirm it before returning his eyes to her face. "Tell me," he repeated, murmuring the words, his mouth barely moving.

"You know," she said, stirring restlessly under his feathery, persistent touch.

He smiled again, and his hand rested on her ribcage while one finger drew a lazy, tantalising circle around the aroused tip of her breast.

"*You know!*" she said again, clenching her teeth against the rising tide of sensation that threatened to engulf her.

His smile taunted. He brought his face closer to hers and whispered, "What? What do you need now, my lovely?"

Her hands reached for him, her fingers in his hair, tugging. "I need . . . your hands," she said, almost against her will. "I need your mouth. . . ." And he allowed her to guide his head down to where she wanted it, and as his mouth closed over her flesh she let out a sighing breath. "I need *you*, Magnus."

Chapter Thirteen

At dawn Jade woke, and lay listening to Magnus breathing beside her. She watched his oblivious face as the light grew gradually brighter, filtering through the curtains. His hair was tousled in sleep, his eyelashes resting against his cheek with deceptive innocence. Wrenching her eyes away, she stirred gently, careful not to disturb him, and eased herself out of the bed, groping for the creased satin robe that at some stage in the night he had hurled carelessly to the floor, and belting it around her before making quietly for the bathroom.

When Magnus woke she was standing by the window, watching the sunrise colour the sea with a faint gold glow, the sky change from a washed-out grey to a fragile shade of blue.

She heard the faint rustle of the covers, and saw his hand slide over the empty side of the bed before he opened his eyes and sat up, leaning on one elbow.

"Jade? What are you doing? Come back to bed."

She took a steadying breath and said, "No . . . not yet."

Magnus sat up further, one hand raking his hair back. "No?" He smiled and thrust back the covers. "Then I'll come to you."

In three strides he had reached her, making to take her into his arms.

Jade stepped back, evading his touch. "Will you put some clothes on, please?"

He glanced down at his blatant nudity and slanted a disbelieving grin in her direction. "I was hoping I wouldn't need to, yet."

"Please, Magnus." She wouldn't look at him, turning her face away.

After a moment he went back to the bed, picking up his discarded underpants and trousers. "Okay," he drawled as he buckled his belt. "I'm decent."

She looked at him and then away, fiddling with the belt of her robe. He frowned and came back to her side. "What's the matter, Jade? I thought last night—"

"I know what you thought!" She still wasn't looking at him.

There was a short, fraught silence before he said, "It wasn't exactly rape, you know."

"I'm not accusing you, Magnus."

"It was good for you, wasn't it? Or were you faking? And if so, why?"

Jade took another deep breath and met his eyes at last. "I wasn't faking. But sex can't solve everything."

Slowly, he said, "I'm not suggesting that it could. It does help, though. What exactly is the problem?"

"The problem is, you think I've been unfaithful to you."

"We've been through all that!" he said. "I have no intention of raking it up again."

"You mean you've forgiven me." There was irony in her tone, but he didn't seem to hear it.

"If it's important for you to hear the words, yes. I forgive you."

Jade shook her head in rejection. "That's what I can't accept," she said. "That you still believe it happened."

"Jade, whether it happened or not, it doesn't *matter!*"

"It matters to me!" she said fiercely. "It matters quite a lot to me." Last night had only confirmed that.

He took her shoulders in a firm grip. "Look at me."

Jade raised her eyes, staring into his sombre, intent gaze.

"I love you," he said. "No matter what you've done or haven't done. As far as I'm concerned that's the only important thing. I was hurt and jealous and angry, and no doubt I've let that show sometimes, but I swear it's *over.* Maybe I had to work through it, and I know I was rough on you at times. But believe me, I never deliberately set out to punish you. Jade—I've waited long enough for you to come home, and I'm bloody thankful that you're here. I don't have any *right* to cavil about—the other."

She ought to accept that and be glad of his generosity, yet she found it wasn't possible. "But you won't forget, will you? Things will never be the same between us."

"If we work at it—"

Jade shook her head, pulling away from him. "I can't, Magnus. I can't just go on as though nothing has happened. If last night was an indication of how things are going to be—"

"You said last night was good!"

"I said I wasn't faking," she reminded him.

"And that it doesn't solve everything," he added impatiently. "I realise that. So what's the problem?"

"The problem is, there's been a shift in our relationship. You are the magnanimous, forgiving husband—I'm the er-ring wife. It isn't a partnership of equals any more. And I don't think I can stomach sex on those terms.''

Magnus made a small, jerky movement with his head, his eyes narrowing to slits. "Just what are you saying?"

"I'm saying that I feel shamed. Not by an act—or acts— of adultery that I don't remember and can't believe really happened, but by the way you made love to me last night."

"You had no complaints at the time!" Magnus said coldly.

"Physically," Jade conceded, "it was everything you thought it was. But emotionally I felt you'd... humiliated me."

"Not by intention!" Magnus denied.

"Perhaps not," Jade said, "but... as long as you believe what you do about me, that's the way you're going to make *me* feel."

Magnus frowned. "Don't you think you're being a bit oversensitive?"

"If I am, I'm sorry. But it doesn't alter my feelings."

"All right. So let's see if you still feel the same next time." He reached for her and drew her towards him again.

She held back, resisting. "I don't think that's the answer."

"Can you come up with a better one?" His arm fastened around her waist. "Well?"

Her hands were against his bare chest, his warm skin. "Magnus, wait!"

"What for?" he enquired. "We can talk about this forever and a day. The only way you're going to know if these feelings of yours are a temporary aberration or a permanent condition is to make love again. One thing is sure. If you brood over it long enough the permanent condition is likely to become a self-fulfilling prophecy."

He could be right. She stopped pushing at his chest and allowed him to lift her face to his, to find her mouth in a kiss that tipped her head back against the curve of his arm, while his other arm imprisoned her so closely that she couldn't be unaware that he was already fully aroused.

His lips left hers and wandered hotly down the curve of her throat, to the hollow of her breasts. She felt his hand tug at the belt of her gown. "Come back to bed," he muttered, and lifted her in his arms, taking her to it and laying her down on the sheets. His eyes glittered over her as he stood shucking off his pants, and then he was lying beside her, one hand caressing her through the slippery satin, while his mouth trailed fire across her skin.

At first she lay quiescent, resentment at his high-handed solution warring with the stirring of her senses under his determined erotic assault. He knew her all too well, she thought as her body moved of its own volition under the deft, intimate touch, and her breathing altered its tempo. Cleverly, he sensitised every nerve under her skin, until the merest brush of his fingers across her breast made her shudder with pleasurable anticipation.

When he moved from his position at her side to poise himself over her, she opened glazed eyes and looked at him beseechingly. "Magnus—please . . . say you believe me."

His eyes were dark gems, on fire with wanting. "I believe you," he said huskily. And he parted her thighs and placed himself between them.

Her own eyes closed as her body opened to him. "I love you, Magnus. . . ." she whispered urgently against his roughened cheek. "Only you, *ever!*"

And then his mouth surged against hers, drowning words, drowning thought, leaving only a warm, rushing cascade of sensation.

* * *

It seemed ages later that the heavy warmth of him shifted, leaving her suddenly cold, and a hand drifted softly over her thigh. "All right?" he asked her, his voice scarcely louder than a whisper.

"Yes." Jade lay with her eyes closed, unmoving. Tiny prickles of remembered pleasure still feathered her skin. There was a faint dampness on her temples and between her breasts.

She felt his breath on her lips, and then he kissed her very gently and lingeringly, as though setting a seal on something. The sheet rustled as he drew it up over her, covering her nakedness.

"Sleep in if you like," he said. "I have to go down."

She didn't answer. After a moment the bathroom door closed behind him and she heard the thud and hiss of the shower. She lay very still, breathing evenly.

He'd said he believed her. Said it in the heat of passion, when she'd demanded it from him as the price of . . . what? Her submission? Whatever—he had said it.

And she knew he had lied.

There was no point in brooding on it, Magnus was right about that. He had promised not to raise the subject again, and she ought to be grateful for that. After all—she made herself review the evidence—no one in their right mind would believe she was innocent.

No one in their right mind . . .

Jade shivered. Perhaps she hadn't been in her right mind, when . . . if . . . anything had happened at all. That might explain the diary, the accident that Magnus believed was no accident. And its long aftermath.

For the first time she made herself consider the possibility that Magnus was right, that her own instinctive rejection of his conclusions was a mere defensive mechanism, a childish denial of wrongdoing. *Oh, come on, Jade!* Lida had said. *What was anyone to think?*

What, indeed, but what they did think—both Lida and Magnus. And, she realised, past conversations, innuendos, taking on new significance, so did his mother and Danella. And heaven knew how many others.

Even if she hadn't been physically unfaithful, there seemed no doubt that she'd been meeting another man secretly, behind her husband's back, that she'd confided to him the most intimate details of her life, that she'd become emotionally, if not physically dependent on him, and had been thrown into a state of desperation and despair when the relationship came to an end.

And there was no way she could prove otherwise, even to herself. She'd been warned that although she might randomly remember things she'd temporarily lost from her consciousness, there was a chance that parts of her memory would never be restored. It was something she'd been prepared to live with.

And so was this. Who Patrick was, exactly what part he had played in her life, she would probably never know.

In the following days she did her best to live in the present. Most mornings she spent some time helping Magnus in his office, gradually establishing a routine. Sometimes she looked up from what she was doing to find him staring at her silently, but when she caught his eyes he would look away and return to his paperwork.

After lunch she would sometimes go down to the beach, to walk or swim or just sit on the rocks watching the water. Once she borrowed the car and went for a drive, trying to renew her knowledge of the district. She found that many things were still familiar to her—the rolling landscape of grassy paddocks populated by the woolly white blobs that were sheep, or by brown-and-white beef cattle; the irregular patches of ragged bush, the narrow streams racing along stony beds between banks of fern.

On the way home she slowed for a couple of youngsters on horseback nearing the gateway of the Mediterranean-style whitewashed house that she'd been told belonged to the Beazleys.

Despite her caution, one of the horses took exception to the car and danced suddenly across the road in front of it, tossing its head as the rider attempted with only partial success to control it.

Seeing the flying hooves coming close to the grille, Jade hit the brake hard and swung the wheel, so that the car slewed sideways and one wheel descended with a jarring thud into the shallow ditch at the side of the road.

The horse had come to a standstill, its hooves planted four-square in the middle of the road, the rider scolding it in a disgusted, girlish voice. The other rider swung over to come to a halt beside the driver's door, and a young, anxious face framed by long blond hair peered in at Jade. "Are you all right?" the girl enquired nervously.

Jade's hands were tightly clamped to the wheel, her temples throbbing and clammy. But she wasn't injured. "Yes." She unbuckled her safety belt and pushed open the door. The other girl, so similar in looks that they must be sisters, had dismounted and was leading her reluctant mount to join them. "I'm awfully sorry," she said breathlessly. "I don't know what's the matter with him."

"He's a pig!" the first girl said witheringly. "He gets spooked at the stupidest things." As Jade warily climbed out and stood on the rough grass verge, the girl backed her horse and said, "I'll get Dad. He can probably pull you out with the tractor. I hope the car isn't damaged."

She cantered up the drive to the house, and her sister said politely, "Would you like to come inside? You look a bit pale." She said hesitantly, "You're Mrs. Riordan, aren't you?"

"Yes," Jade said. "Madeline?" she added as something clicked into place. "And your sister—is that Yvette?"

The girl smiled. "Yes. We'd heard you were home. We wanted to come and say hello, but Mum and Dad said you needed a chance to settle in first. Do come up to the house. Mum will be pleased to see you."

"You've both grown," Jade told her. They'd been about nine and ten when Andrew and their brother had sometimes allowed the two girls to tag along on sufferance.

Yvette came back with her father, who shook hands as though genuinely pleased to see Jade, and walked around the car, inspecting it. "I'll get it out," he said, "but there could be a bit of damage to the suspension."

In the end Jade yielded to their invitation to go inside, and was warmly welcomed by a woman she vaguely remembered, made to sit down and given tea and muffins.

After a while the farmer returned, kicking off his boots at the back door. "Don't think you'd better drive it," he said. "Steering looks a bit rocky. I'll ring Magnus and ask him what he wants to do. Unless you want to?" he queried Jade.

Jade shook her head, reluctant to confess to Magnus that she'd damaged the car, and taking the coward's way out.

In the event, she wished she had made the call herself. She heard Mr. Beazley say, "Magnus—afraid your wife's had a bit of an accident—" and a sharp sound from the other end of the line, clearly audible before Mr. Beazley said hastily, "Just by our place. She's okay—sitting here drinking tea with Glenda and the girls. Do you want—" There was another short burst of sound, and he broke off and put down the phone, looking faintly mystified. "He's on his way."

He was there in less than five minutes, the big car skidding to a halt outside, the back door of the house exploding inwards without ceremony moments later. His eyes went straight to Jade, sweeping over her in one lightning, comprehensive glance. Then he halted in the middle of the floor as though he'd just run into a stone wall. "You're all right," he said.

"Told you she was," Mr. Beazley said.

"It was my fault," Madeline owned bravely. "Monty's, anyway. He jumped out in front of her car."

"It's okay, Maddy," he said absently, without moving his eyes from Jade.

Mr. Beazley cleared his throat. "You'd better take a look at the car—"

"Later." He looked away from Jade at last, his gaze encompassing them all. "Thanks for looking after my wife. I'll take her home now."

He held out his hand, and she stood up uncertainly. He looked as though he was leashing something dangerous that threatened to get out of control. As she hesitated, he leaned forward and scooped her hand into his, scarcely giving her time to thank her hostess before he whisked her out of the room and into his car.

He gave her a hard glance as he climbed in beside her before he turned the key and set the car in motion. They didn't speak until he had driven into the garage at Waititapu. Only when he turned to her as he snapped open his safety belt, she said, "I'm sorry about the car. Will the insurance cover it?"

"Don't worry about that." He paused, looking at her. "You got a fright, obviously. Is that all that's wrong?"

Her hands were clenched in her lap, her back rigid. "I...thought—" she swallowed, her eyes wide open and staring in front of her at the blank wall of the garage ''—just for a second, I felt I was going into the sea . . . It was only a ditch, but I could see the sky, the rocks . . . the water coming over the windscreen. . . .''

''You remembered the crash,'' he said.

Jade shuddered. ''Yes. . . . And, Magnus—I know now that I didn't deliberately do it. I remember parking near the edge, getting out of the car, and standing on the cliff. I was upset, confused . . . I can remember clearly thinking that if I just jumped, it would all be over. . . .''

Magnus drew in a breath, but was silent.

''But I didn't do it,'' Jade said. ''I knew it was a coward's way out, and there was the baby. . . .''

''So what happened?'' He'd turned to look at her, she could feel his gaze, but hers remained fixed.

''I got back in the car, started it up, but . . . I wasn't concentrating, I know I was crying and my vision was blurred. And I must have parked too close to the edge. I had trouble with the gear, and when I thought it was in reverse, it must have been in fifth—I'd had the same problem a couple of times when I first began to drive that car. It jumped forward, and I couldn't do anything—I felt the wheels lurch over the edge, and—'' She bent her head, her face hidden in her hands as she took a deep, shuddering breath.

Magnus leaned over and unfastened her safety belt and took her shoulders in his hands to make her face him. His eyes held hers. ''It's over, Jade. All that's over now. Put it out of your mind. Come along, I'll take you inside.''

At dinner he said to Ginette, ''I'm afraid the Toyota will be out of commission for a few days. If you need anything let me know.''

Mrs. Riordan said, "What's wrong with it? Jade was driving it this afternoon, wasn't she? Did you have some trouble?" she asked, turning to Jade.

Magnus explained briefly, and his mother frowned. "Perhaps you shouldn't allow Jade to drive," she suggested, "if she's going to panic so easily."

"I didn't panic," Jade said evenly. "I might have made an error of judgement, not seeing the ditch, but I didn't want the horse kicking the car. It wouldn't have done either of them any good."

"Driving it into the ditch doesn't seem to have done the car much good," Mrs. Riordan pointed out.

Inwardly, Jade sighed. "No," she had to agree. "In hindsight perhaps it wasn't the best thing to do." Though she didn't know what else she could have done at the time.

Mrs. Riordan looked vindicated, and Jade noticed that Magnus seemed slightly amused. He said, "You need a car of your own, Jade."

Surprised and pleased, she stammered, "They're very expensive. I can do without one."

He gave her a look that she couldn't read and said, "We'll talk about it later."

As they prepared for bed, she said, "It was my fault the insurance lapsed on my car before I wrecked it—otherwise I'd have been able to buy a new one."

"I'll buy it. If nothing else, it will mean one less cause of friction between my mother and you," he added rather wearily.

Jade bit her lip. "I'm sorry we can't get on better."

He shrugged out of his shirt, throwing it down on the bed. "Well, another few months and you won't need to try—at least on a day-to-day basis."

"What do you mean?" Jade paused on her way to the bathroom.

"I hope that by then I'll be able to hand over completely to the farm manager," he explained. "We can afford an extra worker to help out, now. Laurence will be here, too, in the holidays, over some of the busiest times. And in another year he'll have completed his degree and be able to take over. Of course if he wants my advice it'll always be available, but I intend to move out of Waititapu."

"Move out?" Her heart was thundering.

"Yes." He was looking at her intently. "Did you think I was going to keep you here forever?"

"It's your home."

"It was. My home is with you, Jade. We've never had a home of our own, have we? A place where we can be alone? That's another thing we might start shopping for soon. You'd better start thinking about what sort of house you want. Why are you looking at me like that?"

She didn't know how she was looking, but she felt a quite strange combination of a cautious happiness mingled with, perhaps, a kind of trepidation. Buying a home together would be a confirmation of their commitment to the future. A future that they would work out alone together, without the constraints of the presence of his family and other people in the same house. "I think that would be a good idea," she said inadequately.

Later, when he took her into his arms, she found herself responding to him without the familiar small ache of resentment that had previously marred the undoubted pleasure his lovemaking brought her.

Perhaps, she thought afterwards, listening to his steady breathing as she lay wakeful in the darkness, that was a hopeful sign.

* * *

Laurence and Andrew arrived home for the holidays. Laurence was a husky young man, broader and considerably more mature than the gangly sixteen-year-old she had first met here at Waititapu. Andrew had been a grubby-faced twelve-year-old then; now he was a handsome teenager sporting a dashing haircut and topping Jade's height by several inches.

Andrew's greeting was a casual "Hi, Jade. Glad you're back." And Laurence kissed her cheek and smiled down at her, but with a hint of reserve. Whether he was recalling his youthful infatuation or had been regaled by his twin sister with the story of Jade's supposed infidelity, she couldn't ask. Perhaps both were causes for embarrassment.

The day after their arrival, Magnus said at breakfast, "I'm going to Auckland this afternoon to meet a client. I won't have a lot of spare time, but anyone who wants a couple of hours in the city is welcome to come with me."

Laurence wanted to go, and Jade said, "I'd like to visit Annie."

"At the hospital?" Magnus enquired.

"No, she's living in a house in the city. I saw her last time I was in Auckland."

"You never mentioned it."

She'd told him about seeing Lida, and it hadn't seemed the time to mention Annie. She shrugged.

"How is she?" he asked.

"She was fine. Hoping that this time she'll be able to stay out of hospital."

"Great. I'll drop you off there, then, before I go to my appointment. So, Laurence, where do you want to go?"

Laurence was planning to look at a cheap computer deal he'd seen advertised, with an eye to running a new farm management program on it. While they discussed its possible advantages, Jade slipped out of the room. She knocked on the door of Mrs. Riordan's room, and went in. "Magnus is taking Laurence and me to Auckland this afternoon," she said. "Is there anything you'd like me to get for you?"

"If I need anything, Ginette can get it, or take me shopping with her," Mrs. Riordan said. She was sitting in her wheelchair today, staring out of the window at the sea view. Ginette was still in the dining-room. Following her gaze, Jade said, "You never go as far as the beach, do you? I'm sure we could help get you there, if you wanted—"

"Thank you, I have no desire to go to the beach."

"I see," Jade said quietly. "I'm sorry if I've intruded on your privacy."

As she made to leave, the imperious voice said, "Wait, Jade!"

She turned enquiringly, and Mrs. Riordan glared at her for a moment or two. Then she said stiffly, "For all your faults, you're a kindhearted girl. And too easily hurt."

It was probably the nearest thing to an apology she was likely to get, Jade thought. "It's all right. I wasn't taking offence."

"No, you don't, do you?" Mrs. Riordan said thoughtfully. "Perhaps you should have when you first came here." She added, "I know you pitied me. I hated that most of all."

"I'm sorry about that." Jade was astonished at the admission. "But it would hardly have helped if I'd shouted at you."

"Did you want to?"

"Sometimes," Jade said cautiously.

"You hid it well. I decided you had no character at all."

"Did you?" Jade smiled faintly. "You were wrong."

Mrs. Riordan gave her a penetrating stare. "Magnus is a strong character. He doesn't tolerate weakness well."

"Maybe he's learned to," Jade dared to suggest. When she married him, she would have agreed with that assessment. She'd known that he admired her strength, her practicality. It was why she'd hidden from him any sign of frailty, any hint that the burden of helping him care for his home, his business, his family, was more than she could bear. She hadn't wanted to disappoint him in any way.

Face it, she'd been afraid that he would love her less.

"Maybe he has," Mrs. Riordan said. "He must be extremely fond of you."

Jade smiled again at the grudging puzzlement in her voice. "I hope so."

"I would never have thought Magnus would tolerate—"

She broke off as Ginette breezed into the room. Just as well, perhaps, Jade thought grimly. She turned. "I'll leave you, then. Let me know if you think of anything you want."

Annie answered the door herself, enveloping Jade in an enthusiastic hug. "It's great to see you again. You're looking better than ever."

"So are you!" Jade eyed Annie's hair, newly cut in a becoming bob that showed up its fiery thickness and made the most of the curl. "That looks terrific! And the clothes, too—"

Annie grinned, preening ostentatiously. She was wearing a pair of jeans that hugged her rounded behind, and a silk-look shirt casually tied at her waist, instead of one of the shapeless, too-long dresses that Jade was accustomed to. "I'm trying to impress my new shrink. He's quite dishy. A vast improvement on old Half-Specs Turton. Said he'd be here this afternoon."

"If I've picked a bad time—"

"No! A couple of hours or so, you said? He isn't due until four. Come and say hello to the others, and then we'll go to my room."

There were two other women and two men in the house, all of whom Jade had met on her previous visit, and she stopped briefly in the big lounge to greet them.

"You're still having therapy, then?" Jade asked as Annie led the way to her room.

"Once a week we have a visiting therapist to conduct a group session. And we can request a private session if we want." Annie rolled her eyes. "I want!"

"Apart from being 'dishy,'" Jade said, amused, "is he any good?"

"I reckon! He's just got back from two years' study overseas, catching up with the latest methods. And he talks to us about them, even asks our opinion. He reckons we know more than some of the doctors about our own problems, and we should have some say in our treatment. This guy treats us like human beings."

Impressed, Jade said, "He sounds brilliant."

"He is. I think I scared him a bit last time, though." Annie grinned. "Showed him a poem I'd written about him."

Astonished, Jade said, "I didn't know you wrote poetry!"

"I don't—I mean, I didn't. Only he reckons it's 'a healing exercise' to write down your thoughts and feelings, whether it's poetry or letters or just a private journal that you never show anyone. So I thought, what the heck, why not a poem? Anyway, when I showed it to him he got all very solemn and pink and said something about people developing a dependency on a therapist, 'specially one of the opposite sex, and it was normal but of course not to be taken seriously. And then he said he doubted I was in need of therapy any more, anyway. He reckoned I seemed perfectly sane to him—so how about *that?*''

"I'd agree," Jade said, taking a seat on the only chair as Annie bounced onto the bed. "I don't believe there's anything wrong with you."

"Aw, shucks!" Annie put on a gloomy clown face. "I suppose I could say I'm the Queen of Sheba—or how about this?" She dropped her jaw, crossed her eyes and nodded her head idiotically. "Think that might convince him?"

Jade laughed. "Maybe. But it would hardly attract him, if that's what you want to do!"

Annie reverted to herself. "Guess I might as well give up. What professional psychotherapist is going to ever get involved with a professional psycho?"

"They're not supposed to, ethically speaking, are they?" Jade suggested.

"I s'pose not. And Patrick'd never do anything unethical—"

"*Patrick?*"

"He doesn't like to be called Pat. Or Paddy. Y'know, he's not really my type—" Annie broke off. "What's the matter?"

"Nothing." Jade swallowed, the racing pulse in her temple beginning to steady. She tried to concentrate her thoughts. "Did he work at the hospital before he went overseas?"

"No, never. He had his own private practice somewhere, I think. Why? You don't know him, do you?"

Jade shook her head. "I don't think so." There must be dozens—perhaps hundreds—of men called Patrick in Auckland. It didn't mean a thing. "What's his last name?"

"Um—Cowley." Annie looked at her enquiringly.

Patrick Cowley. Did it have an echo of familiarity? Jade wasn't sure. She shook her head but couldn't help asking, "What does he look like?"

"Well, actually," Annie said, cocking her head, "he isn't a real knockout. Not like your Magnus. Brown hair, blue eyes—kind eyes. Glasses. He's just . . . nice. If you stay till he arrives you can meet him, later. Anyway—" she leaned over and tapped Jade's knee "—tell me how things are with you."

Just after three-thirty Magnus rang the doorbell, and Annie dragged him in to meet her flatmates. He shook hands with them all and chatted for a few minutes before saying, "We'd better be going. I told Laurence we'd pick him up at about four."

"Can't you stay a bit longer?" Annie begged. "There's someone I'd like Jade to meet." She winked at Jade, pretending not to see Magnus's enquiring glance.

He looked at his watch. "For a short while."

At five minutes to four he said, "We don't want to keep Laurence waiting."

"He won't mind, will he?" Jade asked, trying to sound casual. "Just a few extra minutes?"

But at four o'clock Magnus was getting restive and she had to concede it was time to leave.

"We can meet your friend another time, maybe," Magnus suggested to Annie, his hand on Jade's waist.

"I'll see you out," Annie said reluctantly, and came with them down the path.

As they were saying their farewells on the pavement another car drew up behind Magnus's, and Annie said, "Here he is!"

Jade turned to see a youngish man with light brown hair and glasses locking his car. He looked up and came toward them, smiling. "Hi, Annie," he said easily.

Jade took a step back and came up against Magnus's shoulder.

The man was coming closer and, as his gaze shifted to her, an uncertain expression crossed his face. "Hello," he said.

The blood had drained from her face. She felt cold all over, then suddenly hot. Her lips parted dryly, and she whispered, "Hello, Patrick!"

Chapter Fourteen

"*Patrick?*" Magnus echoed behind her.

Patrick's blue eyes were warm as they rested on Jade, but his smile had turned apologetic. "I know you but...sorry," he said. "I can't recall your name."

Magnus closed a hand over Jade's arm and she found herself shifted firmly to one side. She heard him say, "*You bastard!*" And then in a blur of movement he'd shoved past her and hurled himself at Patrick, whose expression became startled.

Magnus had grasped his collar and was snarling into his face, "You drove her to the brink of death, and *you can't even recall her name?*"

Jade rushed forward, grabbing his arm with both hands as he viciously shook the other man. "*Magnus, stop!*"

Annie stood with her mouth agape, her eyes wide. Patrick wasn't trying to defend himself, allowing his arms to hang slack at his sides, a look of wary caution on his face.

Magnus bunched a fist, and Jade changed position so that she was facing him, trying to shield Patrick with her body. *"Don't!"* she cried. *"Magnus, for God's sake—"*

Patrick raised a hand and this time it was he who pushed her aside, though his eyes remained on Magnus. "Why don't we talk?" he said calmly.

Magnus gazed at him, his eyes slitted with rage. "I ought to *kill* you!" he said, and then let go, giving the other man a shove that made him stagger.

Jade caught at Magnus's arm again, but this time he didn't move to attack. He was breathing hard, and there was an expression of furious hatred on his face.

Patrick spread his hands in a placating gesture, and said, "I apologise for not remembering. I do see a lot of people, and—" he smiled tentatively at Jade "—I believe it was some time ago, wasn't it?"

Magnus made a sound that was like a low, animal growl, and Jade tightened her hold on his arm. "Yes," she said. "And it wasn't your fault I became ill. You told me when you said you were going overseas that I should see someone else—you even made an appointment for me, but I never kept it."

She felt the sudden rigidity of Magnus's arm in hers as his whole body flexed.

Patrick said, his eyes filled with concern, "You've had treatment since?"

"I was in hospital with Annie, but I'm fine now."

"That's good. And . . ." Patrick cast a speculative, interested look at Magnus. "You two met in the hospital? Are you still in treatment, my friend?"

Annie made a small, choked sound, clapping a hand over her mouth, and Jade cast her an anguished glance and said in an unsteady voice, "This . . . is my husband. Magnus,

Patrick was my therapist—for several months before I— went into hospital."

Annie babbled into the rather blank silence, "What a coincidence, eh? Now he's treating me—us—all of us in the house."

Magnus, looking as though he'd been bludgeoned, said stiffly, "I apologise. I...made a mistake."

Puzzled but polite, the other man shrugged. "No harm done," he said mildly. "Well, Annie—shall we go inside and get started?"

Magnus watched them walk up the path before he moved, going to open the car door as though his limbs were made of wood. His face was pale and he didn't look at Jade at all, didn't speak as he started up the car and drove slowly and with great care to where he had arranged to pick up Laurence. Laurence gave Magnus a brief rundown of the computer demonstration, and of the machine's good and less good features, and made a few other remarks, but after finding that both Magnus and Jade were replying almost exclusively in monosyllables, he cast an unseen, curious glance between them and closed his eyes, apparently going to sleep.

They were held up by an accident that had blocked traffic on the highway. Magnus frowned, drumming his fingers on the steering wheel, and Laurence occupied the time giving a desultory commentary on the progress of the long, crawling column of cars and the arrival and departure of various emergency vehicles, while Jade pretended to read a magazine she'd found in the glove box. The remainder of the journey home was long and silent.

Mrs. Gaines had kept dinner for them, and as soon as they walked in the door she said it would be on the table in five minutes.

Jade went upstairs, expecting Magnus to follow, but he didn't. When she came down again he and Laurence were already in the dining-room and Mrs. Gaines was taking in the first course.

Her nerves jumping, Jade picked at her food and left half of it uneaten, surreptitiously watching Magnus. He cleaned his plate with a kind of absentminded determination, but she doubted if he'd tasted anything.

She helped Mrs. Gaines clear away the dessert plates, and returned to the dining-room to find Laurence alone. "Magnus said he was going out," he told her. "Have you two had a fight?"

Jade shook her head. "No. He's just—preoccupied. Did he say where he was going?"

"Nope. He had a couple of stiff whiskies before he went," Laurence offered, his expression carefully bland. "I don't think he took the car."

Shaken by a spasm of anger, Jade poured herself coffee and made herself sit down and finish it. Magnus and she needed to talk, but he'd taken himself off alone. When was he planning to come back?

It was dusk when she went upstairs again, and she crossed to the window, looking out at the sea, waiting for its calming influence to take over. The long, pale curve of the beach was swept clean and empty, the dark rocks bounding it bleak and rugged. There was something different about them. She knew them so well that she discerned an extra hump that had never been there before. It took a second or two to realise what it was. Someone was sitting hunched on the rock, shoulders bowed and head down. His whole attitude spoke of a depth of despair.

She stood at the window watching for a long time, until darkness hid the figure from her. And in all that time it hadn't moved. Perhaps she was mistaken. Perhaps it was just another rock after all that she'd never particularly noticed before.

The sand was still warm under her feet when she removed her shoes. She walked down to the firmer, cooler sand where the waves had recently smoothed it, and the white, uneven lines of foam rose out of the darkness, hissing onto the beach. A slight breeze stirred her hair and ruffled the hem of her skirt about her knees while she walked steadily to the headland, and paused to replace her shoes before climbing onto the rock.

Magnus remained as still as stone, though now she could see a faint movement as the wind plucked at his sweatshirt. The tumbling boom of the waves covered the sound of her approach. A curling white crest lipped the edge of the jutting rock promontory and fine, cool spray spattered her face. Coming to a halt beside him, she saw that Magnus's hair was beaded with tiny droplets, and the shoulders of his sweatshirt were wet.

She touched his hair, feeling the dampness on her fingers, and knelt at his side, letting her arm slide about his shoulders. She felt his breathing momentarily stop, and then begin again, the muscles under her hand stiffening.

Quietly she said, "He was treating me for months. I wasn't coping as well as I pretended, and I knew if I didn't get help I'd crack up. I looked up counsellors in the yellow pages. Patrick was in private practice then, and quite expensive. That's where the money from my account went, in fees. But I thought it was worthwhile. It helped, being able to talk to someone."

Magnus had raised his head, but he didn't look at her. Another wave hit the rock face and showered them with spray. He took no notice. "Why not me?" he asked, his voice oddly muffled. "Couldn't you have talked to me?"

"I didn't want to add to your burdens," she explained. "You were worried sick about Danella, and relying on me to look after the rest of the family. I didn't want you to know that I was a broken reed. Then, when I realised I was pregnant—I knew it was the last thing you needed at the time. Another responsibility to add to those you already had. I didn't know how I was going to tell you I'd been so careless. I knew you'd be upset, even angry."

"If I'd known it was our child—" He took a deep breath. "Did you really think I would reject it—reject *you?*"

"I was in such a state I didn't know what to think. I just couldn't seem to find the words to discuss it with you. Then Patrick said he was going away to do post-graduate study overseas, and I felt my one prop had been taken from me. I hadn't realised how fragile my control was at that stage, how much I relied on Patrick to keep me functioning normally. I panicked and...oh, Magnus, I'm sorry I was so weak, when you needed me to be strong."

"*You're* sorry!" he said thickly, and with a convulsive movement he turned to her, his arms going about her as though he couldn't help himself, his cheek rasping against hers, damp and salty, before he buried his face on her shoulder. "*Oh God, Jade!* How can I even ask you to forgive me?"

Kneeling on the hard, cool rock, she cradled him in her arms. "It's all right, Magnus," she murmured, her lips against his wet, sea-scented hair. "You don't have to ask."

He gave a great, shuddering sigh. "I thought—"

"I know," Jade soothed. "I know. What else were you to think? Even *I* had to believe it in the end. Although in my heart I could never accept that I'd been unfaithful to you."

He raised his head, facing her in the gloom. "I should never have accepted it, either. I should have had more faith in you."

Jade shook her head. "It's all right," she insisted. "You'd only met me a few months before we were married, and what chance did we have to get to know each other, really? With your commitments to your family and your work—"

"I should have made time for you," he said. "I should have at least realised that I was asking too much of you. What a selfish, blind brute I was."

"No. Just overworked and overcommitted, and with a strong sense of responsibility."

"To everyone but you. And *you* should have come first! I *wanted* you to, desperately. I kept promising myself that soon I'd make time to concentrate on us and our relationship. Everything kept getting in the way. My mother, my sister, the boys—my obligation to the farms. I felt I had to preserve what I could for Laurence—it had always been understood that he was to run them, because I didn't want to make farming my career but he was dead keen. There never was time for us, you and me. And because it was what *I* wanted most in the world—to take you away somewhere and be alone with you—I never considered how unfair I was being to you in *not* doing it."

"How could you?" Jade asked. "You couldn't turn your back on your family when they needed you most."

"You needed me, too. And I let you down—so badly." He drew another heavy, shaking breath. "Maybe deep down I knew that your breakdown was my fault. And I was too much of a coward to face it. It was too monstrous a thought to admit, that I had done that to you entirely on my own. Blaming the mysterious Patrick was the easy way out. And that way, I could even lay some of the blame on you." His mouth twisted. "How did I dare to say I'd *forgiven* you, when the real guilt was all mine?"

"Neither of us was entirely to blame. It was a combination of circumstances. You were too busy to see what was happening to me, and perhaps you didn't want to see it—"

"I did see," he confessed. "But I never guessed how bad it was, and I kept telling myself that it was temporary, and lashing myself to make more money so that I could afford to pull you out of the situation I'd got us in. I should have realised that it was urgent, that there wasn't time to wait. If I'd known how bad it was, I'd have let the farms go, found a rest-home for my mother, left Danella to sort herself out—"

"I couldn't have allowed you to sacrifice your whole family for me! You did your best—I knew that."

"My best," he groaned. "When I was driving you to a complete breakdown?"

She lifted a hand to his cheek, and wiped some of the moisture from it. "I did that myself. Please, Magnus, stop beating yourself. I love you—till death us do part."

"Jade," he said. His eyes suddenly closed tightly, his face contorted in a grimace of anguish. He said her name again, and blindly reached for her, his fingers trembling as they touched her face, her hair, drew her close until her lips touched his. He whispered her name again, and then his mouth closed almost reverently over hers, and he made an inarticulate sound in his throat as she opened her lips and passionately returned his kiss.

His hands and his lips were cold, and she tasted the salt of the sea on his mouth. She moved hers over it, warming it, hooked her arms about his neck, and felt his hands slide to her waist, her hips, then up again, to cradle her head between his palms. He withdrew his mouth and looked down at her. "I don't deserve you, my love," he said soberly. "On my knees, I promise to love and cherish and trust you with my life, through all the days we have left."

Jade turned her head aside and kissed his hand. "We're both on our knees," she pointed out, as a wave slapped onto the rock and spat white foam over them. "And we should be moving, before we get swept away."

He laughed, and pulled her to her feet. "I have been," he said. "You swept me away years ago when you first walked into my office, and I've been in over my head ever since."

"So it wasn't just for my practical skills that you married me?" she asked as they picked their way across the slippery, uneven surface.

Magnus stopped to look at her. "You never believed that!"

"I did for a while. At least, I wondered—your mother thought that was the reason."

"My mother thinks a lot of things," he said shortly, "and she's wrong about most of them. I married you because I was scared stiff that I'd lose you to someone else while I was sorting out my family's problems."

"And when you learned about Patrick you thought it had happened anyway?"

"It seemed an ironic twist of fate, yes."

He let her go and jumped to the sand, helping her after him. She leapt lightly down, landing with one hand held in his, the other on his shoulder.

She smiled up at him. Their bodies were almost touching. "Remember when this was almost the only place we could be alone?" she asked him softly. They stood in a tiny half cove, the dry, pale sand near the cliff above overshadowed by a huge old pohutukawa dipping its curved branches low.

"When you used to get nervous about making love in our bedroom in case someone overheard us?" He gave a sharp sigh. "You put up with an awful lot, didn't you?"

Jade nuzzled her head into his shoulder. "The boys are home again," she reminded him. Their bedroom was on the same floor.

"So they are," Magnus said slowly. "You mean you're likely to go coy on me again?"

Jade raised her head. "I was not *coy!*"

"You were," he said tenderly, tugging gently at her hair. "But never down here. Here, you felt safe, didn't you? In the dark, by the sea."

A smile lit her eyes. "I feel very safe here."

"Oh, Jade." He put his arms about her waist, loosely, and touched his forehead to hers. "I didn't dare ask—expect..."

"So," she murmured, "are you going to make me ask?"

He drew her nearer. "No," he said. "No." And he gathered her to him, his lips meeting hers with desire, and need, and reckless passion.

Minutes later they were together on the cool, cushioning sand in the shadow of the tree, and the leaves moved against the night, making tiny whispering sounds that echoed their incoherent, loving whispers of endearment. Their final cries of fulfilment were lost amid the thunder of the sea roiling about the rocks and falling on the sand.

Afterwards they lay in each other's arms until the night breeze freshened and intruded on their haven, and then they dressed and wandered back along the beach with their arms about each other, pausing now and then to kiss, and murmur words that hardly made sense, and kiss again.

As they stood looking up at the house, Magnus said, "We're going to start looking for our own house, very soon. You must hate this place."

"No." She shook her head. "It's beautiful, and we were happy sometimes."

His hold on her tightened. "We'll come back for visits," he said, "holidays with our children. It's a family place."

Jade drew a breath. "You've guessed?"

"Guessed?" He looked down at her quickly. "Jade! You mean that you're—"

"Pregnant. Yes, I think so. In a week or two I'll know for sure." Hesitantly, she said, "Are you pleased?"

"Pleased? I'm—oh, Jade!" He pulled her fully into his arms again. "No one in the entire history of the world has ever been so pleased as I am at this moment."

She laughed, and hugged him in return. "I hoped you would be, but I wasn't sure."

"Oh, my darling. I have so much to make up to you." His voice shook, and he kissed her with great tenderness.

"You have the rest of our lives to do it in," she promised, stroking back his hair from his forehead. "And I have the rest of our lives to prove to you that you're the only man I will ever love. Starting now."

* * * * *

Silhouette

SPECIAL EDITION™

COMING NEXT MONTH

#919 MAIL ORDER COWBOY—Patricia Coughlin
That Special Woman!
Allie Halston swore she'd conquer rigorous ranch life, even if it meant taking on all of Texas! Then she faced sexy Burn Monroe—who was more than just a cowboy with an attitude....

#920 B IS FOR BABY—Lisa Jackson
Love Letters
Beth Crandall's single passionate night with Jenner McKee had changed her life forever. Years later, an unexpected letter drew her back home, and to the man she'd never forgotten....

#921 THE GREATEST GIFT OF ALL—Penny Richards
Baron Montgomery knew determined Mallory Ryan would sacrifice anything for her young child. But when her boundless mother's love was tested, could Mallory accept his help and his promise of everlasting devotion?

#922 WHEN MORNING COMES—Christine Flynn
Driven and dedicated, Travis McCloud had sacrificed his marriage for career. Now a chance reunion with Brooke compelled him to open his heart...and to take a second chance at love.

#923 COWBOY'S KIN—Victoria Pade
A Ranching Family
Linc Heller's wild, hell-raising ways were legendary. Yet Kansas Daye wondered if becoming a father had tempered Linc—and if he was ready to step into her waiting arms.

#924 LET'S MAKE IT LEGAL—Trisha Alexander
John Appleton gave up the fast track to become Mr. Mom. Then high-powered lawyer Sydney Scott Wells stormed into his life, and John knew he'd show her the best of both worlds!

MILLION DOLLAR SWEEPSTAKES (III)

No purchase necessary. To enter, follow the directions published. Method of entry may vary. For eligibility, entries must be received no later than March 31, 1996. No liability is assumed for printing errors, lost, late or misdirected entries. Odds of winning are determined by the number of eligible entries distributed and received. Prizewinners will be determined no later than June 30, 1996.

Sweepstakes open to residents of the U.S. (except Puerto Rico), Canada, Europe and Taiwan who are 18 years of age or older. All applicable laws and regulations apply. Sweepstakes offer void wherever prohibited by law. Values of all prizes are in U.S. currency. This sweepstakes is presented by Torstar Corp., its subsidiaries and affiliates, in conjunction with book, merchandise and/or product offerings. For a copy of the Official Rules governing this sweepstakes offer, send a self-addressed, stamped envelope (WA residents need not affix return postage) to: MILLION DOLLAR SWEEPSTAKES (III) Rules, P.O. Box 4573, Blair, NE 68009, USA.

SWP-S1094

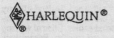 

The movie event of the season can be the reading event of the year!

Lights... The lights go on in October when CBS presents Harlequin/Silhouette Sunday Matinee Movies. These four movies are based on bestselling Harlequin and Silhouette novels.

Camera... As the cameras roll, be the first to read the original novels the movies are based on!

Action... Through this offer, you can have these books sent directly to you! Just fill in the order form below and you could be reading the books...before the movie!

48288-4	Treacherous Beauties by Cheryl Emerson		
		$3.99 U.S./$4.50 CAN.	☐
83305-9	Fantasy Man by Sharon Green		
		$3.99 U.S./$4.50 CAN.	☐
48289-2	A Change of Place by Tracy Sinclair		
		$3.99 U.S./$4.50CAN.	☐
83306-7	Another Woman by Margot Dalton		
		$3.99 U.S./$4.50 CAN.	☐

TOTAL AMOUNT	$
POSTAGE & HANDLING	$
($1.00 for one book, 50¢ for each additional)	
APPLICABLE TAXES*	$ _____
TOTAL PAYABLE	$ _____
(check or money order—please do not send cash)	

To order, complete this form and send it, along with a check or money order for the total above, payable to Harlequin Books, to: **In the U.S.:** 3010 Walden Avenue, P.O. Box 9047, Buffalo, NY 14269-9047; **In Canada:** P.O. Box 613, Fort Erie, Ontario, L2A 5X3.

Name: _____

Address: _____ City: _____

State/Prov.: _____ Zip/Postal Code: _____

*New York residents remit applicable sales taxes.
Canadian residents remit applicable GST and provincial taxes.

CBSPR

"HOORAY FOR HOLLYWOOD" SWEEPSTAKES

HERE'S HOW THE SWEEPSTAKES WORKS

OFFICIAL RULES — NO PURCHASE NECESSARY

To enter, complete an Official Entry Form or hand print on a 3" x 5" card the words "HOORAY FOR HOLLYWOOD", your name and address and mail your entry in the pre-addressed envelope (if provided) or to: "Hooray for Hollywood" Sweepstakes, P.O. Box 9076, Buffalo, NY 14269-9076 or "Hooray for Hollywood" Sweepstakes, P.O. Box 637, Fort Erie, Ontario L2A 5X3. Entries must be sent via First Class Mail and be received no later than 12/31/94. No liability is assumed for lost, late or misdirected mail.

Winners will be selected in random drawings to be conducted no later than January 31, 1995 from all eligible entries received.

Grand Prize: A 7-day/6-night trip for 2 to Los Angeles, CA including round trip air transportation from commercial airport nearest winner's residence, accommodations at the Regent Beverly Wilshire Hotel, free rental car, and $1,000 spending money. (Approximate prize value which will vary dependent upon winner's residence: $5,400.00 U.S.); 500 Second Prizes: A pair of "Hollywood Star" sunglasses (prize value: $9.95 U.S. each). Winner selection is under the supervision of D.L. Blair, Inc., an independent judging organization, whose decisions are final. Grand Prize travelers must sign and return a release of liability prior to traveling. Trip must be taken by 2/1/96 and is subject to airline schedules and accommodations availability.

Sweepstakes offer is open to residents of the U.S. (except Puerto Rico) and Canada who are 18 years of age or older, except employees and immediate family members of Harlequin Enterprises, Ltd., its affiliates, subsidiaries, and all agencies, entities or persons connected with the use, marketing or conduct of this sweepstakes. All federal, state, provincial, municipal and local laws apply. Offer void wherever prohibited by law. Taxes and/or duties are the sole responsibility of the winners. Any litigation within the province of Quebec respecting the conduct and awarding of prizes may be submitted to the Regie des loteries et courses du Quebec. All prizes will be awarded; winners will be notified by mail. No substitution of prizes are permitted. Odds of winning are dependent upon the number of eligible entries received.

Potential grand prize winner must sign and return an Affidavit of Eligibility within 30 days of notification. In the event of non-compliance within this time period, prize may be awarded to an alternate winner. Prize notification returned as undeliverable may result in the awarding of prize to an alternate winner. By acceptance of their prize, winners consent to use of their names, photographs, or likenesses for purpose of advertising, trade and promotion on behalf of Harlequin Enterprises, Ltd., without further compensation unless prohibited by law. A Canadian winner must correctly answer an arithmetical skill-testing question in order to be awarded the prize.

For a list of winners (available after 2/28/95), send a separate stamped, self-addressed envelope to: Hooray for Hollywood Sweepstakes 3252 Winners, P.O. Box 4200, Blair, NE 68009.

OFFICIAL ENTRY COUPON

"Hooray for Hollywood"
SWEEPSTAKES!

Yes, I'd love to win the Grand Prize — a vacation in Hollywood —
or one of 500 pairs of "sunglasses of the stars"! Please enter me
in the sweepstakes!

This entry must be received by December 31, 1994.
Winners will be notified by January 31, 1995.

Name _____

Address _____ Apt. _____

City _____

State/Prov. _____ Zip/Postal Code _____

Daytime phone number _____
(area code)

Mail all entries to: Hooray for Hollywood Sweepstakes,
P.O. Box 9076, Buffalo, NY 14269-9076.
In Canada, mail to: Hooray for Hollywood Sweepstakes,
P.O. Box 637, Fort Erie, ON L2A 5X3.

KCH

OFFICIAL ENTRY COUPON

"Hooray for Hollywood"
SWEEPSTAKES!

Yes, I'd love to win the Grand Prize — a vacation in Hollywood —
or one of 500 pairs of "sunglasses of the stars"! Please enter me
in the sweepstakes!

This entry must be received by December 31, 1994.
Winners will be notified by January 31, 1995.

Name _____

Address _____ Apt. _____

City _____

State/Prov. _____ Zip/Postal Code _____

Daytime phone number _____
(area code)

Mail all entries to: Hooray for Hollywood Sweepstakes,
P.O. Box 9076, Buffalo, NY 14269-9076.
In Canada, mail to: Hooray for Hollywood Sweepstakes,
P.O. Box 637, Fort Erie, ON L2A 5X3.

KCH